# THE RELUCTANT VAMPIRE QUEEN

# THE RELUCTANT VAMPIRE QUEEN

## JO SIMMONS

HOT
KEY
BOOKS

First published in Great Britain in 2022 by
HOT KEY BOOKS
4th Floor, Victoria House, Bloomsbury Square
London WC1B 4DA
Owned by Bonnier Books
Sveavägen 56, Stockholm, Sweden
www.hotkeybooks.com

A CIP catalogue record for this book is available from the British Library.

ISBN: 978-1-4714-1178-6
*Also available as an ebook and in audio*

1

Typeset by DataConnection Ltd
Printed and bound in Great Britain by Clays Ltd, Elcograf S.p.A.

Hot Key Books is an imprint of Bonnier Books UK
www.bonnierbooks.co.uk

*For my beautiful boys,*
*George and Dylan*

# 1

Mo Merrydrew was cycling fast through her village of Lower Donny, her black hair streaming out behind her, her long legs a blur, her breath forming clouds in the chill evening air. One hand was on the handlebars, the other pressing her phone to her ear.

'Hey, Lou. It's me, Mo.'

'You sound excited,' said Lou. 'You've been to the library again, haven't you?'

'Yup,' Mo said, 'where, you'll be super happy to hear, I picked up a ton of extra reading for the science test we have coming up, including a new book about tapeworms that the librarian put aside for me.'

'Yay,' said Lou flatly.

'I also got a biography of the first female welder in Scotland and a book about the Amazon women.'

'The women who work at Amazon?' Lou said.

'No, the warrior women from Greek mythology.'

'What about the Mini Battenbergs?' Lou asked.

'Got them too,' said Mo. 'Whoops! Sheep! Just missed it.'

'Mo, are you cycling *and* on your phone, in the pitch black? Seriously? That's so dangerous.'

'It's totally fine,' Mo puffed. 'I can handle it. I am a clever, independent woman, who is an expert at biking and holding my phone and . . . Aarrggghhh!'

Lou heard bike brakes squealing, then a crunching, rustling sound.

'Mo? Mo?'

'Sorry, went into a hedge,' Mo explained. 'Now, open the door, will you?'

'Which door?'

'Yours! I'm outside.'

Lou ran downstairs and found Mo on the front step.

'So you rang me while cycling *to* my house?' Lou said. 'Even though you could have said everything you just said once you got here and also not fallen into a hedge. For someone intelligent, you're really stupid.'

'You are,' said Mo.

'No, you are,' said Lou. 'And you've got twigs in your hair.'

'It's cool to wear twigs in your hair,' said Mo.

'Like you'd know anything about being cool,' said Lou, hugging her friend and then heading upstairs. Mo followed Lou into her bedroom, dumped her backpack of books on the floor and collapsed backwards onto Lou's bed, in a star shape.

'Can we eat some Mini Battenbergs now, please?' she said. 'I can't stay long. I just wanted to drop off the tapeworm book. Then I need to get on with science revision.'

'You need to take a break, that's what you need,' said Lou. 'You look tired. I'm taking Nipper to dog training this evening. *Nipper!*'

Nipper didn't appear.

'See, no recall,' said Lou. 'Come with me. Take the night off. It'll be fun.'

'You sound like my parents. Always on at me to study less.'

'You need people in your life,' Lou went on.

'There are people in books.'

'Real people like me.'

'I can't, Lou, I'm sorry. There's too much work to do,' said Mo, sitting up and looking into her friend's big blue eyes, which sat in a round face, like a manga hamster. She smoothed Lou's fringe and tucked a stray lock of her blonde hair behind her ear, affectionately. 'I also need to write up the minutes of today's debating-society meeting.'

'Did anyone go?' Lou asked.

'No, but I should write it up anyway. I'm president, after all. And founder.'

Lou opened the Mini Battenbergs and handed one to Mo, without looking at her.

'Don't be cross with me,' Mo said. 'We're still best mates – have been since we were three, remember? Our eyes met across the sand tray at nursery. You were fighting

3

with Marco Pettini over a plastic dinosaur. Pretty sure it was a diplodocus. Anyway, I got you both to share it.'

'That's when our friendship started,' said Lou, beginning to smile.

'That's probably when my interest in conflict resolution started too,' Mo added, taking a bite of cake.

'That's definitely when my interest in Marco Pettini started,' Lou said. 'I was so into him. Wonder what he looks like now. Bet he's good-looking.'

'I haven't thought about Marco Pettini since he left Lower Donny years ago,' said Mo.

'He had lovely dark eyes,' Lou went on. 'I love dark eyes in a boy, don't you?'

'I haven't thought about that either,' said Mo.

'Mo, you're like a robot,' Lou said, putting on a computerised voice. '*Scanning for feelings. Negative. Does. Not. Compute.*'

'I just take my education seriously,' Mo said. 'Knowledge is power. That's what I use my brain for. Not for thinking about Marco Pettini who, by the way, always had a snotty nose. Now, I really need to get going.'

Mo grabbed her backpack and the two of them went downstairs.

'See you tomorrow,' she said, and they hugged goodbye.

Lou nodded, opened the door and watched Mo climb onto her bike and pedal away.

# 2

It was a short ride home from Lou's house, round the village green with its duck pond and benches, past the local shop and the Drowned Rat pub, and out towards the wide, flat fields on the other side of Lower Donny where Mo's house stood alone, flanked by a handful of poplar trees. Mo hardly noticed the journey, it was so familiar, but when she turned down the quiet lane that led to her house she gasped suddenly and slammed on the brakes, stopping just in time. A man had walked out in front of her. Walked out? Appeared, more like, as if from nowhere (or, perhaps, the hedge). A stranger. Mo knew everyone in Lower Donny, but she'd never seen him before. He said nothing. He stood perfectly still, staring at Mo with hooded black eyes. She felt goosebumps ripple over her skin.

'Sorry, excuse me,' she muttered, turning her handlebars to cycle around him. He moved and stood squarely in front of her bike again, blocking her way.

'Can I help you?' Mo asked.

'Yes, by becoming Vampire Queen,' said the man in a deep, rich voice. 'You are the Chosen One.'

Mo blinked hard.

'Sorry, what? Chosen One? Chosen to do what?'

'Rule this entire land, as queen of all the vampires.'

'What vampires? I didn't know there were any vampires.'

'Vampires are everywhere,' said the man. 'They live among you humans, on the margins of life, in the dark corners and flickering shadows.'

'Really?' said Mo.

'Yes, really,' the man spat back. 'And you have been chosen to rule over them. With you as leader, there can be more vampires, better vampires. This can become great and glorious vampire stronghold! Proud vampire homeland! You can pep it all up, yes?'

'But vampires don't exist,' Mo said, shaking her head. 'This is a joke, right? A prank?'

She glanced over her shoulder, expecting to see someone with a camera, capturing this hilarious gag.

'No joke,' the man replied. 'I am Bogdan, chief emissary to the great and mighty Vampire King of the East. It is an honour to meet you, Mo.'

Oh my god, he knows my name, Mo thought. How does he know my name?

'The Vampire King gave me a task,' he continued, becoming chattier. '"Bogdan," he said, "go see what's happening in Great Britain. It's so far away and the weather's rubbish, but there must be some vampires there. Take a look. If you think it's worth adding to my territory, find a king that can rule there on my behalf." This is what I have done.'

'Wait, you said "king". *Find a king,*' Mo said. 'You've found me. A fifteen-year-old schoolgirl.'

'Well, yes, traditionally vampire leaders are male, but we can make exception.'

Mo bristled. 'Women can work in senior positions too, you know. This is the twenty-first century. Ever heard of equality?

Bogdan shrugged.

'So if you wanted a king – so predictable, by the way, pick a man for the top job – why have you chosen me?'

'I see something in you,' Bogdan replied.

'That's a first,' said Mo. 'Mostly no one sees me at all.'

'I have been around long time, worked with many powerful vampires. I have talent for discovering Chosen Ones,' said Bogdan. 'Olaf the Sucker who ruled here in the 1700s? I found him. Bran the Thirsty. Also me. Geronimo the Unquenchable. Me too.'

'All men,' Mo muttered.

'All exceptional,' Bogdan replied firmly. 'I knew they were Chosen One first second I saw them. I know the same for you, Mo. I sense something deep within you, a strength, a force. I can almost smell it.'

He leaned towards Mo and inhaled deeply. She ducked backwards, away from his pale face and piercing dark eyes.

'Are you sure it has to be me? I mean, there must be lots of other possible Vampire Queens out there. Why don't you advertise the role and see who applies? I could help you with the interviews.'

'No!' exploded Bogdan, making Mo jump. '*You* are Chosen One. *You* must be Vampire Queen. *You* and *only* you. Use your strength, Mo. Use it! Become the queen you should be!'

Then he thrust out his hand and clenched his fingers, like he was milking something.

'You will have so much power. More power than you can dream of. Be as ruthless as you like!' he said.

'Rulers should be fair, not ruthless,' Mo muttered.

'You will have eternal life too. Nice, yes?'

'I guess,' Mo said. 'I do have a lot I want to achieve. University, an internship at the UN, and I'm thinking a job in politics or a human rights lawyer . . .'

'Yes, yes,' said Bogdan, waving away Mo's words impatiently. 'I am talking about a life of *real* power and riches and everyone in the land fearing you. Also, immense physical strength. Don't you want that?'

Mo shrugged.

'You could rip someone's head off.' He clicked his fingers. 'Like that!'

'That's a horrible idea. Why would I want to do that?'

'Don't knock it till you've tried it,' Bogdan said, winking and smiling. 'Come now. Leave this sad, damp, tragic little village –'

'Lower Donny is not sad and tragic!'

'No, believe me, it is,' said Bogdan, 'and I should know. I've seen a few sad, tragic villages in my time. Anyway, enough! Leave this dingy, miserable . . .'

'I was born here, you know,' Mo fumed. 'Yes, I am looking forward to growing up and leaving it one day, but still. How dare you turn up, literally out of nowhere, and say mean things about my home?'

'Ha ha, yes! This!' Bogdan exclaimed, grinning and clapping his hands. 'This spirit! This fight! This is what we are looking for. This is why you are chosen. Claim your throne and lead this land into a new era of vampire greatness. One bite, and you will be transformed. You will be majestic! Invincible! Unstoppable!'

Bogdan threw his arms wide and tipped his head back, laughing. It sounded like someone squeezing a crow.

'Well?' he said, finally. 'It's a pretty cool-smart offer, yes? What do you say?'

Mo sucked in a deep breath, folded her arms across her chest and frowned hard. Her eyes flickered over Bogdan, taking in his intelligent pale face, his neat hands and well-manicured nails. Then she spoke.

'I'd like to see some ID, please.'

'ID?' said Bogdan. 'What is this ID?'

'Identification,' said Mo. 'How do I know you are who, or what, you say you are?'

'I am Bogdan!' said Bogdan, looking hurt.

'You don't look much like a vampire,' said Mo. 'I don't see any fangs.'

'Oh, sorry, I have little switch here, on back of neck, makes them come down.' He reached behind his head and fumbled around in his hair for a second, and then collapsed into laughter.

'I am making little laugh with you is all,' he said. 'No, there's no switch. Ha ha ha! Humans always fall for that. In fact, fangs naturally appear when they are needed, at mealtimes. Otherwise, normal teeth, see?' He grinned.

'But your clothes look so ordinary,' Mo said.

'You were expecting a cape? I never wear capes. So sixteenth century,' Bogdan sniffed. 'Also, my luggage containing all my finest clothes is still on its way here from the East. My familiar is bringing it.'

'But why a suit? A dirty one. There's a stain on the left lapel,' said Mo, pointing. 'Looks like ketchup.'

'When I first arrived here, I was unsure how to dress,' Bogdan explained. 'So I looked for a great and powerful human man, to discover what such a masterful figure wears. I saw a huge image of a mighty ruler, standing by many splendid vehicles. He was called the Used Car King! Ah yes, I said to myself, I must dress this way.'

'The Used Car King? You mean Clive Bunsworth from Middle Donny? Posters of him in all the bus shelters?' Mo said, trying not to smile.

'Clive, yes,' said Bogdan. 'A most delicious man. *Delightful* man, I mean.'

'He gave you his suit?'

'Not exactly *gave*,' said Bogdan, smiling awkwardly. 'Let's just say he doesn't need it any more.'

Mo shivered. Her eyes wandered back to that ketchup stain . . .

'Anyway!' Bogdan exploded, suddenly impatient. 'Enough talk of Clive Bunsworth! Forget Clive Bunsworth. Clive Bunsworth is nothing to us. Let us talk of you, the Chosen One. Becoming the Vampire Queen of these islands is your destiny.'

'Well, I think you'll find getting amazing GCSEs, then excellent A levels and then going to a top university is my destiny.'

'Nonsense!' said Bogdan firmly. 'To rule is your destiny. Do not fight it!' He stared intently at Mo, his eyes blazing, the moonlight gilding his grey hair.

She cleared her throat. 'Well, thank you very much for your kind offer, Mr Bogdan,' she said. 'Obviously, being unstoppable and majestic sounds interesting, but I would like some time to think about it. It's a big decision, after all. Could you come back tomorrow?'

Bogdan sighed. 'Really? This is super-excellent offer. I don't see problem here.'

Mo didn't budge.

'All right! If I must,' Bogdan said. 'I will await you here, tomorrow.'

Then he bowed deeply, clicked his fingers and was gone, as though he had evaporated.

Mo let out a long breath. She laughed nervously and looked around her. Had anyone else just seen this vampire guy? What a joke, right? But there were no other witnesses. She was alone. Maybe she'd been dreaming. Or she was dehydrated. She'd been in the library too long, hadn't drunk enough water. That would explain it, wouldn't it?

After all, vampires didn't exist. Fact. (Mo loved facts.) They belonged in folklore, stories, films and TV. And in all the folklore and stories and films and TV, the vampires were exotic and alluring and the humans fell under their power in two seconds flat, and no one asked the vampires for ID and the vampires did not dress as used car salesmen. So, Mo reasoned (Mo loved reason), as the person she had just met looked and behaved nothing like how a vampire should look or behave, he absolutely definitely couldn't be one.

And yet . . . And yet . . . While Mo told herself that what had just happened could not have happened, it had – happened, that is. It shouldn't have, but it had. Deep down inside, Mo sensed that she had met a vampire. It was unexpected, hard to believe and definitely not part of any plan – and this was a problem, because Mo loved plans.

The plan Mo loved, tended and nurtured the most was the one she had made for her life – The Plan. She was working towards a bright future completely of her own making. Getting there involved ignoring Tracey Caldwell when she called her a neek. ('That's a cross between a nerd and geek,' Lou had explained, with an apologetic smile.) It meant not listening to her dad, when he said she should work in his carpet business after GCSEs, or her mum, when she said Mo should never leave Lower Donny because 'it wasn't safe out there'. It meant keeping her head down, studying hard and showing the world how strong, smart and brilliant she was.

What it absolutely did not mean and had never meant was signing up for a future as Vampire Queen, a future offered up on a Tuesday evening in October by some allegedly undead creature of the night in a dodgy suit, who may or may not have jumped out of a hedge.

Mo shook her head, but still the words 'Chosen One' seemed tattooed on her brain. This is crazy, Mo thought. I spend my days trying not to be noticed, getting on with my life, sticking to The Plan, and then – BAM! I'm suddenly spotted, selected, *chosen*. Me! Mo Merrydrew. How weird is that?

Weird and also wrong, Mo quickly told herself. Yes, wrong. And unfair too. To get anywhere in life, you had to work hard. That's what she believed. That's what The Plan was about. You couldn't be picked out at random and launched into greatness. That wasn't how it worked. That wouldn't be right.

With that thought, Mo plonked her bike helmet firmly on her head and zipped up her high-visibility cycling gilet with slightly trembling fingers. Then she fixed her eyes on the lights of home, twinkling through the trees up ahead, and pedalled towards them, fast.

# 3

'Bill had me in stitches again today,' Mo's mum said.

She was standing by the oven, stirring a pot of pasta sauce. Her wavy brown hair was tied up in a loose ponytail and she was still wearing her pink uniform from the care home where she worked.

'He was telling me about how they used to steal apples from the orchard in Donny Under Oak Manor, when they were kids,' she said. 'The gardener would chase them with a rake, swearing. Bill did an impression, complete with all the colourful language. Mrs Kumari spat her false teeth out on her wordsearch. It was that level of colourful.'

Mo smiled weakly, as she set out the knives and forks for dinner.

'What's up?' her mum asked, coming over and stroking her arm.

'Nothing,' Mo said.

'Sure? You seem quiet. Problems at school? Friends?'

'School's fine,' Mo said, 'and I don't really have friends, plural – only Lou, and she's fine too.'

'OK, but remember you can tell me anything, you know,' Mum said.

'Thanks,' said Mo, thinking, Er, no, no, I can't, not today.

The front door banged and her dad came into the room, lobbed his keys into a bowl on the worktop and kissed Mo on the top of her head.

'What's for dinner? I'm famished,' he said, giving Mo's mum a kiss too. 'Tough day. Supply-chain issues again. We're low on underlay, which is a worry. I know I've said it before, but the world of carpets can be physically and emotionally demanding.'

'You have said it before,' Mo's mum said, winking at Mo.

'It is a great career though, Mo. You should seriously consider it. You get to travel, and it keeps you fit too. Look at these guns?' He flexed one arm proudly. 'You don't get that being a human rights lawyer.'

Mo rolled her eyes, noticing how unlike her parents she was – her mum, who was so confident and easy around people, her dad with his stocky build and physical strength. They sat down to eat and Mo's dad changed the subject.

'Did you hear Clive Bunsworth's gone missing?' he said.

'The Used Car King?' said Mum.

'Apparently he took some fella on a test drive to Upper Donny yesterday and he's not been seen since.'

'Are the police looking for him?' asked Mum.

'Yes, they're treating it as suspicious.'

Mo dropped her fork. It clanged against the plate.

'You OK, Mo?' he asked. 'You've gone awfully pale. Paler than usual. What's up?'

Mo could have said, 'I've just met a vampire who says I'm the Chosen One and has offered me immortality and unlimited power as Vampire Queen.'

She didn't though.

Instead she said, 'I'm not very hungry.'

She could have added, 'It now seems likely he's done something very unpleasant and possibly terminal to Clive Bunsworth.'

She didn't though.

Instead she said, 'I have a big science test to revise for.'

She could *also* have said, 'I have to decide whether to become a member of the undead community and run Great Britain as its leader.'

She didn't say that either.

Instead she said, 'I'm going to get started on my homework.'

'At least finish your meal first,' Mo's mum said. 'Come on, eat a bit more before you do your revision. That's if you really must revise. You're always working so hard. You need to relax too.'

'Mum's right,' said her dad. 'It's important to have balance in your life. Get a hobby, play some sport. You don't want to burn out.'

'You always say that, Dad,' Mo said, feeling her cheeks flush. 'You always go on about burnout.'

'I worry about you, that's all,' he said. 'We both do.'

'Well, thanks, but I can take care of myself,' Mo said, standing up and heading for the door.

Typical, she thought as she sprinted up the stairs, I have to decide whether to become a vampire – an absolutely colossal decision, by the way – and all my parents want to do is have the same old row about how much I study and the risk of burnout.

In her room, Mo closed the curtains quickly, without looking outside, and then settled down at her desk. She opened her biology textbook, but for once she couldn't focus. She wondered if she should contact the police about Clive Bunsworth, but then she imagined the call.

'Hello, officer, I believe the person you are looking for in relation to the disappearance of Mr Clive Bunsworth is a vampire . . . Yes, that's correct . . . Yes, his name is Bogdan . . . About five foot eight, grey hair, deep-set eyes . . . What do you mean, I'm "having a laugh"?'

Instead Mo tidied her stationery collection, colour-coordinating her pens, rearranging her stack of sticky notes (pink ones on top) and sharpening her many pencils. Still she felt jumpy. She began pacing her room, thinking about Bogdan's offer, of power and authority as Vampire Queen. Not as Vampire Princess, or Vampire Third in Line to the Throne, or Vampire Assistant to the CEO to the Vampire Queen. The actual queen. Top dog.

Ruler. Big boss. A woman in a position of power. That was good, right?

Then Mo's mind strayed towards the practicalities, but came up against a worrying number of blanks. What were the hours? Nights, presumably. Where would she live? Probably a castle, but maybe she could keep her bedroom here. It had only just been recarpeted, after all. Was there a dress code? She glanced down at her school uniform – dreary grey V-neck, maroon nylon tie, pleated skirt. Might be fun to wear something a little more, well, regal. Something more suitable for the Chosen One.

Chosen One. Those two words again, bouncing around her mind like a six-year-old on a sugar rush. Bogdan had seen something in her, some power, some force. Could he be right? Really? Mo got up and glanced in the mirror, not something she usually enjoyed doing. While Tracey Caldwell was drawn to mirrors like a dog to a dropped kebab, Mo preferred to avoid them. She told herself, 'It's who you are, not what you look like, that matters,' but deep down she wasn't crazy about her milk-pale complexion and raven-black hair – nothing like her mum's brown curls or her dad's thick salt-and-pepper locks.

'I'm being stupid. A mirror isn't going to help me – research is. Before making any big decisions, you do your homework first,' she said.

She dived back to her desk, flipped open her laptop and punched the word 'Vampire' into the search box.

Hundreds of images came up. Vampires with pale faces and spiky fangs, blood dripping from their lips. They all looked furious, like they had anger management issues and someone had just insulted their mother.

None of these vampires had the greying hair and wonky smile of Bogdan. Bogdan, who had gone to the trouble of coming all the way here, from the East, to find her. She couldn't just dismiss his offer based on a few cheesy images. She had to read more.

The facts came thick and fast. Vampires can be destroyed by beheading or driving a wooden stake through their heart.

'Yes, yes, we know,' she muttered. 'They also fear crucifixes and sunlight. Yup, know that too. Oh, hang on, it says here they have no reflection. I did *not* know that. Finally, something I can at least relate to.'

Mo carried on reading.

'There are many vampiric figures in world history, but the one common trait is that they are all sustained by a living being's life force,' she read aloud, feeling the hairs on the back of her neck rise.

Here it was, the one detail she had been avoiding. The one practicality she didn't want to stare down. No more Mini Battenbergs for her, if she agreed to be turned. A diet of human blood awaited.

Mo clicked back to the images and again saw the pale faces and piercing eyes. Some vampires were shown biting the necks of their victims, who lay there, swooning. She thought quickly of Clive Bunsworth, still missing. Is that what had happened to him, with Bogdan? She slammed the laptop shut and stood up quickly.

'I can't be a part of this world. It isn't me,' she said. 'It's violent. It's horrible. It's definitely not suitable for a vegetarian.'

She grabbed her oldest teddy, Mr Bakewell, and hugged him to her chest. Then she messaged Lou.

**Bus? Tomorrow? Need to talk. I have BIG news.**

Lou pinged back: **You've got a boyfriend?**

Mo replied: **No. I don't want a boyfriend, remember? A girlfriend?**

**Not that either. Bigger news than that.**

Lou pinged back: **OMG there is nothing bigger than those two things. TELL ME NOW!!**

Mo sent a 😊 and wrote **See you tomorrow**, then turned her phone to silent and climbed into bed.

# 4

The cold wind made Mo's hair whip up around her face, as if it were waving, while she waited at the bus stop. She hunched into her coat. She hadn't slept much. Vampires had floated through her dreams, chasing her down corridors that stretched out like elastic. One resembled her maths teacher, Mr Chen, wearing one of his hand-knitted cardigans. Another looked like a cute baby koala, but when Mo picked it up, it hissed and revealed enormous teeth made of plastic cutlery.

The bus pulled into the stop. Mo climbed on and breathed in the familiar smell of musty velour seats, overpowering body spray and the cheese-and-onion crisps that a kid called Emir always ate for breakfast. Tracey Caldwell was in her usual position on the back seat, from where she could survey the entire bus, like a Roman emperor at the Colosseum.

'Oh, here she is, the neek, the lanky pale kid,' Tracey shouted.

Head down, Mo hurried towards Lou and sat down next to her.

'So tell me your news then,' Lou said, manga eyes twinkling, but before Mo could even speak, she was interrupted.

'Did I give you permission to get on my bus?'

Tracey Caldwell had stalked her way down the aisle and was now looming over her. Mo tried to ignore her. This wasn't easy, because Tracey was pushing her index finger into Mo's pale cheek.

'Didn't you see the sign on the front of the bus? "No geeks. No freaks." Did you miss it? Great big sign in yellow letters.'

Mo stared at her lap and said nothing. Tracey Caldwell seemed to block out the light and suck up all the oxygen. She was tall and powerfully built – her party trick was to break an apple in two with her bare hands – and her abundant wavy brown hair cascaded over her shoulders like a chocolate waterfall.

She looked healthy and wholesome, like a country wench from a Victorian novel, brought up on unpasteurised milk and honest labour in the fields, but there was nothing healthy or wholesome about what came out of her mouth. Tracey was fluent mainly in the language of gossip, about her friends, and insults, aimed at those less Caldwellish than herself.

'You are ruining my journey to school, you know, Merrydrew,' Tracey said.

'Leave her alone,' said Lou.

'She can speak for herself, can't she?' snapped Tracey.

'She doesn't want to talk to you,' said Lou.

Mo tapped Lou's thigh, urging her to stop. It was sweet how loyally Lou defended her, but it was making things worse.

'Well, guess what, I don't want to talk to you, Lou Townsend. I want to talk to the Square, not the Spare.'

Tracey began picking up strands of Mo's black hair to examine it, like she was holding up a particularly grim exhibit in a murder trial.

'Go away, Tracey,' Mo said, then cringed. *Go away . . .* Was that the best she could do? Really?

'Trace, what are you wasting your time for?'

It was Jez Pocock, the most handsome, popular boy in the year and Tracey's sometimes-boyfriend, calling from the back seat.

'Get back here,' he shouted, frowning his trademark frown. Perhaps he thought it made him look manly and complex. Mo thought it made him look like he was struggling with the last line of an eye test.

'Remember to ask permission next time you want to get on my bus, Square,' Tracey said, sharply tousling Mo's hair, before loping back to her seat.

Mo smoothed her hair down.

'Got properly Caldwelled there,' Lou said.

'Anyway, it's really not her bus,' Mo muttered. 'It belongs to Terry of Terry's Coaches, so she's wildly inaccurate about . . .'

'Mo, shut up and tell me your news,' Lou said.

'I can't shut up *and* tell you my news,' said Mo, a smile creeping across her lips. 'Unless I use telepathy, to transfer *my* news to *your* brain without opening *my* mouth.'

'You know what I mean!' said Lou in a frustrated whine. 'Stop chuntering about who owns the bus, ignore stupid Tracey Caldwell and tell me your big news. Please!'

Mo took a deep breath. 'You're not going to believe this, but . . .' she said, 'I met a vampire yesterday.'

'What?' Lou said.

'Shh, keep your voice down!' Mo hissed.

'Sorry, wait, what?' Lou said, quieter now. 'Vampires don't exist.'

'That's what I thought, but then one appeared suddenly, in front of my bike.'

'Did he jump out of the hedge?' Lou asked.

'I don't know,' said Mo. 'Possibly. Anyway, that's not the point.'

'How did you know he was a vampire? Are you sure it wasn't just Danny Harrington, dressed up in a cape and pointy teeth, trying to frighten you?'

Mo glanced at Danny, sitting on the back seat with Tracey and Jez, pulling some chewing gum out of his hair. Danny, who had once eaten a whole roast chicken for a dare; who thought April was a sign of the Zodiac; who believed you could be allergic to skiing.

'No, this guy was much older, with grey hair. He's called Bogdan. He's from the East, which admittedly could mean East Donny, or it could mean Siberia, but I think more like Eastern Europe. He had a cool accent. And no cape.'

'Did he bite you?'

'No, we just talked.'

'What? Vampires don't stop people on dark lanes for a nice chat,' she said. 'They suck their blood. This was not a vampire, Mo.'

'I know it's hard to believe, Lou, but I'm telling you it was,' Mo went on. 'He said I was "chosen" to be Vampire Queen.'

'Vampire Queen?' Lou said, her eyes wide with disbelief.

'I know! Me! I'd take youngest female prime minister, but I don't know about Vampire Queen,' Mo said.

'But what is it? I mean, what would you have to do, as Vampire Queen?'

'Rule and, you know, be in charge,' Mo said. 'He talked about making a new vampire stronghold here. I'd be queen of it, and I'd have immense power, apparently.'

'Wow,' said Lou. 'That's a lot to think about, isn't it? A. Lot. And you'd have to be an actual vampire to do this, would you?'

'Yeah,' said Mo, frowning quickly. 'I guess so. He did mention something about one bite and I'd be transformed, but we didn't really get into details.'

Lou screwed up her tiny hamster nose. 'You'd have to drink blood,' she said, her voice small and hesitant.

'I guess,' said Mo. 'I mean, it's not like you hear of many vegan vampires, is it?' She laughed nervously.

The two of them fell silent for a few moments.

'Sorry, Mo, I can't get my head round this,' said Lou eventually. 'I didn't even know that vampires were real, and now you say they are and you're top of the list to lead them. It's unbelievable!'

'I know!' said Mo.

'This definitely wasn't in your plan for your life.'

'I know that too!' said Mo.

'How would our friendship go, if you were Vampire Queen?' Lou asked. 'You wouldn't bite me, would you?'

'No!' said Mo.

'Are you going to do it then?' Lou asked.

'I don't know. I don't think so, no. I'm confused,' Mo said.

'Uh-oh, that's not good. You're hardly *ever* confused,' Lou said.

'Exactly!' Mo said. 'It's weird. Everything's weird. Maybe I just need to find out a bit more about it all, before I decide. Bogdan really believes I'm the one to do it, you know? Not that I have to take on the role just because he says I'm chosen. That would be stupid.

Plus, he was looking for a king really, not a queen. The whole vampire thing seems very white male, you know?'

'When do you have to decide?' Lou asked.

'He's meeting me again tonight,' Mo said.

'Is it safe?' Lou asked. 'He didn't bite you yesterday, but he might today.'

'I hadn't thought of that,' said Mo, chewing her lip, thinking suddenly of Clive Bunsworth. 'He seemed sort of decent though. He bowed. Would someone who's not decent bow?'

'Not sure,' said Lou. 'Maybe. Was he scary though? Surely he was scary.'

'Scary? Who's scary?'

It was Tracey Caldwell again, standing next to Mo as the bus swung in through the school gates.

'Are you scared of me, Merrydrew?' she asked, looking satisfied by this idea.

Mo stood up and squeezed past her, dragging Lou with her, feeling Tracey's eyes burning into her back as she jumped off the bus.

'If you were Vampire Queen, you could shut Tracey Caldwell up,' Lou said, linking arms with Mo as they walked towards the entrance. 'That's tempting, isn't it? I'd pay money to see her face when you whipped out your fangs.'

'I was thinking that too,' said Mo, a tiny smile flickering at the corners of her mouth as she imagined actually *being* Vampire Queen. Yes, it would mean lording it over other vampires (so undemocratic) and being ruthless (undemocratic and morally wrong), but it also meant everyone in the land fearing you. Everyone! Even Tracey Caldwell. Who had singled her out for years now, picking on her, laughing at her . . . What might it feel like to be respected, feared even, by her? And not in the future, when Mo had worked her way to the top, but tomorrow, on the bus, on the way to school.

'It would be against everything I stand for though,' Mo said. '"When they go low, we go high" – that's what Michelle Obama does.'

'Yeah, but Michelle Obama hasn't been hassled by Tracey Caldwell day in, day out, has she? If she had, she might be more, "When they go low, we get our fangs out and scare them to Upper Donny and back."'

Mo laughed, and pictured herself shutting Tracey Caldwell up with one flash of her vampire smile.

'Oh my god, you *are* tempted!' Lou said, studying Mo's face, reading her mind.

'No, I'm not, not really,' said Mo. 'Obviously it's nice to be asked to do an important job, and Bogdan picked me specifically to be leader, a woman, not a man like he originally planned. So that's definitely progress . . .'

'But you'd have to be an actual vampire, Mo.'

'But I'd have to be an actual vampire, yes, and I don't want to be a vampire – of course I don't. And honestly, the whole vampire world sounds just like the actual, human patriarchy, but even more violent and with fangs. No, thank you. Plus, of course, it's not part of The Plan. It's a totally random, bonkers thing that just happened. I didn't ask for it and it doesn't fit. At all. I really don't think I can do this. I'm sure Bogdan will understand.'

# 5

Bogdan didn't understand.

'What do you mean, you don't want to be Vampire Queen?' he roared.

He had appeared in front of Mo, just like yesterday. She had caught the bus back to Lower Donny after studying in the library, was walking down the lane and, suddenly, there he was. Maybe he really had been hiding in the hedge. Mo still couldn't quite tell.

'This is very excited offer,' he said. 'You are Chosen One. Just you. It's not Chosen Three or Chosen Sixteen. It's one. You. Only you! In all of land.'

Mo bit her lip. She felt her belly tense with fear. Bogdan had been fairly pleasant yesterday. Today he was angry. He sighed hard, paced up the lane and then returned and glared at her.

'What is problem?'

'I'm not comfortable with all the blood eating. I'm a vegetarian,' Mo explained.

'You don't eat it, you drink it,' Bogdan said. 'And it's delicious. Like fine wine, only meatier.'

Mo shuddered and tried another tack.

'I don't like the idea of unelected power either,' she said. 'Shouldn't the actual vampires of Great Britain get a vote? It's not very democratic, is it?'

'What is this "democratic" you speak of?' Bogdan asked.

'Well, I might have been "chosen", but who by? Nobody voted for me,' said Mo.

'So?' said Bogdan.

'Plus you haven't explained the role to me at all. I don't really know what the queen would do?'

'I told you: create nice vampire stronghold over here,' Bogdan said. 'Make Great Britain centre of excited vampire times. You can do it how you like. I recommend being ruthless, plenty of violence, not so much chatting. Actions are speaking louder than words. But anyway, you are Chosen One, you do it your way.'

Mo shook her head, frowning. 'I'm sorry, but this is just not the sort of role I'm looking for,' she said. 'When I'm older I want a real job, in politics or a charity or as a lawyer. That's my plan, and I don't want to give up on it. I've never considered being able to rip someone's head off as a career ambition and if I'm going to reach a position of influence it'll be because I worked for it, not because some crusty vampire from the East in a suit belonging to Clive Bunsworth says I'm chosen.'

Bogdan was silent. Mo bit her lip again. Had she said too much? She was prone to speech-making when agitated. (She was president of the debating society, after all.)

'I am not crusty,' Bogdan muttered eventually. 'I have some little eczema. It's the damp October weather here. I don't know how you stand it.'

'I can get you some cream for that,' said Mo.

'Thank you, I would appreciate that,' said Bogdan. His shoulders sagged and he sighed, as if all his earlier anger had melted away, like ice cream by a bonfire.

'Now, where were we?' he said. 'Ah yes, you didn't expect to be the Chosen One, and you have a plan for your future. I understand, but, my dear Mo, life doesn't always go how we planned it.'

'Really?' said Mo.

'Of course,' said Bogdan. 'Do you think I wanted to be made a vampire?'

Mo shrugged.

'I was happy farming my tiny strip of land on shores of Black Sea, back in the 1380s. Yes, the land was rocky and poor. Yes, my parents, six brothers and five sisters had died of plague. OK, my treasured cow Ruxandra had been stolen by that wormy little thief Petru from the village over the mountain –' he broke off to spit on the ground – 'but on the whole, I was happy.'

'What happened?' Mo asked.

'I was turned! Suddenly. I had been dozing on the beach one evening, then I woke – *gah!*' Bogdan grabbed his throat, making Mo jump.

'A sharp scratch on my neck. I thought it was a mosquito – you know they can be bad at that time of year; it was August. But no! It was a vampire, feasting on my artery.'

'Gross,' Mo said, 'and wrong. That vampire should never have bitten you without your consent.'

'He drank much of my blood. I was powerless. Then he looked at me with his black eyes and told me I had two choices. Which I thought was nice of him. Everybody likes choices, right?'

'What were they?' Mo asked.

'One, he could drink the rest of my blood and I would die, or two, I could have some of his blood and become a vampire too,' said Bogdan. 'I felt it was – how you say? – a "non-brainer". So I drank of his blood and here I am.'

Bogdan spread his arms wide, grinning. 'Sure, it's not what I planned, but sometimes you have to go with the flow,' he said, chuckling. 'Pardon my tiny joke.'

Mo and Bogdan had been slowly walking down the lane as they talked, and now as they got close to Mo's house, her mum was clearly visible, drinking tea at the kitchen table.

'Your mother looks like nice lady,' said Bogdan in a low voice, sniffing the air once, twice, like an animal tracking prey. 'Vampires can scent humans from far away. She smells almost familiar.'

Mo felt a chill creep over her.

'Don't look at her,' she said. 'You won't touch her either. Ever!'

'Relax,' said Bogdan. 'No need for angry. She's safe.'

'Why should I trust you? You made Clive Bunsworth disappear,' said Mo. 'The police still haven't found him. Is he dead?'

Bogdan shrugged. 'He wasn't quite dead when I left him.'

Mo's eyes grew wide as dinner plates.

'Anyway, I don't eat women, usually. I don't care for the taste.'

Mo's mum glanced out of the window, towards where Mo and Bogdan stood. Had she spotted them?

'In the shed, now!' said Mo. 'I don't want her to see you.'

She walked quickly through the garden towards her dad's shed-slash-man-cave, which lay at the far end, partly hidden behind bushes. Inside, it was part practical space – saws and chisels and bits of wood, flowerpots, a wheelbarrow – and part den, with an old armchair, a lamp, boxes of vinyl records and books about bands from the 1960s.

Mo pulled open the door and went in. 'Quickly, come inside,' she said.

'You have to invite me in,' said Bogdan. 'A vampire cannot enter a home unless invited by the owner.'

'This isn't a home, it's a shed!' said Mo. 'Look – no plumbing!'

Bogdan fidgeted from one foot to the other, but wouldn't step through the open door. Mo sighed.

'All right then. Please come inside, Mr Bogdan.'

He grinned and hopped over the threshold, sinking into the armchair and sighing happily.

'I don't understand why I have to invite you in,' Mo said.

'It's just the rules,' Bogdan said.

'What rules? Whose rules?'

Bogdan batted Mo's questions away like they were midges and then sat forward in his chair, his expression suddenly focused and serious. Mo didn't like the way Bogdan flip-flopped between chatty, jokey, let-me-tell-you-about-vampire-life Bogdan, and staring eyes, you-are-the-Chosen-One, give-me-your-decision Bogdan. She wondered quickly if his hormones were out of balance, or his gut flora. Probably all that blood he ate. Pretty much the definition of an imbalanced diet. No wonder he was so moody.

'Mo, I can give you one more night to consider my offer,' he said. 'But only one. I must get Vampire Queen organised quick sharp. No time to lose. Tomorrow, Luca, my familiar, will be here with my luggage, but he will also bring news from Vampire King of East who, I fear, is getting impatient. I told him I would find suitable leader. Now he wants it all done and fixed up nice.' Bogdan rubbed his eyebrows and sat back in the armchair. He looked suddenly tired.

'Does he get impatient often? The Vampire King of the East,' Mo asked. 'What's he like?'

'He is most powerful vampire in all of Europe,' said Bogdan, shrugging.

'Was he elected?'

'Elected? Why are you always chatting about elected? No!' said Bogdan. 'He has power, because he is Chosen, like you. Well, sort of. He was actually chosen to be previous Vampire King's deputy.'

'He got promoted?' Mo asked.

'Not exactly. He killed the original Vampire King, soon after he was turned,' said Bogdan. 'Was a bit nasty. We vampires don't like to talk about it. You shouldn't kill the king, you know. We put it down to inexperience. He was new to job, a little confused and *boom!* He ripped previous king's head off. Anyway, never mind, he's great ruler. He won power with force, and he keeps it with more force, and big fat temper.'

'Scaring people isn't the right way to keep power,' Mo said. 'You do that through fairness, decency, balanced leadership. I've read enough political biographies to know that. You need to be able to communicate too. Good people skills are essential.'

'Well, his people skills are mainly to do with eating them, but yes, he's very good at that. He once ate four men in one evening. Four! Fully grown adults. Amazing achievement. He has enormous appetite, will drain anyone with pulse, you know?'

Mo gulped but pressed on. 'But is he honest and fair? Are you happy working with him, and with your employment contract?' she asked. 'Do you get days off, sick pay, a lunch break?'

'I don't usually eat lunch,' Bogdan muttered. 'But to answer your questions, Mo, there's no contract. It's simple. I do his bidding, this is all, and I try to keep him happy, or else . . .'

'Or else what?' Mo asked. 'Could he sack you?'

'You mean put me in a sack and drown me in well? No, we don't do that any more.'

'But you have employee rights, surely,' said Mo.

'Rights?' Bogdan gave a dismissive snort. 'There are no rights. Vampire King of East has all the rights – can do whatever he likes. Why you not understand? I thought you were brainy person. He is great mighty vampire lord. The end.'

'He sounds like a nasty macho old-school tyrant,' Mo said. 'You should have a woman running things. She would do it right. Wait, why are you smiling?'

Bogdan raised his eyebrows, nodded at Mo.

'Oh, I get it. I could be that woman, you mean? Running things as Vampire Queen.'

'Precisely,' Bogdan said. 'You, the Chosen One.'

'Chosen One, Chosen One, that's all you keep saying,' Mo snapped, her cheeks suddenly blazing chicken-tikka red. 'If I am the stupid, so-called Chosen One, why give me any choice? If it's got to be me, why haven't you just turned me into the Vampire Queen already?'

'Mo, stop this,' Bogdan said.

'No, I want to know,' Mo persisted, breathing fast. 'Why don't you just bite me, since I'm chosen and don't really have a say? Just get it over with. Go on, I dare you, do it. Bite me.'

'Enough!' Bogdan roared, leaping up and glaring at Mo. She stumbled backwards.

'I may be undead,' he said slowly, 'but I am not a monster.'

The two of them stood in silence, eyes locked, for one second, two, then Bogdan turned away.

'Look, Mo, this is my last job for King of East,' he said, his voice quieter now. 'I am old – over six hundred years. I am tired. I want to go to Caribbean to retire. Warm air, sea breezes . . .'

'The sun on your face,' Mo muttered sarcastically.

Bogdan ignored her. 'So please, think very carefully about my offer. It is good one, for me, and for you.'

He pushed the shed door open and walked out onto the grass.

'Aren't you going to do that evaporating thing?' Mo called after him. 'Like yesterday, when you sort of puffed away.'

'It's called materialising,' said Bogdan. 'It takes some effort though. I can't do it when I'm tired. I will walk instead. Fresh air is nice. Might pick up snack on way home. See you tomorrow, Mo.'

*6*

Mo didn't eat much dinner, couldn't study, didn't want to watch a documentary about the Nobel Prize on TV when her mum suggested it. She lay in bed, staring at the ceiling, replaying what had happened in the shed, how she had urged Bogdan to bite her. She winced for the millionth time. What was she thinking? She wasn't, that was the point. She was stressed, confused, agitated – all the things she hated to be – and she could have been attacked.

There was a knock at her door. Mo leaped like it was gun fire.

'Brought you a hot chocolate,' her mum said, coming into the room. 'What's up? You look like you've seen a ghost.'

If only, Mo thought. Ghosts sounded a doddle compared to vampires.

'Everything all right, love?'

'Yes, just thinking about something,' Mo said, taking the mug. 'Thanks, Mum.' Her mum sat on the bed and she sat down next to her. 'Well, trying to decide something really.'

Her mum said nothing, just smiled in a 'go on' way.

'OK,' said Mo, taking a deep breath, 'what would you do if someone wanted you to do something, which he said would be really great, and which he also said only you could do because you were so special, but you just weren't sure you wanted to?'

'Is someone pressuring you . . . ?'

Mo's mum took the hot chocolate, set it down on the desk and then knelt in front of her daughter.

'Mo, listen to me,' she said, clutching her daughter's hands urgently. 'No boy has the right to put pressure on you to do anything with your body that you're not completely comfortable with. You're not even sixteen yet.'

'God, Mum!' Mo shrieked, yanking her hands away. 'I'm not talking about *that*.'

'I mean it. There has to be consent, always, and you have to feel, deep inside, that it's what you want, that it's right for you, that there's trust.'

'Please, stop talking now,' Mo said, standing up.

'When I met your father, I just knew that –'

'Oh my god, Mum!' Mo yelled, slapping her hands over her ears. 'I am not talking about sex and please, please, don't talk about it either. Especially not with Dad!'

'All right,' her mum said, holding her hands up in submission. 'I just think it's important to look at these things.'

'Well, we've done that now,' said Mo quickly.

'Probably should have done it sooner,' Mo's mum went on. 'You're growing up so fast. Anyway, I hope that was helpful. It was good to chat, Mo. Love you.'

She went back downstairs and Mo slumped on her bed. Good to chat? Was it? Really? Horrifying, yes. Embarrassing, definitely. Good? Er . . . Not so much. Mo felt caught between wanting to laugh hysterically and the urge to curl up in a ball on the bedroom floor. At least all that 'don't do anything unless you feel it's what you want', icky, earnest, total cringe parent sex talk had been a distraction from the real problem – what to tell Bogdan.

Mo thought about his description of the Vampire King of the East. 'The Spoilt Brat Bully of the East, more like,' she muttered to herself. Violent, greedy, angry – that's what he was. Did she want to work alongside him? Really? Then she thought about Bogdan, sent to do his bidding. Not a monster, he had said, but he was pressuring her to take a huge step, one there was no going back from. Was that right? Was it fair? Was it, to quote her mum, what she wanted deep inside?

Mo sat up suddenly.

No, it's not what I want, she decided. I won't do this. I'll tell Bogdan and he will go away and the Vampire King won't ever come here and I can get back to The Plan for my life. That's it. That's what I'll do. Sorted. The end.

Mo imagined saying no to Bogdan next day, in her dad's shed-slash-man-cave. He would probably be sitting in the armchair again; he would probably be angry, leap up, shout at her. She would stand firm; she would not be guilt-tripped into changing her mind. He wouldn't bite her either; he had promised her that. It would be OK.

Then she remembered there might be a witness too. Bogdan's familiar, who was arriving soon. Hang on – what even was a familiar? Mo could only picture a black cat, like a witch might have. More of a pet really. How could a pet transport luggage? Could it drive a van? Or something smaller maybe – a golf buggy? Maybe a vampire pet could. Vampires did weird freaky stuff like materialising. They probably had pets that could drive golf buggies too, why not?

There was a knock again.

'Mum, I really don't want to talk any more, thanks . . .' Mo called out.

'It's me,' her dad said, putting his head round the door. 'Mum told me about your chat.'

He grinned.

'Shut up, Dad,' Mo muttered, throwing Mr Bakewell at him.

'Was it useful?' he asked, still beaming.

Mo sighed and pulled the duvet up over her face.

'I can tell it was. I can tell you got a lot out of it. That's great. You sleep tight now. Love you.'

'Love you too,' Mo murmured from underneath the covers.

Next morning, Mo ate her breakfast in calm silence. She had made her decision – no to being Vampire Queen – and it felt good. Making decisions always made her feel good.

'I'm going to the flooring conference today,' Dad said, picking up his car keys and kissing her on the top of her head. 'I know you're jealous, but try to get a grip on it. I'm delivering the keynote speech on the only three things that matter to carpet layers: underlay, underlay, underlay.'

'Cool, Dad,' said Mo.

'I'll be back tomorrow evening. Be good. Stay safe. Love you.'

Mo's mum walked with him to the front door. Mo heard them muttering to each other before hugging goodbye. When Mum came back to the kitchen, she was holding an envelope.

'This was on the doormat,' she said, passing it to Mo. 'Must have been delivered in the night. Handwritten. Very fancy.'

Mo took the envelope. Her name was written in a beautiful, swirling hand. She stroked her thumb over it. The ink was deep scarlet and so thick she could sense the shape of the letters against her skin. She pulled out the note inside.

*Mo, you must become Vampire Queen. If you do not, Vampire King of East will come here and make harm. Much harm. To me, definitely, but to you too.*

*Maybe also to people you love – your mother, your little friend Lou. As I explained, he is very powerful. He hates feeling disappointing. He extra plenty hates betrayal.*

*I didn't tell you this yesterday, because I hoped you would decide it was super-cool offer anyway. But instead, always so many questions from you . . . So I must speak plain. You must say yes. Much harm is coming otherwise.*

*Bogdan.*

Mo felt her knees become liquid. She felt her hand fly up to her mouth. She collapsed onto a chair, blinking hard, struggling to reread the letter.

'Mo, are you all right?' her mum asked.

Mo didn't answer. She ran to her bedroom and, with shaky hands, stuffed the letter deep inside her desk drawer and slammed it shut. Then she hugged her sides and tried to slow her breathing. Bogdan had said that Mum was safe. Safe! But now this. And how did Bogdan know Lou? Had he been watching them? Most importantly, what the heck did 'harm' mean?

Mo slumped down by the side of her bed, knees pressed up against her chest. Perhaps she should tell someone. Mr Chen? Her maths teacher and also her favourite teacher. Would he be able to help? He knew his way around a quadratic equation, but navigating the world of vampires . . . ? No, he wouldn't have a clue. Maybe her parents? They always said she could tell them anything, but would they believe her? Of course not. What about the police – maybe she should go to the police after all –

'Mo, you're going to miss the bus if you don't leave now,' Mum called up the stairs. 'What are you doing? It's not like you to be late.'

Mo grabbed her backpack, raced downstairs and sprinted out of the front door.

# 1

Bogdan's letter colonised Mo's mind all day, forcing everything else out. Mr Chen handed last week's maths test back. She had scored 98 per cent. She didn't notice. Her English essay was 'superlative'. She didn't care. Her science project on Marie Curie was 'in-depth and fascinating'. She felt nothing. How could she? She was paralysed by fear – of what the Vampire King would do if she didn't become queen, and what she'd do if she did.

In PE, Mo was picked to play defence in hockey, which meant guarding the goal as Tracey Caldwell thundered towards it like a rhino on steroids, her lips pulled back in a grimace, revealing her black gumshield. At least if I am Vampire Queen, I won't have to do PE any more, Mo thought, desperate for something, anything, positive to cling to, as Tracey raised her hockey stick like a medieval weapon and 'accidentally' slammed it into Mo's shins, sending her thumping face down into the mud.

By lunch, Mo could barely find the strength to walk to the end of the playing field, where she and Lou met each day to eat their sandwiches.

'Mo, you look terrible, what's happened?' Lou asked as Mo plodded sadly towards her.

Mo shook her head.

'It's that vampire, isn't it? Did he hurt you? Oh no, don't cry. Why are you crying? You never cry. You're a strong, independent woman, remember? What's happened?'

'Bogdan said that if I refuse to be Vampire Queen, there may be consequences,' Mo said, in a shaky child's voice that went up at the end of the sentence.

'What kind of consequences?' Lou asked.

'Bad ones,' Mo said, tears now streaming down her face. 'I had just made up my mind to say no, I was really certain, but now I think I should say yes.'

'But you'd have to be a real vampire,' Lou said.

'I know!' said Mo, more tears falling. 'I wish Bogdan had never shown up in my life. I wish I'd never been the Chosen One!'

She buried her face in Lou's coat, where she snuffled and snotted as Lou patted her back. Eventually she looked up and smiled weakly at her friend.

'Kind Lou. Loyal Lou. Friend for life, Lou,' Mo said.

'OK, you can stop stroking my face now,' said Lou. 'It's a bit weird. Look, maybe that Bog-off bloke is just putting a bit of pressure on so he gets his own way.

Maybe it's a bluff. You don't have to do anything you're not OK with.'

Mo nodded weakly.

'Now eat your sandwich. You need the energy. What kind is it?'

'I think it's cheese,' Mo said in a tiny voice.

'Good, cheese is good,' said Lou.

The two of them ate in silence, Lou with her arm around her friend, until the bell rang for lessons and they made their way to the French classroom. As the teacher explained the past imperfect tense, Mo thought about what Lou had said. Maybe Bogdan was trying to spook her into doing what he wanted. It was blackmail.

I can't let threats and nasty suggestions from a six-hundred-year-old vampire frighten me or distract me from The Plan, Mo told herself, feeling a tiny flicker of strength returning. Bogdan just wants to retire to the Caribbean. This is all about him. Besides, the Vampire King of the East couldn't be bothered to come to Britain in the first place, so there's no way he'll make the effort to come over to Lower Donny to hassle a schoolgirl and her family.

'It's going to be OK,' she told Lou after lessons. 'I'll say no and get on with The Plan. Worst-case scenario, if the Vampire King of the East does show up, I'll reason with him. I am president of the debating society after all. I'll persuade him I'm not actually the Chosen One, there's been a mistake, and offer to help him find an alternative.

I can get him set up on some dating apps or put an ad online. It'll be fine. I'll handle it, and then I'll get on with my life.'

'Sounds like a plan,' said Lou. 'And we all know how much you love plans. Can I help?'

'Thanks, Lou, but no – I have to do this alone,' Mo said, squeezing her friend's hand gratefully, then rushing for the bus.

She found a seat near the front and sank down into it. She was thinking about how she'd break the news to Bogdan, when a loud voice grabbed her attention.

'Oh, look – Merrydrew's here alone. The Square but no Spare.'

Tracey Caldwell.

'What are you doing on my bus at this time of day? Shouldn't you be at your after-school club for super-geeks? That must be where Townsend is, right? Maybe you've got to rush home to your mum. Or maybe you've got someone to see?'

Mo's head spun round. Did Tracey know something? Had she seen her with Bogdan?

'What do you mean?'

'Ooh, calm down,' said Tracey, her eyes flashing with glee. 'I was only joking, but maybe you *do* have a hot date. Go on, tell me, what's he like? Is he as minging as you, or more minging than you?'

Mo stared out of the window again, willing the driver to get moving.

'Trace, you coming?'

Jez Pocock had got on the bus. Danny Harrington was behind him. Someone had written 'BIN MUNCH' on his forehead. Jez nudged Tracey towards their usual seat at the back, and then nodded, ever so slightly, at Mo.

The bus rumbled to life and pulled out through the school gates. Mo sank deeper into her coat and stared out at the fields and hedges whipping by, wondering if Bogdan was already waiting for her, but when she turned onto her lane there was no sign of him. She walked fast, expecting him to materialise in front of her at any second, but he didn't show up. Odd. He was usually so reliable. Maybe it wasn't quite dark enough yet.

At home, Mo ran from room to room, closing all the curtains, relief washing over her like warm custard. When her mum got in from work, she rushed up to her and hugged her.

'Nice to see you, too, sweetie,' said her mum, looking surprised. 'You've cheered up since this morning.'

Over her shoulder, through the open front door, Mo could see it was now pitch-black outside. Bogdan could be out there, right now, waiting, watching. She slammed the door and locked it. She went back to the kitchen and started to make some tea, but then she made a sound, a peculiar yelping squeak, like a startled guinea pig, when she heard . . .

*DING DONG!*

The doorbell.

'I'll go,' said her mum.

'No!' shouted Mo.

'It's all right. It's probably just a package. Dad was waiting on a delivery. A new stain-resistant carpet sample, I think.'

'Don't invite whoever it is in,' Mo shouted urgently, and then reversed into the corner of the kitchen by the fridge, her hands clasped nervously together.

She could hear her mum talking to whoever was at the door, and a soft voice replying. It sounded masculine. Bogdan? Bogdan?!

Then the voices got closer. Mum *had* let him in! Why? What was she thinking?

Mo felt her whole body begin to shake. She heard her mum say, 'She's just in here,' and before Mo knew what she was doing she opened the fridge door and tried to hide behind it, her top half covered, her legs visible below.

'Well, she *was* just in here,' said her mum. 'Mo?'

Mo pushed the fridge door with one finger and stood perfectly still as it swung slowly shut and revealed her standing in the corner.

'There you are! This young man has come to visit you,' said her mum. 'I'll be in the living room if you need me, for anything at all. Just there, across the hall, OK? Help yourselves to biscuits.'

The 'young man' stepped forward, his hand outstretched. Mo looked at him for the first time, blinking hard. He was wearing jeans and a black top under a thick shirt in deep-grey check, and he carried a backpack. Then Mo looked at his face, took in the soft, dark hair with a slight wave, the olive skin, the bright white teeth and deep brown eyes that twinkled like sunlight on golden syrup.

'Hi,' the young man said, in a voice that almost purred. 'I'm Luca.'

## 8

Mo walked unsteadily out from her hiding spot and took Luca's offered hand. It felt warm, strong and huge, encasing her tiny, white hand like a bear hugging a chipmunk. She shook it – badly. Mo had seen on TV how real people shook hands – world leaders and movie stars and important businesswomen. They used a firm grip and a confident up-and-down motion, but Mo could only manage a limp wobble before snatching her hand back, convinced it must have felt like raw chicken to Luca, or a bag of cold gravy. She forced a smile, smoothed her hair and offered him a seat.

Then she said: 'What can I do for you?'

The words tumbled out and crashed onto the floor, like embarrassing ball bearings. Mo felt an internal cringe so powerful she thought she might shrivel up on the spot. Her cheeks burned like a radiator. Luca could probably melt marshmallows on the heat coming off them, Mo thought.

*What can I do for you?* Why did I say that? Why? What is *wrong* with me? I'm not working on the hosiery counter of a department store in the 1930s . . .

'I am Bogdan's familiar,' said Luca, laying out the words slowly, as if he was dealing cards. 'I have just arrived. I was transporting his luggage from our home in the East. It was a long journey.'

Mo gulped and nodded, barely able to concentrate. So a familiar was not a black cat, or any sort of pet, but a real human. An actual human with eyes so extremely dark and soft – the colour of a conker, or a sticky-toffee pudding, or expensive honey – that they made her blink like she had snorted pollen.

Mo, stop being so lame! she told herself. Just because I've never had a boy standing in my kitchen before, doesn't mean I need to fall apart. Strong, independent woman, remember?

Mo sat down, cupped her face in her hands and rested her elbows on the table, trying to look nonchalant while also hiding the fact that her cheeks were threatening to burst into flames.

'I think I was travelling for twelve hours in total today,' said Luca, smiling faintly, his gaze wandering towards the biscuits Mo's mum had left on the worktop.

Suddenly Mo understood.

'Oh, sorry, you must be starving, and thirsty. Let me get you something to eat, and a drink. Tea? Water? Squash?'

Luca grinned broadly. 'Thank you, that's kind,' he said.

Mo felt that cheek heat again. He said she was kind. That was nice. And very new. She had been told she was a neek and square by Tracey Caldwell, a lot, and she had been told by Bogdan that she could be majestic and invincible. Neither felt great, but being told she was kind . . . Wow, that made a nice change.

Mo pushed her chair back, making it grate noisily against the floor tiles, and lurched over to the worktop. She scattered some biscuits on a plate, her hands jittery. Did biscuits go on a plate? she wondered. Was that too uptight? Too old-fashioned? Never mind, they were on a plate now. She passed it to Luca, avoiding eye contact, and then mixed him a big glass of squash. Did vampires' familiars drink squash? Perhaps they drank vodka from bejewelled goblets, or manly flagons of beer. How was she to know? Someone should write a book on vampire-familiar etiquette. Maybe she would. But not now. She was too busy making squash.

By the time Mo set the glass down in front of Luca, he'd eaten three biscuits and was half way through a fourth.

'You were hungry,' she said.

'Sorry, yes,' said Luca, quickly brushing crumbs from his mouth.

'It's fine, have as many as you like,' said Mo, feeling a rush of tenderness towards him that made her blush some more. What is happening to me? Mo screamed silently at herself as she tried to arrange her face into a calm expression.

Luca finished his biscuit, gulped the squash back in one and then smiled at Mo again. She gasped, quietly, quickly. She couldn't help it. It was like she had lived in the dark her whole life and suddenly, right here in the kitchen, she had been picked out by a lighthouse beam that illuminated every cell of her body with dazzling brightness and Ready Brek warmth.

Then Luca spoke.

'I bring a message from Bogdan.'

Mo blinked hard, jolted by the return to reality. Those six words really killed the vibe.

'He says . . .'

'Yes?' said Mo.

'He is in the shed.'

'Oh,' said Mo. 'I thought I had to invite him into the shed.'

'It's only a shed, not a proper building. No plumbing.'

'That's what I told him!' said Mo. 'Did he say anything else?'

'Yes. He says, can you come and see him, please? In the shed.'

There it is, thought Mo. The summons. Time to tell him I'm not going to be Vampire Queen. He's not going to like it . . .

'Are you OK? You look pale suddenly,' said Luca.

Great! Either blushing or blanching, Mo thought. My cheeks are really letting me down right now.

'I'm totally fine,' she lied. 'Shall we go?'

Mo pulled on her coat and walked across the garden towards the shed, with Luca alongside. As they walked, she steeled herself. This had to be done. She would say no and then life could get back to normal. No point putting it off. She had to face Bogdan, stand up to him, get it over with.

Mo opened the shed door. Inside, Bogdan was asleep in the armchair, snoring faintly. The grubby grey suit and pink tie he had 'borrowed' from Clive Bunsworth, the Used Car King, were gone. He was now wearing a black woollen coat, dark trousers, tall boots, a white shirt and a rather bling gold waistcoat and cravat. Kind of Victorian gentleman meets circus ringmaster, Mo thought.

Luca cleared his throat softly and Bogdan opened one eye, then the other.

'Sir, Mo is here,' he said.

'I can see that,' Bogdan barked. 'I may be over six hundred years old, but I'm not blind.'

Luca bowed and stepped backwards.

'I have news from the Vampire King of the East,' Bogdan said, waving a letter. It was written in the same red ink as the note Mo had received from him earlier, but the handwriting was messier. 'He hopes I have already turned the future Vampire Ruler of this land and installed them on throne.'

Bogdan stared meaningfully at Mo for a few seconds. She looked at the floor and bit her lip.

'Hmm, yes, well. He *also* says he has big problems to deal with. His old enemies, the vampires of the Real East –' here Bogdan broke off to spit on the floor – 'are moving into his territory. This is not good. They need to be shown lesson, slapped in face. So he is raising a vampire army to push them back.'

'Which means he'll be busy, fighting for, what, ages, I guess?' Mo asked. 'No chance of coming over here then?'

'On the contrary, Mo,' Bogdan replied. 'He will squash vampires of Real East –' he spat again – 'like tiny weakling beetle under his boot, quick-sharp. Maybe take a week, maybe two. Vampires of the Real East –' and again – 'are not that scary. They could not arrange poetry reading in a library, you know? Isn't that right, Luca?'

Luca nodded and smiled.

'After that, he will come. He is eager to be here. He wants the Vampire Ruler in charge – all nice and sorted – and soon new vampire territory going strong. I must make this happen. No more shilly and shally from you, Mo. I need you to say yes now. So, off you go, say it . . . Say it . . .'

Mo's eyes locked with Bogdan's. She could hear her pulse in her ears. She parted her lips to speak, but then her hand closed around something in her pocket.

'Eczema cream?' she said.

Bogdan frowned sharply.

'I brought you some eczema cream,' said Mo, holding the tube out. Bogdan stared at it angrily, then took it and rubbed some cream into his hands.

'Thank you,' he said, stashing the tube in his waistcoat pocket. 'Now, where are we? Yes! All that remains to do is the thing many lives depend on – become the Vampire Queen of these lands. Come now, Mo, take the destiny that is before you. Grab it! Seize it!'

# 9

Bogdan had thrust his hand out dramatically as he spoke. His fingers curled slowly into a fist, which he held in the air just centimetres from Mo's nose. She stared at it for a few seconds and then cleared her throat.

'Sorry, Bogdan, but my destiny lies in another direction,' she said, in a quiet but calm voice. 'I can't accept your offer to be Vampire Queen.'

Bogdan snatched his fist away. His face contracted into a furious glare. He opened his mouth to roar at her, but instead, a gasp of pain exploded out and he doubled over, clutching his sides.

'Sir? Are you all right?' Luca said, rushing to his side.

'Was it me saying no? Or maybe the eczema cream?' Mo asked.

'It's my stomach,' Bogdan groaned. 'I think I had a dodgy human last night.'

'What does he mean?' Mo said.

'He drained someone who had eaten a lot of garlic, or had a cold, probably. It's made him sick,' Luca

explained quickly, easing Bogdan back into the chair.
'It happens.'

'Should I do something?' Mo asked.

'Get a bucket,' groaned Bogdan.

'What?'

'A bucket – I might be sick,' said Bogdan.

Mo covered her mouth with both hands.

'Grim, grim, grim. I cannot watch a vampire being
sick, no way, no. Too much!' she said, running for the
door.

'Please, Mo,' Luca called.

His voice was urgent. Mo froze. Bogdan was now
making a weird barking sound, like someone was doing
the Heimlich manoeuvre on a fox. She spotted a box of
old beach toys and pulled out her little red bucket and
spade set.

'This?'

Luca shook his head. 'We're going to need a bigger
bucket.'

'Oh, double grim, triple grim, grim to infinity,' Mo
said. 'Please don't spray vampire sick all over my dad's
shed.'

'Find something then,' Luca pleaded.

Mo spotted the wheelbarrow. She grabbed it and
pushed it up against Bogdan's knees, where he was
doubled over on the armchair. Then, without looking
back, she fled, racing through the garden and out into
the lane, her fingers wedged into her ears, her puffing

breath condensing into frosty clouds in front of her. She counted to twenty, then thirty, then all the way to two hundred . . .

'How long does it take for a vampire to throw up in a shed? And then how long does it take for his familiar to clean up after him?' she muttered to herself, pacing anxiously.

After about ten minutes, Mo tiptoed back across the garden and opened the shed door a crack. Inside, Bogdan was asleep in the armchair. The wheelbarrow had disappeared.

'Can I come in?' Mo asked.

'You don't have to ask – you're not a vampire already, are you?' said Luca, smiling.

Mo edged inside. Bogdan looked extra pale. Luca was spreading an old picnic rug over him and tucking it in gently around his shoulders.

'Will he be all right?'

'Yes, he just needs to rest,' said Luca. 'I'll move him back to our lodgings before dawn, once he's feeling better.'

'OK, that's good,' said Mo. 'I thought I'd killed him when I said I didn't want to be queen.'

'It takes a lot to kill a vampire,' said Luca.

'Stake or beheading, right?' said Mo. 'That sounds like the specials in a really bad restaurant. "Would you like the stake or the beheading?"'

Luca laughed. Mo almost jumped with shock. She smiled quickly at him, then smoothed her hair, suddenly aware that they were effectively alone together again. She spotted the letter from the Vampire King of the East on the floor and picked it up.

'Why don't vampires use mobile phones?' she asked, handing it to Luca. 'It would be way more efficient.'

'They can't work the touch screens,' he said. 'No electrical current in their fingers.'

'Right, of course,' said Mo. 'Do you have a phone though? Might be handy for keeping in touch with your family back home.'

Luca shook his head.

'Or you could set up an Insta account called TheRealFamiliar or ThisVampireLife or something? Bogdan probably wouldn't like that though. Would draw attention to the whole vampire thing,' Mo joked, and Luca laughed again.

'I'm sure my dad has an old phone in the house somewhere,' Mo offered. 'Do you want to come in and I'll find it?'

'That would be amazing, but I can't, sorry. I must go and unpack and get our lodgings prepared, while my master rests,' said Luca.

'Oh, of course, absolutely,' Mo said. She made for the door.

'But I can meet you tomorrow, after school, if you're free?' Luca said. Mo stopped in her tracks. 'I have a little time before he wakes up.'

'Really? I mean, sure, yes,' Mo said.

'Perfect,' Luca said.

'Perfect,' Mo replied. 'Although, could we meet in town? My mum has the day off work tomorrow, and if she sees you here again, she won't shut up about it. How about 3.30 p.m., by the clock tower in the market square in Middle Donny?'

'It's a date,' said Luca, smiling.

At the word date, Mo blushed. Was it? A date, that is. Or did he just mean, it's an arrangement, that we've both agreed on, like sensible people do when they're organising their lives . . . ?

Luca held the shed door open for Mo. She tried to make herself small as she squeezed past him, breathing in a waft of purest Luca, which contained delicious notes of toast and coconut.

Once out on the grass, Mo turned to face him. His full-beam smile was directed her way again. She wanted to hold his gaze, wave confidently or give him an ironic salute. Instead she blinked twice, nodded awkwardly and ran back to the house.

'There you are,' said Mum. 'Where's that guy?'

'Luca,' Mo said.

'Is he the one who's been pressuring you?'

'No, Mum!' Mo exclaimed. 'That's not him. And "that" isn't what you think, anyway.'

'Fine, OK,' her mum said. 'I have to ask, that's all. He said he was a friend, so I just wondered. So long as he's a nice guy, that's all I care about.'

'He's nice,' Mo said.

'He certainly looks nice,' Mum replied. 'What? Why are you rolling your eyes? I'm just saying.'

'Well, don't,' said Mo.

'How come you never mentioned him before, this new, secret, very handsome friend?'

'I hardly know him,' Mo replied.

'But you're hoping to get to know him?'

'Mum!' Mo said.

'All right, sorry. It's just all very mysterious. Good-looking strangers calling at the house. Makes me wonder what other secrets you've got going on.'

Wouldn't you like to know? Mo thought, but she said nothing.

# 10

Mo spent the next day in school feeling distracted and agitated. Or, as Lou put it, 'weird'.

'I'm not being weird,' Mo protested. 'I just didn't get to tell Bogdan last night that I don't want to be Vampire Queen. He got sick, so I couldn't.'

'OK,' said Lou. 'That sort of makes sense, but I'm sensing some extra weirdness on top, Mo.'

'Well, maybe you're sensing wrong,' said Mo. 'I'm a bit worried about telling him tonight, that's all.'

'But you keep checking your reflection in the classroom windows,' Lou pointed out, 'which you don't normally do, and you've got your tie a bit undone, in a sort of relaxed way that I've never seen before.'

'Really?' Mo said, her fingers fluttering over her tie knot briefly.

I can't tell Lou that the extra weirdness is because of Luca, Mo thought. Toast-scented, beautiful-eyed Luca. Or admit to her that I'm distracted because of a boy. Me! Losing focus over a boy! Arggh! I need to get a grip.

Lou wasn't the only one to notice Mo acting strangely.

'Mo, stop staring out of the window,' Mr Chen said during maths. 'Pay attention, please – this is not like you.'

He looked both cross and concerned. He also looked like he had bypassed the modern age, thanks to the sleeveless cardigan he was wearing. He had knitted it himself. It was a disturbing shade of pale brown, like something you might find in a baby's nappy. He had other hand-knits too, the colour of mould, curry stains and bruises.

Mo mumbled an apology, but her brain quickly drifted off equations and towards Luca again. That smile! Like liquid ... Mo couldn't complete the analogy. Liquid honey? Liquid Mini Battenbergs?

'Mo!' Mr Chen barked.

'Sorry,' she muttered again.

Then the bell rang, the bell that signalled freedom and – yes – Luca! Mo raced out of the classroom and towards the exit, but a hand on her arm stopped her.

'Hey, weren't we going to do science revision together in the library?'

It was Lou, her blue eyes burning with questions.

'Can't come, sorry,' Mo panted. 'Something important to do.'

'What?' Lou asked.

'Just, you know, something.'

'What is it? Why are you being all secretive? You usually tell me everything. Is it vampire stuff?'

Mo shrugged, shook her head, frowned, blushed a bit, muttered, 'Got to go,' and rushed off.

'It *is* vampire stuff,' Lou said, as she watched Mo disappear.

Mo's school was on the outskirts of Middle Donny. It only took five minutes to walk into the town, five minutes that Mo used to try out some facial expressions, ready for her meeting with Luca. She tried serious and businesslike, and then super positive and happy, but she settled on calm and assertive.

Calm and assertive dissolved into flustered and blushing (again – Damn you, cheeks!), when Luca tapped her on the shoulder. He had approached from the opposite direction. Mo had not expected this. She cursed this basic rookie error in the second it took to spin around and face . . .

Luca. In daylight. Mo tried to take him in. Had he improved overnight, like leftover curry? Again Mo told herself to get a grip, but how could she, when he was bathing her in his full-on, resistance-is-useless, mega-watt smile. It was as if a bomb made of caramel and bubbles and kittens had exploded all over her insides.

'Hi,' she squeaked.

'Hi,' said Luca, still beaming.

'I've got the phone. It's pay as you go, and there's still some credit on it. I've added my number into the contacts just, you know, in case . . .'

Stop gabbling, she told herself as she handed the phone to Luca. He took it, and she thought that would be it. He'd start noodling about on it and ringing his friends back home, maybe even his *girlfriend*, and she would slope off. But he didn't. He thanked her and slipped the phone into his pocket.

'I have some time now – before nightfall, when Bogdan wakes up – if you do.'

Mo blinked and nodded.

'Maybe we can go for a drink?'

'I'm too young for alcohol, sorry,' Mo spluttered. 'I'm fifteen and you can't get served here until you're eighteen anyway . . .'

Luca's smile got wider.

'Oh right, argghh, stupid me. You mean, like tea or something.'

'Tea or something, yes,' he said.

'Of course, yes, let's do that,' said Mo.

Mo guided Luca to what she understood was the best cafe in town, The Diner. She had never been, but lots of kids went there after school, or so she heard from Lou, who heard from her mum, who worked there as a waitress.

The Diner had booths with padded wraparound seats. Mo sat down, expecting Luca to sit opposite her, but instead he slid in beside her, putting her in full range of his delicious toast meets coconut aroma. She also detected a hint of cinnamon there today, which was positively intoxicating. Cinnamon was her favourite smell.

'Hiya, Mo – how are you, luvvie?'

Lou's mum was standing by the table, notepad and pencil in hand. She was squeezed into a red-and-white striped waitress uniform with a ruffled apron round her middle.

'Oh, hi, Mrs Townsend,' said Mo. 'Fine, thank you.'

'Now, what can I get you two?'

They ordered milkshakes, and when Lou's mum brought them to the table, Luca offered to pay.

'Oh, don't worry, you can have those on the house,' Lou's mum said, looking approvingly at Luca. 'Keep it quiet though, or all the other kids will want free shakes. Lovely to see you, Mo, and nice that you're taking a break from your studies too. Come round to the house soon. Lou's been stockpiling Mini Battenbergs for you.'

Mo took a long sip of her drink. The cool of the ice-creamy milkshake seemed to trickle through her body like an advert for indigestion medicine, soothing the intense warmth she felt when Luca was near her. I can do this, she told herself. I am a strong, independent woman, who can handle sitting next to a very attractive guy and not be immediately overwhelmed with complicated and unhelpful feelings.

'That's superb,' said Luca, after gulping some of his milkshake.

'Superb,' Mo repeated, softly, feeling complicated and unhelpful feelings surge through her yet again. No boy she knew had ever used that word before.

'Is it wrong?' Luca asked, anxious. 'My English isn't so good.'

'No, no, your English is perfect.'

'Is it? I hope so. I study hard.'

'I study hard too,' said Mo.

'I want to go to university, maybe become a doctor.'

'I want to go to university too, but I'm thinking international development or law, probably.'

'But I have no money, and the universities back home are expensive, so no university for me,' Luca said.

'Oh,' Mo said.

'It's OK though, because now I work for Bogdan,' said Luca.

'And he pays you, and you're saving up and you'll be able to go to university in a few years, right?' said Mo.

'He doesn't pay me much, no, just an allowance for food, but I am glad of the job. It's full time, regular hours. Admittedly, mostly nights, with some daylight errands, but I get to travel, see the world, and my parents don't have to support me any more. They're really proud that I have a job already, at sixteen, and I've left the village where I grew up, where Bogdan grew up, too, centuries ago obviously.'

Mo wanted to launch into a speech about how Luca shouldn't accept so little pay when he worked night shifts and was expected to clean up vampire vomit. She wanted to urge him not to give up on his dream of university. But she didn't. She took another sip of milkshake.

'I read that some familiars do the work because they want to be turned into vampires one day,' Mo said. 'Is that what you want?'

'Well, I can see why some think being a vampire is a good path,' he said, 'but for now I am just pleased to be working, that's all, and besides, Bogdan isn't so bad. He was a human once after all. He's not a monster.'

'That's what he said to me!' said Mo. Then she did an impression of Bogdan's drawling accent – 'I am not a monster' – and added in his trademark nonchalant shrug, which made Luca roar with laughter.

'You're funny,' he said.

'Am I?' said Mo.

'Yes. That was a brilliant impression of Bogdan,' he said. 'Did you know he started learning English in the 1500s, from Henry VIII?'

'How did he know Henry VIII?'

'He turned him,' said Luca.

'Wait, Henry VIII was a *vampire*?'

'Of course,' said Luca. 'How do you think he got through so many wives?'

Mo gasped. Now this was the kind of gossip she could get behind. Historical gossip. Tudor gossip. She felt her nerves ebb away.

'Tell me more. Who else in history was a vampire?' she asked.

'Who wasn't, more like?'

Mo's eyes lit up, but before she could ask another question, someone slunk onto the bench opposite.

'Who said you could come into my cafe?'

Tracey Caldwell. Her top lip curled as she looked across the table at Mo, but then she turned her gaze to Luca.

'Aren't you going to introduce me?' she asked.

Mo tensed her jaw but said nothing. No, she was not going to introduce Luca to Tracey stinking Caldwell. What, so Tracey Caldwell could claim ownership of him too? My bus, my café, my Luca.

Tracey was focused purely on Luca now, a coquettish smile creeping over her lips, one hand playing with her dark brown locks.

'I haven't seen you around before,' she said. 'Like your earring.'

She reached across the table towards Luca's left earlobe.

'It's actually a mole,' said Luca. 'I'm worried it might be infected. I wouldn't touch it if I were you.'

Tracey Caldwell pulled her hand back sharply. 'You're joking, right?' she said.

Luca gave the tiniest shrug and continued gazing calmly at her.

Tracey Caldwell laughed loudly and then looked around, to see if everyone else had heard the joke. 'You *are* joking,' she said, summoning her trademark Caldwellish authority.

Then she seemed to notice Mo again and her smile turned back to a sneer.

'Did I say you could look at me?'

'No, Tracey, you didn't,' Mo sighed.

Then Tracey Caldwell snapped her gaze back to Luca. 'Do you want to come and hang out? A bunch of us are going to the park in a bit.'

Luca shook his head and Tracey's mouth twitched slightly with irritation. People didn't generally say no to her.

'Why are you with her?' she snapped, flicking a dismissive hand towards Mo. 'Is she making you? Is she paying you or something?'

Luca smiled slowly at Tracey Caldwell but didn't reply. Instead he slowly lifted his left arm and stretched it along the top of the bench behind Mo. Then he dropped it gently onto her shoulder and left it there, as Tracey Caldwell's eyes grew bigger and bigger.

'Actually, she's my girlfriend,' said Luca, in his treacle-slow voice.

Mo froze. She stopped breathing. Tracey Caldwell's mouth dropped open, stunned, just for a second, then she laughed again, loud and urgently.

'You are really funny. Good one. Like it. You, dating Mo Merrydrew? That's hilarious. See you around, funny guy.'

She slid back along the bench and walked away.

Mo exhaled like a bike tyre with a bad puncture, but Luca continued to calmly watch Tracey Caldwell as she disappeared out of sight. And he didn't move his arm.

# *11*

After what seemed like hours but was probably seconds, Luca moved his arm and the two of them finished their milkshakes. Mo could still feel the sensation of Luca's warm hand on her shoulder as she drank and, not wanting to break the spell, didn't say a word to him about what had just happened. Eventually Luca pushed his empty glass away and stood up.

'Please excuse me, Mo,' he said. 'I must go now. It's almost dark. Bogdan will be waking. He will probably want to see you later, to speak about your decision.'

'Oh yes, that,' Mo said, grimacing.

'I'll be in touch,' Luca said, patting the phone in his pocket and smiling.

Mo smiled back and watched him leave, noticing how effortlessly he swung his backpack onto his broad shoulders, and how the light found the golden notes in his dark brown hair. Her smile still played around the corners of her mouth as she sat there for a bit longer, savouring everything that had just happened.

She had always imagined that the best moment of her life would be her university graduation ceremony, or seeing off two hundred candidates to become the first female head of some impressive but environmentally responsible global organisation. She had never imagined this – Luca saying she was his girlfriend, to Tracey Caldwell.

Maybe that was actually the best moment of my life, Mo thought. It's certainly a contender for best moment so far anyway. Which is wrong, isn't it? I'm a feminist – I don't need a man to validate me. But oh my god, Tracey's *face*! Ha! Caldwell got Caldwelled. She looked so shocked, and Luca looked so cool, and even if I'm not actually his girlfriend, what the absolute hell, it was amazing. Just totally off-the-chart brilliant.

Eventually Lou's mum came over to say The Diner was closing. Mo thanked her for the milkshakes and wandered around the town for a bit, in no rush to get home. The realisation that she would soon have to tell Bogdan about not being Vampire Queen kept bubbling up, but she shoved it down, preferring to picture Tracey Caldwell's shocked face again, over and over.

Mo was just climbing onto the bus when her phone pinged. It was Lou.

OMG. Mum says she saw you in diner with a super-hot boy. WHAT IS GOING ON????

All true, Mo messaged back, smiling.

SHUT YOUR MOUTH. Who?

Bogdan's familiar.

**Bogdan's familiar what?**

**His assistant. He's called Luca. Tracey Caldwell saw us and he totally Caldwelled Caldwell.**

**This is unbelievable! Is he really hot? 😊 😳**

Before Mo could answer, her phone began vibrating with an incoming call. A name popped up on the screen: Luca.

'Hey,' she said, trying to sound relaxed and summery.

'Hi, Mo,' said Luca. He did *not* sound relaxed or summery. 'I don't think Bogdan will want to meet tonight. He's too busy.'

'Busy?'

'He's got his appetite back.'

Luca sounded out of breath. Was he running?

'What do you mean?'

'He's out there now – feeding. I need to catch up with him, but he's moving fast. Are you at home?'

'No, I'm on the bus. Why?'

'Get home as fast as you can, Mo. Stay indoors. Please be careful.'

He hung up. Mo felt goosebumps prickle up her back and across her scalp. She peered into the darkness beyond the bus window, but could see nothing beyond her own face reflected in the glass – two frightened eyes dotted in a white oval.

Mo clutched her coat tighter around her. When the bus doors opened at the Lower Donny stop, she jumped off. The lights inside the Drowned Rat glowed and she could see a few people sitting at the bar. Everything else seemed quiet as usual. Maybe Luca was overreacting. Bogdan was probably miles away. Maybe he'd stopped 'feeding' by now too. Mo took a deep breath and began walking towards home.

She had reached the edge of the village and was approaching the turning to her lane when her phone rang again. She hoped it would be Luca. It wasn't. It was Lou.

'Hey,' said Mo.

Lou made a weird gulping noise.

'Lou? What is it?'

'Have you heard the news?' Lou gasped, and then her voice took on a pleading tone. 'I know I hated maths and joked about his stupid hand-knitted jumpers, but I didn't know this would happen, did I?'

'*What* would happen?'

'Mr Chen. He was found on the school playing fields, down the far end near the willow trees, where we eat our lunch.'

'What do you mean, found?'

'His body. Everyone's talking about it. They're saying he was murdered.'

Mo stopped walking. She felt herself swaying slightly. Her mouth went dry and there was a hissing sound in her ears.

'Mo? Are you there?'

'I need to get home,' Mo whispered. 'I'm sorry, Lou.'

'Why are you sorry?' Lou asked, but Mo hung up.

She dropped the phone into her coat pocket and blinked into the night. She wanted to run, as fast as her long legs would take her, but she also wanted to become small and silent and invisible. The result? She began a sort of hurried crouched tiptoeing – part running, part walking.

'I just need to get home, quickly, then I'll work out what to do and what to think and what to feel, once I'm safely inside,' she muttered in a breathy whisper to herself. 'I am a tiny bit scared right now, even though I don't usually get scared, but I'll make tonight the exception.'

Mo turned onto her lane and paused. There were no more street lights here, only a half-moon to light her way. The rain on the road's surface reflected its silver light. The hedges either side rose up like fat, strong arms, hugging the route. Mo peered into the distance and saw, with a rush of gratitude, that her mum must be safely at home. The lights were on. She moved towards them, trying not to make a sound.

She could see her breath forming clouds in front of her and tried to slow her breathing. She gripped the straps of her backpack. She willed herself forward, refused to think of Bogdan, out there somewhere, 'feeding', or of Mr Chen, lying dead under a tree. Occasionally, though, an image would flash before her eyes, his mustard knitwear glowing in the dusk, the rest a terrifying blur.

Then, up ahead, a figure. Not an imagined one, a real one. Mo stopped. It was a man. He was solidly built, like

Bogdan, and in the exact spot where she had met Bogdan twice before. Mo stared hard, peering through the night. The man was standing still. No, scrap that – now he was moving, walking fast towards her. Mo yelped. Her breath became an animal pant. Adrenaline surged through her veins – the fight-or-flight hormone. I choose flight, Mo's brain decided without hesitation! Flight, flight, flight! Flee! Run! Go! Now! Now!

At that exact moment, the figure flicked on a torch and shone it right into her face.

'That you, Mo?' it said. The voice had a soft Donny accent. 'It's Jez.'

Mo sagged with relief and watched, motionless, as Jez started running towards her, his torchlight bouncing on the rainy tarmac. He was soon standing right in front of her. Mo could hardly take in this latest surprise. Why was Jez in her lane? He lived in Upper Donny, three miles away.

'What are you doing here?' she stuttered.

Jez lifted the torch and shone it towards Mo's face again. She flinched from the light.

'Sorry, I was just passing,' he said, lowering the beam. 'And I wanted to check you were . . .'

Then the light shone in Mo's eyes again, just for a split second, only this time Jez had not pointed the torch. Instead, the beam had flicked over Mo's face as the torch flew upwards and landed with a crack on the road. Then the light went out.

Darkness. Silence.

'Jez? Where are you? What happened?' Mo whispered, blinking into the darkness, her eyes still dazzled from the torch light.

Then she heard movement, a muffled dragging sound. 'Who's there?'

No answer. Mo dropped onto all fours and began feeling for the torch, her throat so tight she knew she couldn't scream even if she wanted to. She patted the wet road frantically, and then, at last, her hand closed around it. She clicked on the light and flung the beam around. It danced across the road, across the grassy verge, towards the hedge where . . .

'Arrggh!' she screamed.

Jez Pocock was lying on the grass and, crouching over him, a dark form. Indistinct. A soft, animal grunting seemed to be coming from it. The beam wobbled in Mo's trembling hand and the black shape moved suddenly. A face spun round, eyes crazed and teeth shining like sharpened knives.

'Bogdan!' Mo gasped.

He didn't seem to recognise her, didn't seem to care that she was watching. He turned back to Jez. Mo could see that he had loosened Jez's collar and exposed his neck. So this was it. This was what Luca had called 'feeding'. This was how a vampire survived, by springing out on people in the dark and feasting on their blood by the roadside.

Mo suddenly felt hot anger pulse through her body. The flight instinct turned to fight. The image of Mr Chen under the willow tree leaped once more into her mind in vivid colour, and there, right in front of her, was Jez, about to become dessert. She took a huge breath and roared.

'Stop it, Bogdan!'

It came out louder than she expected, furious and sure, hardly her voice at all.

Still crouching over Jez, Bogdan spun to face her, hissing and baring his fangs like a cornered tiger. Mo had never seen him like this before, so full of rage and terrifying energy. Then he turned back to Jez. He was not going to stop, she could tell. He would not listen to reason. He was in full feeding mode and Mo could sense that coming between a hungry vampire and his human meal would be stupidly dangerous.

'I have to do something,' she muttered. Did she have any garlic in her backpack? A sharp stake? No, but she did have an enormous chemistry textbook. She found it, gripped it in both hands and raised it above Bogdan's head.

'You asked for this,' Mo said as she brought it down on the back of his head with as much force as she could manage, and then sprang backwards.

Bogdan swore in his native tongue – it sounded like 'Yanoz blad!' – and slumped across Jez's body. Would he squash him, suffocate him? How much do vampires weigh? Have I made things worse? Mo wondered. But then Bogdan stood up unsteadily, staggered a little and turned to look at Mo.

'Leave him alone, Bogdan,' she said. 'Or I'll hit you again.'

For a second Mo thought he might show his fangs again and attack her, but instead, like a sulky drunk after a pub brawl, he limped away and was gone.

Mo dropped the textbook and rushed over to Jez. She sank to her knees next to him, her thick black tights soaking up the cold rain. With fluttering, terrified fingers she felt his neck, expecting to touch the warm, liquid seep of blood, but there was nothing there. She had hit Bogdan just in time, but what to do now?

Jez was unconscious, lying on the cold, damp ground. Could she load him into the wheelbarrow and get him home that way? But where was the wheelbarrow after Bogdan threw up in it? And where was Bogdan? Had he gone for good, or was he nearby, waiting for a chance to finish his meal?

Then Mo noticed the faint sound of footsteps, running down the lane from the direction of the village. She fumbled for the torch and its beam picked out a figure, sprinting fast. Mo crouched small, terrified . . .

'Mo, it's me, are you OK?' a voice shouted.

It was Luca.

# *12*

Luca ran up to Mo and knelt down next to her. Mo said nothing; she was struggling not to cry. His face was transformed by worry as he looked at her.

'You're all right? He didn't hurt you?'

Mo shook her head.

'Thank goodness,' Luca said. 'Who is this?'

'It's Jez Pocock – he goes to my school. Bogdan was about to feed on him, but I hit him with my chemistry textbook,' Mo said in a shaky voice. 'Why isn't he moving?'

Luca felt around the back of Jez's head and pulled out fingers stained with blood.

'He must have hit his head. Did Bogdan come at him from behind? He usually does. It's his signature move.'

'I think so, it was dark, it all happened really fast . . .' She felt her shoulders begin to shake, her mouth begin to pull down at the corners . . .

'It's OK, Mo,' said Luca softly, resting his hand on her arm. 'Now, let's get him to your house.'

Mo stood up slowly, wobbling like a newborn foal. Luca heaved Jez up off the ground and tucked himself in under Jez's flopping arm. Mo supported Jez on the other side and together they dragged him down the lane and into the house.

'Lie him down in the sitting room,' Luca said, once they were through the front door. 'Good evening, Mrs Merrydrew.'

Mo's mum was standing in the middle of the room, talking on her phone, but she hung up with a hurried 'I'll call you back' and watched, mouth open like a tunnel, as Luca heaved Jez onto the sofa.

'What happened?' she said.

'Jez hit his head in the lane,' said Mo.

'How?'

'He fell,' said Mo. 'Backwards. He'll be OK.'

'It could have been worse,' Luca said under his breath.

Mo glanced at him and he shot her an apologetic smile. She smiled back, quickly. It wasn't funny, it really wasn't. A vampire, freshly arrived in her village with an unusual work proposition for her, had tried to kill Tracey Caldwell's sort-of boyfriend, and Mo had saved him. You really couldn't make this stuff up. What has happened to my life, Mo thought? Up until a few days ago, the most exciting thing was Mini Battenbergs and the chance to write up the geography field trip for the school magazine. Now this!

'Mo, go and get the first-aid kit from the bathroom,' said her mum, checking Jez over as he, blearily awake now, moaned softly on the sofa.

As Mo rummaged through the bathroom cabinet, she heard a car crunching over the gravel outside. The police? She peeped out. No. It was only her dad, back from his flooring conference. She watched him rush into the house, heard the front door slam and his voice, angry and agitated.

'What's going on? Is that Jez Pocock? What's happened to him? And who the hell are you?'

Mo ran back downstairs, and saw Luca smiling and holding out his hand to her dad.

'I'm Luca,' he said.

Mo's dad didn't shake Luca's hand; he just stared at him, taking him in with narrowed, suspicious eyes.

'*Dad!* Please,' Mo whispered.

'Actually, I should be going,' Luca said, pulling his hand back.

Mo followed him to the front door.

'Sorry about my dad,' Mo whispered. 'He's not usually that rude.'

'It's no problem,' said Luca. 'I'm sorry to leave so soon, but I have to find Bogdan and stop him.'

'Can you do that? Is it safe?' Mo asked.

'Just about. Vampires don't generally bite their familiars, although they can get a bit aggressive when they're in feeding mode, but it's OK. I've done this before. It's my job after all,' he replied.

'You can borrow my chemistry textbook if you like,' Mo said, smiling awkwardly.

Luca grinned back, his full-beam smile. It was like brandy to a buried-by-an-avalanche skier. 'See you soon,' he said, and ran off up the lane.

Mo watched him disappear into the darkness, then returned to the sitting room. Mum had patched up Jez's head and given him some painkillers. He looked dazed and a little embarrassed.

'Sorry, I don't really know how I got here,' he said.

'Good,' Mo blurted. 'I mean, that's OK. You tripped in the lane and fell backwards. So I brought you here to have a sit-down. Simple. Could have happened to anyone. Nothing to worry about.'

'Actually I think we should take Jez to A&E, get him checked out,' said Mo's mum.

Jez touched the back of his head tentatively and winced.

'Are you sure?' Mo asked. 'It's cold outside and maybe it's going to rain again. Perhaps you guys should just stay here, where it's nice and warm and safe.'

At the word 'safe', Mo's dad looked sharply at her.

'Mo, is there something you're not telling me?' he asked. 'There have been terrible things going on this evening. You've heard about Mr Chen, I'm guessing.'

'Yes, of course,' she shot back, hating to be reminded. 'But this was just an accident. Jez tripped, like I said.'

'But why was I in the lane?' Jez piped up.

'You said you were passing, and then you passed out,' said Mo, forcing a laugh.

'Which is why we definitely need to take him to A&E,' Mo's mum said firmly. 'Blacking out is serious. You could have concussion, Jez. Come on, let's get you up. You can call your parents from the car, let them know what's happened.'

Mo's mum and dad helped Jez across the gravel of the driveway and into the back of the car. Mo watched from the doorstep, chewing her lip and glancing around nervously. As soon as the car began to pull away, she ducked back inside, locked the front door and ran up to her room, where she crawled under her duvet, curled into the shape of a comma and plummeted into a deep, deep sleep.

# 13

Mo was woken by a tapping sound. Something was hitting her bedroom window. She struggled to work out what day it was – eventually landing on Saturday, yes, but it was early. Still dark.

Mo put on her dressing gown – pink, extremely fluffy, with pandas on it – and pulled back the curtain. An acorn bounced off the glass. She looked down at the lawn and saw Luca, just visible in the gloom. She smiled, broadly, instantly, and felt heat pulse through her. He beckoned her to come down.

'You could have texted me,' Mo said, trudging across the frosty lawn to where he waited, her pyjama trousers tucked into her wellies.

'Yes, but I've always wanted to wake up a young woman by throwing stones at her window. It's a classic move.'

'Bit old-fashioned, isn't it?' Mo said, a smile flickering at the edges of her mouth. 'And anyway, you threw acorns, not stones.'

'Even better,' said Luca. 'Who doesn't like acorns?'

He grinned and looked genuinely delighted – by the situation? The acorns? Where did he get his good humour from? Mo wondered. It was very early on a cold October morning. He worked for a homicidal vampire who kept him up all night, doing any number of deeply unpleasant jobs (the wheelbarrow!) and yet he was still in a great mood.

'Love your dressing gown,' said Luca. 'I hear all the best-dressed women in Paris are wearing panda dressing gowns this season.'

Mo knew she was being teased. She tried not to smile, but it was impossible. Wow, she thought, being teased by Tracey Caldwell never felt this good.

'Did you wake me up to tell me that?' Mo asked.

'Ah, no, I woke you up to say Bogdan wants to see you,' said Luca. 'Don't worry – he's stopped feeding.'

Mo felt the smile slide from her face, she felt anger clench her brow, as she remembered what Bogdan had done to Mr Chen – poor, kind Mr Chen. How could she even consider being part of this disgusting vampire world? Bogdan was ridiculous to ask her, ridiculous to imagine it was a 'cool-smart offer'.

Mo stomped off towards the shed, her fists clenched in her dressing-gown pockets, but Luca called her back.

'He's this way,' he said, leading her down the lane a little to a parked car. 'Hop in. I'll take you to him.'

'You can drive?' she asked.

'Bogdan got lessons for me, back home. A vampire friend of his runs a driving school, called Tasty Wheels. Its catchphrase is – "We Don't Suck – at Driving",' said Luca. 'Here, let me put the heating on for you, so you're not cold.'

'Where did you get a car from?'

Luca smiled awkwardly. 'Are you forgetting Clive Bunsworth, the Used Car King?' he said. 'Bogdan said he paid for it, before he, you know . . .'

Mo shivered and sank deeper into the passenger seat. She pulled her dressing gown around her, as Luca performed a perfectly smooth three-point turn and then drove out through Lower Donny, towards the main road. Mo felt lulled by the motion of the car and the warm air. She had been asleep for almost twelve hours and still felt woozy from it. Outside, the landscape seemed hushed. Motionless trees. Dense black hedges. Fields spread out like frosty blankets. Only a glimmer of silver in the east suggested morning was on its way.

'Where are we going?' Mo asked.

'To our lodgings,' Luca replied.

Mo pictured a deserted castle, high on a hill, black windows like knocked out teeth, but after a few minutes they pulled into the car park of the Premier Inn in North Nollerton.

'We like the Premier Inn – excellent value,' Luca explained. 'Free hot chocolate too!'

Luca breezed through reception, calling out 'Morning, Kimberly,' to the woman behind the check-in desk as he strode over to the lifts. Kimberly smiled back, then caught sight of Mo, hair unbrushed, pink dressing gown, wellies. A look of surprise followed by disdain twitched across her face.

They took the lift to the third floor and walked down the quiet corridor. Outside room 304, Luca paused and then knocked once.

Bogdan's unmistakable voice replied: 'Enter.'

Bogdan was lying on the bed, propped up against pillows. He was no longer wearing his thick overcoat and boots. Instead he was in a white towelling robe and quilted slippers. Wrapped around his neck was a brightly patterned scarf.

'Ah, Mo!' he said, when he saw her hanging back near the door, keeping her distance. 'Come in, come in. Also wearing very nice dressing gown, I see. So comfortable, aren't they? And what do you think of my scarf? Exquisite, no? Armenian silk.'

Mo wished she had got dressed quickly before she left the house. She didn't want to be bonding with a six-hundred-year-old vampire over leisurewear. After all, she could still picture, very clearly, that moment yesterday when he crouched over Jez Pocock, about to feed on him, that ferocious look on his face.

'I am sorry for draining your maths teacher,' Bogdan said.

'Mr Chen,' said Mo, shooting a venom-soaked look at him.

'Yes, yes. And also, I am sorry for attacking the boy.'

'Jez. His name is Jez, OK? A person. A human being. Jez. He banged his head badly when you pulled him down. He blacked out. My parents had to take him to hospital.'

Bogdan shrugged. 'Well, it could have been worse.'

'That's what I said,' Luca chipped in, smiling.

'Anyway, you hit me plenty hard on back of head so we're all even now, yes?' said Bogdan.

Mo folded her arms and glared at the floor. Bogdan pulled his dressing gown collar further up around his pale cheeks and set his jaw obstinately. Luca glanced between the two of them, like a parent trying to encourage siblings to make up after a fight.

'How could you?' Mo said eventually. 'How could you do what you did last night?'

'I have to feed,' said Bogdan. 'Besides, British people are so tasty. It must be all the potatoes you eat.'

Mo grimaced.

'Where is your humour sense, Mo?' Bogdan asked. 'Anyway, I was hungry, and I was also angry.'

'I believe you call that hangry?' Luca offered.

'I'm the one who should be angry,' Mo snapped back. 'Mr Chen was my favourite teacher. He didn't deserve to die.'

'Well, I was angry that you hadn't agreed to be Vampire Queen,' Bogdan replied. 'I was feeling frustrating, you know? I want to sort everything for Vampire King of East – keep him happy and then retire in warm-nice Caribbean.'

'Well, sorry for messing up your plans, but frankly, that's exactly what you've done to *my* plans,' Mo stormed. 'I mean, look! You think you can just march into my life and my village with a fixed idea about my "destiny", turn me into a vampire and then disappear off to some tropical island to laze about in a hammock all night long. Did you ever think that I might not want to be Vampire Queen? That I might at least have an opinion about it? Did you imagine I'd just do as you say, the second you show up? Why, because I'm young? Because I'm a woman?'

'No, none of those things,' Bogdan protested. 'You are the Chosen One, this is all, and I thought being Vampire Queen was cool-smart offer and you would want opportunity. Plainly simple. I know you have plans for your life, but I thought you could be flexible. I understand now – it's a big step.'

'Big step? Big step?'

Mo was shouting now. She'd never expressed herself so forcefully before, not even in the debating society, and she couldn't stop.

'You can say that again. I have my entire life planned out, do you realise? The A levels, the university course, the internships . . . Then you leap out of a hedge . . .'

'Materialised.'

'. . . and offer me a completely different plan, a completely different life, and not even a human one, but as a creature of the night who can rip people's heads off. Wow. Way to make a girl confused. It's a lot to take on board. A *lot*.'

Mo took a deep breath, but she wasn't finished.

'Then, while I'm trying to decide, trying to do what's right so I don't anger the Vampire King of the East and put you or my family or Lou at risk, you go on the rampage and eat half the village. Not doing yourself any favours there, are you? "I am not a monster," you said to me, but I saw how you looked when you were about to eat Jez. Totally wild. Like a horrible, freaky, starving animal who has maybe actually got rabies!'

'I was extra hungry after being ill,' Bogdan said. 'That was unusual for me. Normally I have strict diet and only drain one human every two days. It's how I stay so trim.'

He patted his belly.

'Perhaps you could apologise one more time, sir,' Luca whispered, nodding towards Mo, who was glaring at the floor again.

'Mo, I'm sorry you had to see that.'

'Sorry I had to see it? If I agree to be turned, I will have to *do* that. It's disgusting!' She turned away, arms folded tightly across her chest. 'I should go to the police, turn you in,' she muttered.

'Police are powerless against a vampire,' Bogdan said quietly. 'Silly little men in silly uniforms . . .'

'Excuse me, master,' Luca said, pointing out of the window, 'but it will be light very soon.'

Bogdan raised his hand in a stop sign. He fixed his eyes on Mo.

'So what is your final decision, Mo?' he asked, swinging his legs off the bed and standing up. 'Last chance to change your mind. Tell me now.'

'It's still no, obviously,' Mo fumed, spinning around to face him. 'No to being Vampire Queen, no to drinking human blood, no to killing maths teachers, no to looking like a wild animal. No to all of it.'

Bogdan rubbed his throat slowly. 'This is plenty risky, Mo. Remember, Vampire King of East is extra dangerous. He must not be crossed.'

'I don't care. I'll stand up to him,' Mo said. 'I refuse to be pushed around by stupid vampire bullies.'

'Master, the sun,' said Luca, looking nervously towards the golden-yellow rays that were filling the horizon. He pulled the curtains closed quickly.

'All right!' Bogdan snapped. 'All right.'

Bogdan walked towards Mo, who eyed him suspiciously, then he held out his hand. Slowly, cautiously, Mo extended hers, expecting a handshake, but instead he raised her fingers to his lips and kissed them.

'You would have made a spectacular queen,' he said quietly, 'but I must write to Vampire King of East and tell him you refuse. He will not be happy. I will try to keep him away. I will try to reason with him, to protect you, Mo, but I don't know if I can . . . I have failed, and Luca will now lose his job and his promotion, the job of his dream . . .' Bogdan bowed deeply. 'It has been great honour meeting you, Mo.'

Then he went into the bathroom and locked the door. Mo stared at it for a few seconds.

'He sleeps in the bath,' Luca said, appearing next to her, smiling awkwardly. 'He finds coffins a bit claustrophobic. Plus they're bulky to transport, you know?'

Mo said nothing.

'It works for him,' said Luca, shrugging.

Still Mo said nothing.

'Come on, let's get you home,' he said, opening the door for Mo. Mutely, she followed him into the corridor and out of the hotel.

# 14

They drove much of the journey home in silence, until Mo eventually turned to Luca.

'What did Bogdan mean, you'll lose your job *and* promotion?'

'Well, I can't work for him if he's terminated by the Vampire King of the East,' he said.

'What? He'll be *terminated*? Like, killed? But he's not even alive, is he?' Mo shrieked. 'Does that mean the same for me? What about my family or Lou? Bogdan said the Vampire King *might* cause them harm, and harm can mean a lot of things, but he didn't actually, specifically spell out, you know, deadness . . . Oh no, no, no, what have I done?'

'Breathe, Mo, breathe,' said Luca. 'You're panicking. Come on, slow your breathing down.'

Mo gripped the car door handle and slowly brought her breathing under control.

'That's better,' said Luca. 'Now listen, try not to worry. The Vampire King of the East may not come over for a long while. He may not come at all. He's still busy with the vampires of the Real East uprising. He may even pardon Bogdan. It will be OK. Anyway, you just stood up to Bogdan in there. You can stand up to the Vampire King of the East.'

'I'm a strong, independent woman,' Mo muttered, feeling hot tears prickle her eyes.

'Right, but I suspect you're strong in here,' Luca said, pointing at Mo's heart, 'and not just up here.' He pointed at her head.

Mo blinked hard, said nothing.

'But, of course, whether he terminates Bogdan or he lets him retire to the Caribbean, I'm out of a job.'

'And the promotion?' Mo asked. 'What promotion?'

'Ah yes,' Luca smiled faintly, still staring ahead at the road. 'Bogdan said that when you became Vampire Queen, he would retire and I would, well, I would be promoted to your familiar.'

'Working with me?'

'Working *for* you,' said Luca. 'Your faithful companion. We would have been together all the time. A familiar always sticks by their master, no matter what. You wouldn't get rid of me.'

He glanced at Mo.

'Don't look sad. Please. I can find another job somewhere. Maybe not serving a queen, but another vampire might take me on. I'm sure Bogdan will give me a good reference.'

The sun had peeped above the horizon now and the frosty grass on the fields sparkled. Mo tried to concentrate on how pretty it looked, tried to squash down the question howling inside her *What have I done?* She had lost Luca his job and he'd have to go home. His parents would be disappointed. He was disappointed and, Mo had to admit, she was too. Sure, she didn't love the idea of him 'serving' her – not very equal, not very fair – but being together all the time? Mo felt a pang, unusual and new to her, of longing and loss. He was going. It was over. Whatever 'it' had been, or might have been, or could have been . . .

The sound of tyres on gravel told Mo she was home. She opened the car door and stepped out, then bent down to peer in at Luca.

'Would you like some tea?' she asked.

'I should get going really,' he said.

'Squash? Biscuit?'

Luca shook his head and smiled softly at her. 'It's been really good to know you,' he said. 'Good luck with your life, Mo.'

She nodded faintly, but couldn't speak. She could only blink rapidly, shut the car door and wander back inside.

Mo spent the day feeling sapped of energy, unable to think straight. When Lou came over in the afternoon, she found Mo still in her bedroom, still in her bed, still wearing her pyjamas.

'Oh, Mo. Not up yet, pyjamas on, toast crumbs everywhere – you never normally eat in bed – school bag not even unpacked. Emergency, emergency!'

Silently Mo lifted up a corner of her duvet and Lou scooted in next to her.

'Your mum says you haven't spoken to her all day. She says she's never seen you so quiet. Are you upset about Mr Chen? I am. He wore terrible knitwear. Those cardigan-slash-tank-top things sucked. What did he call them?'

'Tardigans,' said Mo.

'And he smelt of soup, didn't he? But he didn't deserve to die. I can't believe it.'

Mo nodded silently.

'You should see it out there, Mo – police everywhere,' Lou went on. 'They reckon the same person is linked to Mr Chen's murder and Clive Bunsworth the Used Car King going missing. It's mad. Nothing ever happens in the Donnys, usually, but in the last couple of days you've met a vampire *and* there's been a murder and a disappearance.'

'You don't think they could be connected, do you?'

Lou's mouth dropped open. 'OMG, I had not thought of that,' she gasped. 'Your vampire – Bogspam, is it? You're saying he killed Mr Chen. Seriously now?'

'Yes, and it makes me feel terrible,' said Mo.

'Why? Did you tell him to do it?'

'No, of course not!' Mo shrieked. 'I don't know why he picked Mr Chen.'

'Maybe it was the smell of soup?' Lou suggested. Unfortunately she wasn't joking.

Lou reached into her bag and pulled out a box of Mini Battenbergs, took one and then passed the box to Mo. They chewed their cakes slowly, both lost in thought.

Mo decided not to tell Lou about Jez Pocock being attacked in the lane. It was too frightening, too *weird*. It didn't feel good, hiding stuff from Lou, keeping the truth from her, but Mo didn't want her to be more worried than she already was.

Once Lou had popped the last bite into her mouth, she rubbed her hands together briskly to brush off the sugar and said, 'Anyway, let's try to forget all that grim stuff, just for a moment. Let's focus on the positives here. You were in The Diner with a hot guy! Bogflan's familion.'

'Bogdan's familiar.'

'That's what I said. Anyway, that's unreal! Tell me everything. Tracey Caldwell is saying that *he*, the Hot Guy, said he was your boyfriend, which is just SOOO cool, I can hardly believe it. I wish I'd been there.'

'He's not my boyfriend,' said Mo. 'He was pretending.'

'Tracey Caldwell believed him,' said Lou. 'I'd be happy with that.'

'But it's not true,' said Mo.

'So what?' Lou shrugged. 'Tracey Caldwell thinks that you, the squarest person she knows, is dating a gorgeous guy. Enjoy it.'

'Well, it won't last. He's going away, back to the East,' said Mo.

'What? When?'

'Soon, I think. I finally said a definite no to being Vampire Queen this morning, and so he's leaving. That's that. The end. No more Chosen One stuff. No more Luca.'

Lou frowned so hard two deep vertical creases appeared above her nose, like train tracks.

'But don't you want to see him again? He sounds amazing. Good-looking and . . .'

'Kind,' said Mo.

'And capable of Caldwelling Caldwell. The guy is off the chart. Can't believe my mum got to see him and I didn't! I can't believe he's going away either.'

Mo sighed heavily. 'It's fine. Really it is.'

'Is it? I mean, yes, I'm super relieved you're not going to be a vampire,' Lou said. 'I can't lie. It did sound rank and I know it would have come between us, but then again, it is a massive shame that you can't go on seeing this boy.'

'It's just the way it is,' said Mo. 'The sooner I forget all about the last few days, the better.'

'If I was you –' Lou said.

'*Were* you,' Mo muttered.

'Shut your mouth. If I *was* you, I would never let him get away. Guys like this Luca don't come along very often in our world. Guys full stop don't come along very often. And he was into you.'

'Well, I don't know about that –'

'From what my mum said, I think he was,' said Lou firmly, 'and that has never, ever happened before. I know it wasn't in your life-story spreadsheet thing –'

'The Plan,' said Mo.

'Yeah, that, but then again, who cares?'

'Arrgghh,' Mo growled, scooting down under her duvet so only her nose and eyes were visible. 'Stop talking. Stop confusing me. I hate feeling confused, you know that. Look, I made my decision. I'm sticking to The Plan. Don't roll your eyes. Why would you do that? You think The Plan is boring, right?'

'Maybe a bit,' said Lou. 'You do all that work now, for stuff you're only going to get to enjoy in millions of years' time, and it does get in the way of us hanging out sometimes. It might even get in the way of you having a boyfriend.'

'But it's my life!' said Mo, sitting up sharply. 'Everything I do is for The Plan – all the study and work and putting up with being picked on by Tracey Caldwell and, yes, sometimes not being able to see you, or anyone in fact. It's all so I can get where I want to go in the future – THE PLAN! It's too important to let go of.'

'All right, calm yourself, jeez,' said Lou, holding her hands up. 'Got it. Good call. Great call. The best call. That must be why you're looking so happy today.'

'What? Lou, what are you doing?' Mo snapped, flushing. 'Why are you trying to make me doubt myself?'

'I'm not. Just saying . . .'

Mo slumped back down, pulling the duvet over her head this time, her outline barely visible beneath the covers. Lou eased the bedclothes back to reveal Mo's flushed, frowning face.

'What's that cross little face?'

'Don't, Lou.'

'Who's an upset little bunny now, eh?'

'Don't do your baby voice, Lou. I am not a baby.'

'No, you're a grumpy little fruit bat, aren't you? All fed up because some boy's come along and messed up your life plan and made you have all these *feelings*. Oh, you poor thing. That is so mean, isn't it?'

Mo grabbed her pillow and thumped Lou with it.

'Ouch, that really hurt!' Lou said, clutching her cheek.

'No, it didn't, and you deserved it,' said Mo.

Lou grinned. 'Anyway, you know what day it is?'

'Saturday.'

'Top marks, genius, but it's also Halloween. So get up and get dressed – we're going to a party.'

## 15

Lou had to drag Mo out of bed and shove her into the bathroom.

'Don't come out until you've had a shower,' she shouted through the door.

Mo reappeared ten minutes later, hair dripping and cheeks pink from the hot water.

'You look better,' Lou said. 'Right, the police made it very clear that people shouldn't go trick-or-treating, because of you know what, so loads of us from school are going to get together in the market square in Middle Donny, for a Halloween party. My mum said she'd give us a lift. We don't have to stay long, but it will be cool seeing everyone's costumes. Plus I thought it might take your mind off things. It'll be totally safe because there's going to be heaps of people there.'

*Totally safe.* Really? Mo glanced out of the window. It was a dull, murky afternoon, and it would be dark in an hour. Where was Bogdan? Just waking in the Premier Inn, ready to do what? He had not promised to leave, when she refused to be Vampire Queen, and she had not asked him to. What a stupid mistake! He had said he would write to the Vampire King, that was all. Which meant he was still around, maybe hungry again, and where better to grab a quick bite than at a large gathering of people – basically the vampire equivalent of a buffet.

'OK, I'm coming,' Mo said. I didn't protect Mr Chen from Bogdan, she thought, but I did protect Jez and tonight I might need to do the same again.

'Cool,' said Lou, a little surprised. 'I thought you'd give me some speech about not agreeing with parties or something.'

Mo shook her head.

'Great, well, I've got a few costumes for you to choose from,' Lou said, rummaging in her bag. 'Can you stop texting and look?'

'Sorry,' Mo mumbled, finishing off a hurried message to Luca, telling him about the market-square Halloween gathering and asking him to keep an eye on Bogdan. She signed off with a single, forlorn x.

'I'm going as a pumpkin. The costume Mum made for me two years ago still fits,' Lou said, holding up a plump orange outfit.

'Then, for you I thought maybe wear your mum's work uniform but accessorise with scars and blood – I've got make-up – kind of like a zombie murderer care-home assistant . . .' Lou said. 'OK, I can see by your face that isn't going to work.'

She looked in her bag again.

'Oooh, how about a ghost?' she said. 'It's dead simple, and quite plain – kind of like you.'

'You're funny,' Mo said.

'I know, I can't help it,' said Lou. 'Anyway, you'd just need to find a sheet and maybe –'

'Lou, you said you had actual costumes for me to choose from,' Mo interrupted. 'So far they rely on using stuff from my house.'

'Costume *ideas*, I meant,' Lou added, rummaging one last time. 'Wait, I do have this.'

She pulled out a long black furry tail and a hairband with two neat ears attached.

'Cat!' she said. 'Witch's black cat. Or just evil regular cat. Or just cat. You'd have to wear some black clothes, to complete the look, but . . .'

Mo put the ears on.

'Cute,' Lou said. 'Let me add some whiskers.'

She whipped out an eyeliner and drew on Mo's cheeks.

'Now close your eyes,' she said, and added a curvy, cat-like line on Mo's top lids.

'Oh wow, now you look like foxy cat, smokin' cat. Mee-ooowww!'

'Shut up, Lou,' Mo said. 'I'm not interested in how I look. I just want to be sure that the only vampires I meet tonight are six years old, wearing shiny capes and plastic fangs. Now get your pumpkin on and let's go.'

Mo sat quietly in the back of the car as Lou's mum drove them into town. When they passed the school, her stomach flipped. She glimpsed blue police tape flapping in the breeze, cordoning off the bottom of the playing field. Then, further into town, she saw police officers. Lots of them: on foot, driving, talking to people, talking into their walkie-talkies, talking to each other, looking serious.

'See, police everywhere,' Lou said, squeezing her fat pumpkin body out of the car. Mo followed, and then they both clapped their hands over their ears and looked up as a police helicopter thundered overhead. Mo watched its bright searchlight scanning the town below, then felt Lou tapping her arm excitedly.

'Check out all the costumes. So cool!'

Mo stared at the busy scene ahead, a dizzying mass of green-faced witches, black-eyed zombies, toilet-roll mummies, gurning clowns, snarling werewolves, evil fairies carrying axes and, well, just axes, so many axes, mainly sticking out of kids' heads.

'How can you tell who anyone is?' Mo asked Lou nervously, as they moved through the crowd.

'You can't, but that's the point,' Lou said. 'It's fancy dress. It's fun!'

It's really not, Mo thought. It's a weapons-grade nightmare. A disaster waiting to happen. How the hell am I going to spot Bogdan in this crowd of freaks? He'll fit right in.

'Oh gross, that kid has a zip fitted in his face,' Mo said, gripping Lou's arm.

'Awesome, isn't it?'

Some staff from the local supermarket, faces painted white and criss-crossed with fat scars, were shaking deep orange buckets filled with sweets. A police officer standing alongside had a plastic knife sticking out of his neck, and some small kids were trying to yank it out, laughing hysterically. The world's gone mad, Mo thought, clutching Lou's hand.

'Wow, your palm is so sweaty,' Lou said. 'Relax. It's all good. Let's go and get a drink.'

They made their way towards the food vans at the far side of the square, Mo's eyes darting everywhere, scanning every face that passed her. A girl with a snake spilling out of her belly. Frankenstein's monster, complete with neck bolts. A man in a shaggy mask – his face looked like it had sprouted grass. Mo winced. Two crows clacking their beaks, a trio of terrible nuns, a ghost, a life-size rabbit carrying a sword (*Why?* Mo found herself thinking) and a frankly terrifying scarecrow with red eyes.

'Impossible, impossible, impossible,' Mo muttered, glancing quickly from left to right, in front and behind, feeling her belly clench with tension. 'I will never spot Bogdan here.'

They queued up behind five hockey players, in school PE kit, who turned to reveal deathly white faces and terrible head wounds oozing blood.

'The Square!' one of them yelled. Mo focused in. Tracey Caldwell. Oh great. 'And you've brought the Spare with you, or fat ginge more like,' she said, pushing her hockey stick into Lou's squashy pumpkin outfit. The other hockey girls laughed.

'What have you come as? A ferret? Actually, I really don't know why you bothered dressing up. You look like a horror show every day of the year, not just Halloween.'

More laughter.

'Hey, look at me when I'm speaking to you,' Tracey Caldwell shouted, sternly now, shoving Mo a little with her hockey stick.

'Sorry, I'm . . .' Mo's eyes continued to scan the crowd anxiously. Bogdan could be here right now. He could be sidling up to his next victim, who could be asking an innocent question, like, 'Hey, what have you come as?' To which he'd reply, 'I'm a six-hundred-year-old vampire.' And the person – so clueless, so sweet – might say, 'But you haven't got any fangs.' Then Bogdan might raise his eyebrows, part his lips and . . .

'Who are you looking for Square? Your –' air quotes – 'boyfriend?' Tracey snarled.

Mo barely glanced at Tracey, before turning her attention back to the crowd. 'Sorry, I haven't got time for this,' she muttered, feeling anxiety pulsing through her veins like hot poison. Failing to stop a vampire attack while being told she looked like a ferret by Tracey

Caldwell was just about the worst thing that could happen this evening.

'You go when I say you can,' Tracey said, shoving Mo backwards with her stick, now gripped in two hands like a weapon.

'Don't, Tracey,' Mo mumbled, but Tracey just raised her eyebrows and pushed again, sending her tottering backwards until she crashed into someone, a body, standing firmly behind her . . .

Mo wheeled around and . . .

'Aaarggh!' she screamed, as a white face lunged at her, pointed fangs glistening. The figure raised its arms, a long black cape flowing down like a screen, almost enveloping her. Mo stared, terrified, her brain scrabbling to keep up, until she saw a smile stretching out from around the fangs, saw a look of glee in the eyes, and realised who it was.

'Danny Harrington, you . . .' She thumped his chest hard, pushing him backwards.

'Whoa, whoa!' Danny yelled, dropping his cape, giggling. 'I was only having a laugh. Keep your ears on.'

'It's not funny,' Mo said, trying to move past him, hearing Tracey snickering.

Danny raised his cape again, blocking her way. 'What's the matter, don't you like vampires?' he asked, leaning in until his face was very close to hers.

'Let me go, Danny,' Mo said, feeling her hands clenching.

'Don't you like creatures of the night, bloodsuckers, the undead . . .'

'Danny, I need to go,' Mo said, trying to duck past, but blocked each time by his sweeping cape.

'Vampires who feed on human blood, with their long, sharp fangs . . .' he went on, leering at Mo, leaning in . . .

And that was it. Mo slammed her hands into Danny's shoulders. She pushed him fiercely and sent him flying backwards. She saw the stupid grin skid from his face and heard a satisfying thud as he collided, hard, against the hot-dog van.

'Vampires don't wear capes,' she hissed at him, her eyes boring into his. Then she dropped her hands and spun away.

'Oh! My! God! What is she doing?' Tracey Caldwell screeched. 'She's totally lost it. Did you see that? I knew she wasn't right.'

The hockey girls were all staring at Mo, mouths open.

'I called it all along,' Tracey went on. 'I said to Jez, but he never believed me – she's out of her box. Stand back, everyone, Mo Merrydrew might be coming for you next!'

Danny Harrington tried to swagger forward if nothing had happened, rearranging his cape, smoothing his hair with shaking hands. Mo heard Tracey ask him what she'd said. Heard Danny reply. Heard them all cussing and gasping and yelling at her, that she was out of control, she had gone too far, she'd pay for this, but Mo was moving away fast, the crowd parting for her, with Lou following behind.

# 16

'Mo, what happened?' Lou panted, finally catching up with her.

'Nothing, I don't know, I just want to go,' Mo said, striding on.

'Are you OK? I've never seen you like that before. Did you mean to do that to Danny?'

'No, I just did it,' Mo said. 'I'm not sure what happened.' She stopped and looked back towards the food vans, her hands knotted together. 'Oh god, this is awful, I can't go attacking people in public. That's what I'm supposed to be stopping Bogdan from doing, and then I do it. What is wrong with me? Tracey's right, I've lost it. Maybe I should go back and apologise to Danny.'

'No, don't do that,' Lou said. 'He had it coming, although he totally didn't expect it.'

Mo didn't move, apart from her hands twisting nervously together.

'Anyway, it looked really cool,' Lou said. 'Did it feel cool?'

'What kind of a question is that?' Mo asked, setting off again through the crowds. Lou, weighed down with pumpkin padding, waddled after her.

'Actually, it did feel quite good,' Mo said. 'Kind of exciting. Not like me, but still me. I can't explain.'

Her phone rang in her pocket, making her jump. She snatched it and saw that it was Luca.

'I'm here, in the square,' he said.

Mo spun around, her black hair whipping out as she looked quickly to right and left.

'Where? I can't see you,' Mo said. 'What have you come as?'

'A vampire's familiar. Well, ex-vampire's familiar.'

Mo winced, though she could hear the smile in his voice.

'Look behind you,' he said, and Mo turned to see . . . A zombie surgeon. Some kind of ghost bride. Three bats eating candy floss and then . . .

'Luca,' she said, her eyes locking with his.

'That's Luca?' Lou whispered, standing very close to Mo, watching as he walked towards them. 'Wow!'

'Thanks for your text,' said Luca. He was standing in front of them now, smiling. 'Bogdan's not here. I threatened to rub raw garlic on his favourite silk scarf if he didn't promise to stay away, so it's safe here tonight.'

'Oh, thank god,' Mo said, sagging with relief. She pressed her fingers to her eyes and puffed out some deep breaths, then dropped her hands and blinked at Luca.

'Are you OK?' he asked.

'Yes, it was just stressful, wondering if he was in among all these people, waiting to pounce. But he's not, so phew! I can relax, can't I? He's definitely not here?'

'He's not here, I promise,' Luca said. 'In fact I'm taking him up to Scotland later tonight. I've booked him onto a mindfulness retreat. I think it will do him good.'

Mo laughed. 'Did he write to the Vampire King yet, to tell him about my decision?'

'Not yet,' Luca said, 'but he will have to let him know soon. We'll stay up north out of the way, in case the king decides to come over. I'm sure Bogdan can appease him. Anyway, I wanted to give you back your phone.'

He held it out to Mo, but she shook her head sharply. 'No, please keep it. In case you need anything.'

'Sure?' Luca asked.

'Sure,' said Mo. 'In fact, maybe you could message me when you arrive in Scotland, just so I know you got there OK?'

'I'll do that,' Luca said, nodding and smiling. 'Bogdan insists on driving, so it could be an interesting journey.'

He mimed someone swerving and shrugging at the same time, which made Mo laugh. Then she felt a tugging on her sleeve. 'Oh, sorry, this is Lou, my best friend.'

Luca held out his hand and Lou rested hers in his for a second.

'Close your mouth,' Mo whispered to her.

'It's my pleasure to meet you,' Luca said, in his slowest, softest voice. Lou wobbled a bit, like she was having an internal earthquake. 'Are you enjoying all this?' he said, waving his hand at the crowds of people.

'Yeah!' Lou blurted, 'and the best part is Mo just pinned Danny Harrington against a hot-dog van.'

'Lou!' Mo said.

'Sorry. It was brilliant. I couldn't *not* say, could I? *So* brilliant.'

Luca smiled at Mo, not his full beam, but a curious smile, one that would raise an eyebrow if it could.

'It wasn't funny,' Mo said.

'I didn't say it was,' Luca replied.

'Why are you staring at me then? Have I smudged my whiskers?' she said, rubbing her cheek.

'You have now,' Lou said.

'It's nothing,' Luca said. 'I should go. Goodbye, Mo.'

He held both hands out. Mo rested hers in his and he lifted them to his lips and softly kissed one, then the other, just as Bogdan had that morning. Only this time Mo didn't freeze. She melted.

'Bye,' she murmured.

Luca turned and left, quickly swallowed up in a crowd of Halloween monsters. Then Mo felt a sharp punch on her upper arm.

'Mo, shut up, shut up!' Lou gasped.

'I didn't say anything,' Mo replied, rubbing her arm. 'That hurt, by the way.'

'I mean, shut up. He's even better-looking than I thought he'd be, and he just kissed your hand. Hands!

He kissed your hands! I've never seen that before, not even on TV. So romantic.'

Mo shook her head faintly and walked away. A small child, dressed in black with horns and a forked tail, hopped up and down in front of her, poking his tongue out, but she hardly saw him.

'I just met Mo's boyfriend,' Lou said to her mum, when they got back in the car.

'Oh, the dishy chap from The Diner.'

'No one says "dishy" any more, Mum,' Lou said.

'You two going steady, Mo?' Lou's mum asked, glancing at her in the rear-view mirror.

'Mum, no one says "going steady" either,' Lou snorted.

'You know what I mean. Are you together, Mo?'

'No, we're not. In fact, he's going away,' said Mo.

'Oh, that's a shame,' said Lou's mum.

Mo didn't reply. She stared silently out at the darkness, unable to think clearly, aware only of the strange new sensations she'd just experienced – the feeling of strength that had surged through her when she flew at Danny Harrington, the delicate warmth of Luca's kiss on her hands, the softness and sorrow it churned in her.

Once home, she snuggled under a duvet on the sofa, her face just visible above her cocoon, staring blankly at the TV and hardly answering her mum's questions about the Halloween gathering. 'Was it safe?' 'Yes.' 'Were the police there?' 'Yes.' 'Did anything happen?' 'No.' 'Did you have fun?' Shrug.

When her phone pinged, she jumped.

It was Luca.

**We've made it to the M5!**

Had a girl ever received such a beautiful message before? Mo read it and reread it, like it was a love poem.

Later Luca texted to say they were on the M6. Mo gazed at this message for a full five minutes. The M6! They were on it!

Not long afterwards, Luca sent a photo of a service station with the caption:

**Just stopped here for a sandwich and a coffee.**

Mo felt like she had been filled with helium and was gently floating upwards towards the ceiling. (She didn't ask if Bogdan was having a snack too.)

Back in her room, Mo curled up in bed, cradling the phone in her hand like it was a newly hatched chick and smiling as more messages pinged in. Now they had passed Lancaster, now Carlisle, now they had crossed the border into Scotland. Eventually, at 2 a.m., when the message 'we've arrived' and a selfie of Luca, smiling his beautiful wide smile, dropped into her inbox, Mo pinged back a ☺, turned her phone to silent and fell asleep.

# 17

When Mo woke up, eight hours later, something felt different. She opened her eyes – and realised it was *her*. *She* felt different. Energy crackled in her limbs, purpose pumped through her veins. She felt as though she had a motor running inside her.

She held her hands in front of her face, the same hands that had pinned Danny Harrington to the side of a hot-dog van. The same hands that Luca had kissed, that she really, really wanted Luca to kiss again. Wow, it had been a big night for those hands, on top of a gigantic few days.

Bogdan had arrived less than a week ago, convinced that Mo was the Chosen One, and since then things had been happening. Bizarre things, terrible things, exciting things. Life had reared up in front of Mo like a magic flaming stallion, dazzling and terrifying and impossible to ignore. How could she turn her back on that? What, to scurry to her desk, to sit alone, study alone, plan only for some theoretical future? When there was a massive horse made of actual fire tossing its blazing mane and snorting out flames right in front of her. She sensed this beast could warm her, burn her, trample her, transport her to strange and thrilling new lands. Any of those things, all of those things, she wasn't sure, but suddenly she felt, with every cell of her body, that she wanted to find out.

The word 'destiny' popped into her mind. That word Bogdan loved to use. *Seize your destiny*, he had urged her in the shed just three days ago. Mo slowly curled her hand into a fist, just as he had, and gazed at it. Then she leaped out of bed and stood in front of her mirror. She stretched herself to her full height, straight and tall, her shoulders back and her chin up. Her long hair shone. Her dark eyes sparkled. Her pale skin glowed like a comet.

Maybe I really do have a little bit of Chosen One in me, she thought, admiring her reflection for the first time in her life. Something a tiny bit powerful . . .

She leaned in to the mirror, pressing her forehead against it and staring hard at her face, while her breath, which was coming quickly now, condensed on the glass. Then she slowly pulled away and stood perfectly still, her eyes sparkling, her hands balled into tight fists at her sides.

'That's it,' she said aloud. 'That's what I have to do. I know it now. I can feel it. I have to change my decision. I have to say yes to being Vampire Queen.'

Mo gazed at her reflection, letting the words sink in.

'Am I really going to do this?'

Her reflection raised its eyebrows and nodded.

'OK, I *am* really going to do this,' she said, feeling her hands begin to shake. '*But!* But, but, but – I'm going to do it *my way*.'

She turned away from the mirror and began pacing the room, her mind spinning like a wind turbine in a hurricane.

It has to be my way, and that means I will agree to become Vampire Queen, but *not* by being turned, she thought. I haven't changed my mind on that. I will not be a true vampire. It's too violent. So instead I'll find a way to fake the turning and then I'll go from there, rule from there, have Luca as my familiar from there, save Bogdan's 'life' and appease the Vampire King of the East and guarantee my family's safety from there . . .

She sat down quickly at her desk and grabbed paper and pen.

This can work, she thought. It can. I'll draw up a plan, just like The Plan, which – ha! – I don't have to give up on. I can do both. I'm a fast reader, I'm smart, this can totally work. Student by day, Vampire Queen by night.

Then she penned, in big letters:

*The Plan – Part Two: HAVING IT ALL!*

But her jittery fingers wouldn't write more and her racing heart wouldn't slow down. She leaped to her feet again, grabbed her phone and called Luca, rocking from her heels to her toes, over and over, as the ringtone chirped and chirped. She was about to give up when she heard: 'Hi, Mo?'

'Oh no, were you sleeping?' she said, noticing the furriness in his voice. 'Sorry, sorry. Of course you were – it's the middle of the morning.'

'Mmm, it's OK,' Luca purred dozily. 'Busy night last night. Bogdan's discovered Scottish dancing. We went to a Highland thing as soon as we got here.'

'A Highland thing?'

'Yeah, a type of dance,' said Luca.

'Oh, a Highland *fling*,' said Mo, and then giggled, picturing Bogdan in a kilt, bouncing around to the bagpipes.

'Do vampires like to dance, on the whole?'

'They *love* it,' said Luca. 'It's a little-known fact.'

'I can't decide if you're telling the truth or not.' Mo smiled into the phone.

'All true,' said Luca. 'Bogdan especially loves dancing. He spent most of the 1970s in New York. Total disco bunny.'

'No!' Mo giggled.

'Yes! Anyway, what can I do for you?'

Mo smiled again. What can I do for you? The phrase she had used the first time she had met Luca, in her kitchen. The phrase that had made her blush to her fingertips. Now, from him, it sounded so natural and kind.

'Well,' she said, taking a deep breath, 'I've changed my mind about becoming Vampire Queen.'

'What?' said Luca, sounding suddenly awake.

'I'll do it. It's not too late, is it?' Mo asked.

'No, no! It's not too late, but I mean, wow, are you –'

'Yes. I'm sure,' Mo said firmly. 'It's good. I'm fulfilling my destiny, right? And you'll get promoted.'

'To be your familiar!' Luca said. 'That's fantastic. It's brilliant. But wait – this is a big change in your plan for your life. You had it all mapped out. What happened?'

'Ummm,' Mo said. 'Hard to explain really, but it's sort of to do with Danny Harrington and that hot-dog van last night and my hands and looking in the mirror and, anyway, it's good and I've decided. It's what I want to do. It's best. Will you tell Bogdan, when he wakes up?'

'As *soon* as he wakes up,' said Luca. 'He'll be so happy. He'll probably want to rush straight back and do the turning immediately.'

'Like, tonight?'

'Maybe, or soon anyway. This is huge, Mo. Bogdan is going to be super, super excited about this!'

'What about you? Are you happy too?' Mo asked, crossing her fingers. Luca said nothing at first, but she could sense his full-beam smile. The warmth of it seemed to reach her through the phone.

'Yes, Mo, I am happy,' he said. 'Really, really happy.'

Mo nodded and closed her eyes.

'Good,' she said quietly. 'Me too.'

They said goodbye, and Mo leaned her head against the cold glass of the window and gazed out across the fields, holding the phone to her chest, breathing softly. Then she flopped on her bed and stared at the ceiling, feeling pleasantly calm and quiet after the energy rush of her decision.

Soon, though, reality showed up, like it always does, stamping all over her peaceful state like an overtired toddler who's been refused a biscuit. She had agreed to be Vampire Queen, but not as Bogdan or the Vampire King of the East intended. She was going to fake it. The question was, how?

Mo sat down at her desk. The first and maybe the biggest problem was the 'turning'. This would have to be a real Oscar-winner of a performance, but how did vampires actually turn a human into one of them? From what Bogdan had said, it was an 'I'll drink your blood, you drink mine' kind of deal. Well, not this time, she thought. There is no way I'm drinking liquid Bogdan, and definitely no way he's getting anywhere near my throat with his hideous pointy fangs.

'I'll tell him we're doing it on my terms. I'll find a way to stage it,' she said, and scribbled a few notes. Then her mind skipped to other problems. What would she wear, as Vampire Queen? Would Bogdan supply the wardrobe? What about fangs? She had to have fangs. Even if fangs only appeared when vampires were feeding – and Mo had no intention of doing that – she felt sure she'd have to flash a bit of fang sometimes, for dramatic effect.

Mo sketched some fangs and wrote more notes – papier-mâché? some kind of dentures? – as another, even bigger thought occurred to her. This decision to fake being Vampire Queen *had* to be a secret. No one could know what she had done. No one. If Bogdan found out, he'd be furious. If the Vampire King of the East found out he might cause all the 'harm' she was trying so hard to prevent. If her parents found out, they'd be distraught that their sensible daughter was taking such un-sensible risks. If Lou found out, she would be in on the mother of all secrets. That was a big responsibility, and Mo didn't want her best friend burdened with that. Plus if Lou accidentally let it slip, and other people knew . . . No, it was too risky. She couldn't tell her. And what about Luca? How would he feel if he knew Mo wasn't a real vampire? She wasn't sure. Perhaps he'd feel betrayed, tricked into serving a faker. He might admire her bravery, but then again, he might despise her willingness to live a lie.

The doorbell rang and a dog barked, shattering Mo's thoughts like a heel through a frozen puddle. Lou was outside with Nipper. Mo dressed hurriedly and ran down to see her.

'Fancy a walk?' she asked.

Mo nodded, pulled on her coat and they set off over the fields towards Middle Donny. Nipper rushed ahead and Mo chased after him, racing across the grass and gulping down the cold air.

'You've got that excited buzz you get when you're about to finish a difficult crossword,' Lou said when she caught up with them. 'What's going on?'

'Guess,' said Mo.

'*Are* you about to solve a difficult crossword?' Lou asked.

'No,' said Mo.

'Did you find that protractor you lost?'

'No.'

'Did your dad carpet your room again?'

'No. Well, not this week anyway.'

'Did the prime minister reply to your letter?'

'No.'

'Did President Obama reply to your letter?'

'No.'

'Did David Attenborough reply to your letter?'

'*Sir* David Attenborough,' said Mo. 'And no.'

'Did the *Middle Donny Examiner* publish your letter?' Lou asked. 'The one about fitting solar panels to sheep?'

'No,' said Mo.

'What then?' Lou asked. 'Oh, I know, and it's classic Mo. You're feeling happy because Luca is going away and you can get back to your plan for your life. You actually think it's totally all right that a massively cute guy who was definitely into you has gone away for ever, so you can concentrate on studying.'

'Actually, you're wrong,' Mo said. 'Luca is coming back.'

'But he was going away, last night,' Lou said. 'What's changed?'

'Things, details, don't worry about it,' said Mo.

'What details? What are you on about?'

'Never mind, it just means he's going to be around again.'

'That's amazing! And are you, you know, actually together?' Lou asked.

'Don't be daft, of course not,' said Mo. 'But we will be spending time together.'

'Mo, this is wild. I am totally jealous, I've got to say, but I'm happy for you, honestly. You'll get to look at him, like, a lot. I love looking at him.'

Lou drifted into a tiny Luca reverie for a few seconds, but then refocused. 'What about Tracey Caldwell?' she said, grinning. 'Oh, brilliant! She is going to be totally destroyed. And probably really confused, like, "How come Mo got the hot guy?"'

'Speaking of Tracey, look. There she is,' said Mo.

They had wandered as far as the playing fields on the outskirts of Middle Donny. A hockey match was underway. Tracey Caldwell was playing. She was Team Donny's captain and star – fast, aggressive, always on the attack. In hockey as she was in life.

Mo watched as Tracey thundered out in front, raised her stick and smashed the ball past the goalie and into the net. Her team roared and hugged her, and then the final whistle blew.

As the players walked back to the clubhouse, Tracey spotted Mo standing on the sidelines. She did a circling motion with her finger next to her head, then pointed at her.

'She thinks you've lost it,' said Lou, 'because you attacked Danny last night.'

'Yeah, I got that,' Mo said, but she didn't care. She was looking at Tracey's gumshield, a frightening black blank where her teeth should be. It gave her an idea.

'Let's follow them,' she said.

# *18*

Inside the clubhouse, Mo marched towards the changing rooms.

'I'm going inside,' she said to Lou. 'Give me two minutes and then let Nipper in. Got it?'

'Why? Wait! What are you doing? Mo!'

Mo stuck her head around the changing-room door and called out: 'Hi, everyone, I was wondering if I could interview the captain for the Middle Donny school newspaper?'

Tracey Caldwell appeared from the shadowy far end of the changing rooms, still holding her hockey stick.

'The Square?' she said, horror and surprise dancing across her face. 'You want to talk to me? What if I don't want to talk to you? I *never* want to talk to you. Especially not after last night, when you attacked one of my friends.'

'It's for the school newspaper,' said Mo, looking straight into Tracey Caldwell's eyes. Admittedly only for a few seconds, but it made Tracey raise her eyebrows just a pinch.

'Fine,' Tracey snarled, then she walked back to her bench. She sat down heavily, took her shin pads out of her long socks and laid them next to her gumshield. Mo clocked it with one glance and sat next to it.

'Don't get comfy,' said Tracey. Mo sprang back up.

'I'm writing the match report,' she said, holding her phone near Tracey's mouth to record her words. 'Can you tell me how you feel about winning?'

Tracey Caldwell stared as if Mo had asked her to reply in Swedish.

'We didn't win,' she said. 'We lost six–four.'

'Oh dear,' said Mo, 'that must be disappointing. Are you disappointed? How do you feel?'

'What is this, a therapy session?' Tracey snarled. 'I'll tell you how I feel: I feel pretty upset that you, the Square – and also now officially a dangerous freak – are in my personal space. Did I give you permission to come into my changing rooms?'

'Well, you kind of did actually,' said Mo, noting mentally that she had – wait a second – just talked back to Tracey Caldwell. And it felt pretty good. Pretty good until she clocked Tracey's glare, which looked deep, dark and dripping with threat.

Mo edged away from her. Where was Nipper? Lou was supposed to send him in now. Come on, come on . . .

She asked another question. 'What is it that you like about hockey? It's quite a rough game – I wonder if you ever get scared.'

Tracey grabbed Mo's phone and held it close to her mouth.

'I. Never. Get. Scared,' she breathed into it, staring at Mo, who was really not enjoying this much eye contact with Tracey Caldwell.

At that moment someone shouted, 'Who let that dog in?' and Mo spotted Nipper darting through the changing rooms, nose-diving into kitbags in search of food, his fuzzy white body scattering the hockey players, who shrieked and laughed and chased around after him.

'Is that your dog, Square?' Tracey said, as Nipper ran towards them. 'He better not touch my stuff.'

Too late. Nipper located Tracey Caldwell's bag, lying at her feet, sniffed it and – bullseye! – peed right on it. A direct hit. Mo could have scooped him up into her arms and kissed him, but instead, while Tracey waved her hockey stick at Nipper like an angry cavewoman, Mo snatched the gumshield and ran out of the changing rooms.

'Nipper's out of control. He peed on Tracey Caldwell's bag,' Mo said to Lou, who was waiting anxiously outside. 'She's not happy. Good luck!'

'Where are you going?' Lou shrieked, but Mo had already left.

Back at home, Mo found some white paint in her dad's shed and, after washing Tracey Caldwell's gumshield under the hot tap for a really long time while pulling a 'yuck' face, she began carefully painting teeth onto it, including two huge, pointy fangs. She set the gumshield down on her desk to dry and stared at it. It grinned back. Could this work?

Mo's phone pinged to life with a stream of messages.

**OMG Mo. Where did you go?**

Lou.

**And since when do you actually speak to Tracey Caldwell?**

**It was bonkers in that changing room. Caldwell tried to Caldwell Nipper, but he nicked her shin pad and ran off with it. I couldn't catch him. Dog training obvs not working.**

Mo sent Lou a ❤ but didn't explain herself. No time. The fangs were dry. She tiptoed over to the mirror and slipped them into her mouth. The weirdness of wearing Tracey Caldwell's gumshield evaporated once Mo stretched her lips into a broad grin. Instead of her usual small, neat teeth, a blaze of white gnashers appeared, complete with vampire fangs, reaching down like stalactites.

Not bad, she thought, pretty convincing, but were they good enough? Would they fool Bogdan? He'd been a vampire for over six hundred years. He'd seen a lot of undead bloodsuckers in his time. Could Mo-plus-gumshield pass for one?

Mo closed her mouth and then grinned to reveal the fangs again, adding a little hiss this time. She did it a few more times, making her eyes blaze. She practised taking the gumshield out, looking normal, and then popping it in quickly to show – *ta da!* Vampire fangs. Out with the gumshield – normal face. In – creature of the night! Out with the gumshield – normal face. In – be afraid, humans! Out – normal Mo. In – majestic and very scary queen!

'I am your queen,' Mo said, trying to look fearless, only it sounded more like 'I mam yorth qweem'. Mo took the gumshield out. Note to self: never speak with fangs in! she thought, then hid them in her desk drawer. They would have to do.

Mo spent the rest of Sunday afternoon drawing up a contract to give to Bogdan, detailing her role as Vampire Queen, all carefully designed to hide the fact that she would not actually, technically, officially, truly, absolutely, one-hundred per cent be a vampire.

She wrote:

*Bogdan agrees that Luca will be the familiar to the queen (me).*
*Luca will supply all the queen's 'food'.*
*The queen will never be required to consume said 'food' in public.*
*The queen will take all meals in private.*
*Banquets are OFF!*

She added in the hours she was prepared to work. Nights, obviously, but starting no earlier than 7 p.m.

'So I can have dinner and get some homework done first,' she muttered to herself.

Then she wrote:

*Two nights off a week, and six weeks leave a year.*

'So I can catch up on sleep, still go on holiday with Mum and Dad every August, plus not miss Christmas.'

What about travel? Mo wondered.

I'll have to do some kind of royal tour, she thought, tapping her cheek with her pen and gazing out of the window, imagining motorcades, impressive speeches, crowds applauding, small children shyly handing her bunches of flowers . . .

Then she shook her head sharply.

That's what real queens get, you idiot, not the Vampire Queen.

But still, some kind of exploration of her vampire realm would be needed, some survey of its strengths and weaknesses. Bogdan had also mentioned creating more vampires which, Mo realised, must mean turning normal regular people into vampires. She shuddered and began writing hurriedly.

*Queen will not engage in the turning of humans, ___ever___.*

She underlined 'ever', twice, then continued:

> *Queen will go on fact-finding mission around Great Britain to establish state of current vampire population and best way forward, re. expansion of vampire realm for Vampire King of East. All expenses paid by him.*
>
> *Queen will be driven in car by Luca.*
>
> *Queen requires accommodation in Premier Inn or better.*

Mo set her pen down. What else was she supposed to do, as Queen? Was there paperwork, important documents to sign, significant deals to be negotiated with, with . . . who? Mo blinked nervously.

I'll ask Bogdan later, she decided. Perhaps he's got some kind of *Dummy's Guide to being Vampire Queen* he can lend me. For now, this will do. A contract. Clear communication is always best, the sign of a good leader. Who doesn't love a contract? Maybe, she worried, Bogdan, especially when he noticed her refusal to turn humans or eat in front of anyone, which would signal a very un-vampiric aversion to blood and violence.

'Well, too bad,' Mo said to herself. 'It's my reign, my way.'

As dusk was falling, Luca called.

'Oh my god, Mo, Bogdan is so happy. He is doing a special dance to celebrate you agreeing to be Vampire Queen! Can you hear him?'

Mo could make out a thumping sound and shouts of 'Yah, yah, yah!' followed by a loud smash.

'He's breaking plates now,' Luca laughed. 'This is a classic vampire way to celebrate.'

Smash.

'Whoa, there goes a teapot. Man, he's really happy.'

Smash.

'That was a mug,' said Luca. 'Anyway, we're travelling back tonight, checking into the Premier Inn and then Bogdan wants to do the turning tomorrow night. He thought in your dad's shed. Nice and private.'

'Tomorrow?' Mo said.

There was another smash in the background.

'That was a milk jug,' said Luca.

'Did you say tomorrow?'

'Yes, oh, hang on, there's someone at the door, shouting. It's the hotel manager. I'd better go. Take care, Mo. See you tomorrow. A new adventure awaits, yes?'

'Yes,' said Mo, a slight quiver in her voice. 'A new adventure awaits.'

# 19

Monday. A perfect autumn morning. Pale blue sky, bright lemon sun. Mo cycled into school instead of taking the bus. She craved the feeling of movement, of chilly air plunging into her lungs. She wanted her legs to be working more and her brain less. She was bubbling with doubt. Yesterday she was determined to fake being Vampire Queen. Today she wasn't even sure if that was possible. Let alone sensible. Let alone safe.

As Mo neared the school, the bus passed her. She could see Jez Pocock on the back seat, the white dressing on the back of his head visible through the rear grimy window. Thank goodness he's OK, Mo thought, despite being almost eaten by Bogdan. Then she spotted Tracey Caldwell leaning up against the rear window, doing her circular 'you've lost it' gesture with her finger, until the bus turned a corner and was gone.

At break, Mo messaged Luca.

**Can I meet you after school? Clock tower? Had a few thoughts about the ceremony tonight . . .**

He messaged straight back, up early while Bogdan no doubt slept in the bath at the Premier Inn.

**Sure, see you at 3.30?**

As soon as the final bell rang, Mo hurried out of school. She was unlocking her bike when Lou ran up to her.

'Hey, give me a backie? Remember when we used to do that? When we were kids? You were always giving me a backie.'

Mo didn't reply as she stashed the lock in her backpack.

'What's the matter?'

'Nothing, sorry. I just need to get going, that's all,' Mo said.

'Going to the library? I'll come with you.'

'No, actually, I'm meeting someone.'

'Someone? That's a bit mysterious. Why can't you just say who. It's Luca, isn't it?'

'Yes, it's Luca,' said Mo.

'Your not-your-boyfriend boyfriend,' said Lou.

'He's not my boyfriend,' Mo said, 'but I do really need to go. He'll be waiting.'

'Can I come?' Lou blurted, then clocked Mo's face. 'Sorry, no, I get it. You want to be together. I haven't got used to this yet. You with him, not with me, or your books.'

'We can study together soon,' said Mo, climbing onto her bike, 'and eat some Mini Battenbergs.'

'When?' said Lou.

'I don't know. Soon. Doesn't matter when, does it?'

'Matters to me,' Lou mumbled, but Mo was already pedalling away, calling over her shoulder, 'I'll see you tomorrow.'

Lou watched her, frowning, then called out, 'Hey, Mo, you're not wearing your helmet! You always wear your helmet!' But Mo was too far off to hear.

When Mo arrived at the clock tower, Luca was waiting, hands deep in his jeans pockets, staring down at the pavement. She studied his profile as she walked towards him – that strong nose, those dark brows – and felt tiny, twinkly fireworks go off in her brain. Maybe I have lost the plot like Tracey Caldwell said, Mo thought quickly, letting myself go to bits over a boy. Not very strong or independent, is it? Then Luca looked up. His smile seemed to lift Mo up and pull her towards him. Next thing she knew, she was standing by his side, smiling back.

Luca bowed deeply and Mo laughed.

'I'm not queen yet,' she muttered.

'Not long now though,' he said. 'Excited?'

Mo laughed nervously.

'Stressed, more like,' she said.

'Don't be, you'll be brilliant,' he said.

Mo handed Luca a piece of paper.

'I drew up a little contract, for me and Bogdan,' she said. 'Will you give it to him? You're in it too. As my familiar, you'll be entitled to six weeks off a year and bank holidays.'

'I don't know what bank holidays are, but thanks,' said Luca, tucking it into his coat pocket.

'And for the turning ceremony, I've had some ideas, like I mentioned,' she said, chewing her lip nervously.

Luca rested a hand on her arm. 'I know, and it's OK. You can talk to Bogdan about it all later,' Luca said. 'It will be fine. He's a vampire, but he's not a monster, remember?'

'OK. Sure. You're right. It will be fine,' Mo repeated. 'But what should I wear? I can't wear jeans, can I? Or can I?'

'This is also fine. Bogdan has given me money for your clothes. We will go shopping.'

'Now?' Mo asked.

'Why not?' Luca said.

Why not? Why *not*? Because I've never been clothes shopping with a boy before, because I never pay that much attention to what I wear, because I've no idea what a good look for a fake vampire queen might be, because I'd normally be in the library now . . . *That's* why not.

'Middle Donny doesn't really have any clothes shops,' she said. 'Only a few charity shops, but then, you know, buying second-hand is more environmentally responsible, cheaper too, so . . .'

Luca's calm smile silenced Mo's babbling. She took a deep breath and walked towards the biggest charity shop on the high street.

Once inside, Luca paused. 'Now, you want something regal and elegant, to fit the role,' he said.

Mo nodded and began exploring.

'This?' she said, pulling out a crumped black suit jacket.

'Too boring,' said Luca. 'You're going to be Vampire Queen, not an estate agent.'

'Sorry,' said Mo. 'Maybe this? Bit more cheerful?' She held up a loose top with a bright green-and-purple pattern.

'Vampire Queen, Mo,' said Luca, shaking his head.

'OK then, how about this?'

Mo showed him a yellow collarless jacket with brass buttons and matching skirt.

'Again, *Vampire* Queen, not *the* queen,' said Luca.

Mo nodded eagerly and rummaged some more, until Luca appeared at her side wearing a top hat.

'I really want this,' he said, pointing at it and grinning.

'Look, we're shopping for me, OK?' Mo said, trying to look stern.

'Sorry, Your Majesty,' he said. Then he dived over to another rail and pulled out a Hawaiian shirt.

'How about this?' he said. 'Only joking!'

Mo poked her tongue out at him and turned away and that's when she spotted it, hanging up at the other end of the shop – a long black dress. Something in its simple shape appealed to her – a neat round neck, long sleeves, a fitted body. Mo went over, stroked the fabric. It was soft and thick.

'I'm trying this on,' she told Luca, and disappeared into a changing room.

The dress slid down Mo's body effortlessly, as if it had been made for her. She looked at herself in the mirror. She had never worn anything like this before. Her go-to outfit was jeans and a hoodie, but this was entirely different. Its clean lines accentuated her height, its soft black fabric matched her ink-black hair. Her pale face hovered above it, like a moon.

'What do you think?' Mo said, pulling back the curtain and taking one nervous step into the shop.

Luca yanked off the sunglasses he had tried on and walked towards her, without blinking. He took off his top hat and bowed again, only this time he looked serious. 'It's perfect,' he said.

Mo felt suddenly self-conscious. Her cheeks reddened and she reversed back into the changing rooms.

'Keep it on!' Luca said. 'I'll go and pay for it.'

Mo stuffed her school uniform into her backpack, then found Luca waiting outside.

'Here, I got you this too,' he said, passing her a long black coat with a pattern of leaves and vines in gold thread stitched on its cuffs. Mo slipped it on.

'Do I look the part?' she asked.

'You're ready,' he said, nodding approvingly. Then he raised one finger. 'Listen!'

The sound of the Donnys Brass Band, playing in the market square, bounced through the crisp evening air.

Luca took Mo's hand and ran towards it, pulling her along.

'What are you doing?' she squealed.

'Let's dance,' Luca said.

He stopped in front of the band, and before Mo had time to melt into a hot puddle of embarrassment, Luca put one hand on the small of her back and pulled her in close.

'Vampires love to dance, remember?' he whispered in her ear, and then he spun her around twice, her long coat flaring out from her sides.

Mo shrieked as Luca continued to spin her out then pull her back into him, over and over, until she felt dizzy and delirious. She was amazed that her body knew how to move, smoothly and easily, in a way it never had before. As the music came to an end, Luca slid both hands to Mo's back and gently dipped her down. She felt her hair tumble towards the pavement and saw the stars twinkling around Luca's head as he leaned over her, just for a second, before pivoting her back up.

The little audience that had gathered to watch cheered. The band leader clapped and Mo opened her mouth and laughed, breathless and bewildered. Luca bowed to her again, and Mo blushed and giggled. It was only once the crowd had drifted away that she spotted a familiar figure among them.

'Wasn't that the girl from The Diner?' Luca asked, following Mo's gaze.

'Tracey Caldwell,' Mo muttered. 'She looked really angry.'

'Jealous probably,' Luca said. 'You're a great dancer.'

'Thanks. Not something I'm used to doing,' said Mo, grimacing. 'I'm surprised I didn't fall flat on my face.'

'I'm not,' said Luca. 'I hope I get to dance with you again, but actually, right now, I ought to get going. Sorry to race off, but Bogdan will be waiting. Please be in the shed at 1 a.m. We will be there. Bogdan will perform the turning ceremony, and then your new life as Vampire Queen will begin.'

Mo nodded and watched Luca as he walked away, and then, suddenly feeling alone and exposed, she hurried over to her bike, unlocked it and pedalled towards home.

Back at home, Mo hung her new clothes up carefully in her wardrobe and checked the time. Six o'clock. Still seven hours to go until the turning ceremony. So long, but also not long enough. Stay calm, Mo told herself. I'm Mo Merrydrew, the Chosen One. I've got this. No, really, I have.

At dinner, she mechanically spooned soup into her mouth, squishing any thoughts of fluffing the ceremony and of the Vampire King of the East's hot temper the moment they floated up, like a child popping bubbles.

'How was the first day back since Mr Chen, you know . . . ?' Mo's mum asked.

'OK,' Mo said.

'OK? Weren't people still in shock?'

'I guess so.'

'How about you?' said her mum. 'Are you all right? You seem distracted.'

'I'm fine,' said Mo. 'I didn't have maths today, so –'

'We'll find who did it, you know,' Mo's dad said. 'The police will, I mean. Try not to worry.'

'I'm OK, honestly,' Mo said, finally looking up and noticing her parents' anxious faces. She stood up and kissed them, and then, pleading tiredness, went to her room. The clock on her bedside table said 8 p.m. Five hours to go. Just five hours until the turning ceremony.

Mo climbed into bed, hoping to grab a few hours' sleep, but she would have had more chance of dozing off if she'd drunk three espressos and taken an ice bath. She was still awake when she heard her parents go to bed at eleven, and at midnight she gave up. This was it. One hour to go. Time to prepare.

First the dress – again it seemed to envelope Mo like a second skin – and then the coat. Mo looked at herself in the mirror, hoping for that jolt of 'damn, I look like a queen' that she'd felt earlier. It didn't come. Her face looked less like a beautiful moon, more like a nervous pancake; her body language was more 'waiting for the bus in the rain' than 'about to seize my destiny'.

Mo repeated affirmations in a whisper – 'I've got this, I've got this . . .' – as she brushed her hair. Next she tried slipping her fake fangs into her mouth, but her fingers were jittery as horses in a high wind.

Come on, Mo, get it together, she thought and then practised getting the teeth in and out until she could finally do it smoothly.

At about twelve forty-five Mo thought she heard voices outside. She gasped and clutched her chest. Her heart was rattling like an old tractor. She peeped into the darkness. Nothing. She checked the time – ten minutes to go. She brushed her hair again, in hurried, urgent strokes. She patted her pocket, checking the fake fangs were there. Then, suddenly . . .

'A note,' Mo squeaked. 'I must leave a note, for Mum and Dad, explaining what I'm doing, in case something happens . . .'

She rushed over to her desk and grabbed a pen, but her hands were shaking too much to write. She blinked back tears, squinted at the clock – twelve fifty-seven! She had to go. Now. It was here. It was time.

Mo glanced around her room, anxiously. Would someone leap out of the wardrobe and stop her? Would her parents burst in and refuse to let her go? No, there was no one there except her teddy, Mr Bakewell. She touched his soft head for luck, then took a deep breath, opened her bedroom door and tiptoed downstairs.

# 20

Mo put on her trainers and opened the front door. The cold outside slapped her cheeks. The darkness seemed absolute. She paused on the front step for a heartbeat, then pulled her coat around her and padded quietly across the grass towards the shed.

Mo knew exactly where it was, of course, and yet it seemed to have been completely swallowed by the night. By the time she could pick out its shape, she was almost close enough to touch it. It seemed deserted. Did it really contain a vampire and his familiar, waiting to perform an ancient turning ritual on her?

Mo pulled the door open slowly and peered in. The old picnic rug had been hung up over the window so the light from hundreds of candles, spilling a golden glow over her dad's old records, the flower pots and wheelbarrow, did not escape.

Mo stepped inside. The candle flames flickered in unison. The shed was silent, except for the sound of her breathing. Where was Bogdan? Where was Luca? What was going on? Was the turning ceremony off?

'Hello?' Mo whispered.

Silence.

She spoke a bit louder. 'Anyone here?'

BANG! Two party poppers exploded through the air, draping Mo in streamers. She leaped back against the shed door, blinking rapidly, as Bogdan and Luca sprang up from behind the armchair.

'Surprise!' they yelled, before hooting with laughter.

'Oh no, we scared you, so sorry,' said Bogdan. 'We are feeling so exciting! This is a happy event, yes? A party. A celebration. A great moment in all our lives. If there were plates here, I would definitely be smashing them.'

Mo was gasping for breath, clutching her chest. Luca rushed round to her side and helped her into the armchair.

'You gave me a shock,' she stammered.

'A happy shock!' said Bogdan, throwing his arms up gleefully. He looked jollier than Mo had ever seen him before. His dark eyes shone as brightly as the silver waistcoat he was wearing.

'My dear Mo, you look quite splendid,' he said. 'Luca told me you had found a most beautiful, excellent outfit. Elegant but also comfortable. It is – how you say? – spots on. And so, my dear Mo, as soon you are ready, we can begin the ceremony. It's quite simple. I will drink a little of your blood – well done for not wearing a polo neck, by the way – and then you will drink a little of mine. I can help you get access to a vein. You may experience a slight headache, you know, or some other little side effects while the turning takes place, but this passes pretty quick sharp and then – wow! hooray! – you are a vampire. Great, yes?'

Mo gulped and raised a single finger. 'First, can I check you got my contract?'

Bogdan nodded, digging it out of his pocket and passing it to Mo.

'Here,' he said. 'It's a little boring, but anyway I signed it. Now, let's go, yes? Turning ceremony time!'

'Wait, don't you have anything for me?' Mo asked. 'No royal manual, no brief, no dos and don'ts of being the Vampire Queen?'

'Mo, you know all this,' said Bogdan. 'Just be spectacular. Make Vampire King proud, turn Great Britain into Great Vampire Britain, yes? Now, let's go again! Turning ceremony time!'

'Actually,' said Mo, 'I wondered if we could just tweak a few details of the ceremony too.'

Irritation twitched across Bogdan's face. Mo glanced quickly at Luca, who nodded faintly at her, as if willing her on.

'I know you don't like to bite women, usually,' Mo said.

'Correct,' said Bogdan.

'So I was thinking we could just, you know, skip that bit,' said Mo.

'Skip it?'

'Yes, just leave it out,' Mo said. 'I did some research and found lots of cases, particularly from the eighteenth century, when people were turned without the vampire drinking even a drop of the human's blood. It seems that the turning can work perfectly without you feeding on me.'

Bogdan folded his arms and narrowed his eyes, but said nothing.

'Then, I thought, I could drink your blood from a cup or a ladle or something, rather than suck on your neck,' Mo continued. 'It's much more hygienic. I know that's how you were turned, back in the 1300s, but it's the twenty-first century now. Let's not take any chances. We need the strictest hygiene measures if we're going to start opening up veins all over my dad's shed.'

'You are about to become immortal. I don't see how this is necessary,' Bogdan said.

'It's my turning, my way, I'm afraid,' Mo said, trying to sound tough, but gripping the fake fangs in her pocket so hard they left teeth-marks in her palm.

Bogdan sighed deeply. 'I should have guessed this would not go simply straight,' he muttered. 'Always have something to say, don't you, dearest Mo? Always some little opinion. Never mind. As you wish. I will give you my blood to drink, as you suggest, but if it doesn't work, I will drink yours too. And don't tell Vampire King of

East we messed around with ceremony. He will find this not impressive. This is not how it's usually done.'

'I won't say a word,' said Mo.

'Very good. Now, what shall I put it in?' Bogdan asked.

Mo looked blank.

'My blood, what shall I put it in?'

'Oh,' said Mo, blushing suddenly. 'I totally forgot to bring anything.'

Luca stepped forward, holding the little plastic bucket that Mo made sandcastles with as a little girl. The same one that Mo had offered Bogdan when he was sick.

'Perhaps this, master?' Luca said.

Bogdan's lip curled as he took the red bucket.

'This again,' he said. 'I would prefer finest Murano glassware from Venice, but all right.'

'Perhaps you would like to sit, before you begin,' Luca said to Bogdan.

Mo sprang up and rushed to Luca's side. Bogdan eased himself into the armchair and then, with absolutely no warning, his fangs shot down like daggers and he plunged them, hard, into his wrist.

Mo shrieked and flinched backwards. Only Luca's hand on her back stopped her collapsing. Bogdan held Mo's gaze as he withdrew his fangs, now red with his own blood, and then held the plastic bucket beneath his punctured wrist. Blood trickled down into it, the darkest, stickiest blood Mo had ever seen. She couldn't take her eyes off it until, a few seconds later, Bogdan swept his wrist back up to his mouth. He sucked and licked the wound – it sounded like a dog drinking from a puddle – and when he took his wrist away from his lips, there was nothing to see but clean, pale skin.

'It is done,' Bogdan said, standing up. He smiled faintly at Mo – his fangs had disappeared – and held the bucket out to her.

'Now, my dear, it is your turn.'

Mo stared down into the plastic bucket. Her pale face was reflected in the puddle of Bogdan's blood. This was it. This was the moment. She had to get it right. Drink it – or appear to. Sprout fangs – or appear to. Morph before their eyes into a powerful queen – or appear to. Get it wrong and . . . Mo wasn't sure. It would probably involve violence. It would definitely involve losing Luca. Luca – whose hand still steadied her, warm against her back.

'Drink up, Mo, your destiny awaits,' Bogdan said.

She raised the bucket to her lips. Bogdan leaned forward a little, eyes shimmering with excitement. Luca held his breath. Then Mo lowered the bucket again.

'Would you mind if I did this in private?' Mo said.

Bogdan let out a frustrated 'Gah!' and slapped his forehead with the palm of his hand. 'Mo, Mo, Mo,' he said. 'Always this playing and changing and editing. Let it all go. You are on the doorstep of a new glorious existence. What do you care if we watch you drink blood or not? From now on, that's all you'll be drinking!'

'It was in my contract. I will never consume blood in public,' Mo replied. 'Take it or leave it.'

'Perhaps, master, you could simply return to your seat, to give Mo some space, and I will look the other way,' said Luca.

'Arrgggh!' Bogdan growled. 'If I must. All right!'

He stomped back to the armchair and thumped down into it.

'But hurry, Mo! At this rate it will be morning and our ceremony will be kaputs.'

Mo nodded and then looked at Luca.

'Sorry, yes,' he said, and turned to face the shed wall.

'Thank you,' said Mo.

She spun around shakily and crouched down in the corner of the shed, putting the bucket on the floor in front of her. Her long coat created a tent around her huddled form. She was certain Bogdan could not see anything and Luca, standing a little way off with his back to her, well, he wouldn't look round; Mo trusted that he wouldn't.

'I will drink it now,' she said, over her shoulder.

Then, with a shaking hand, she dabbled her fingers into Bogdan's blood and suppressed a gasp of horror. It was cool and oily. Still trembling, she slowly raised her fingers to her mouth and smeared blood on her lips, then she dipped her fingers in the bloody pool again and this time dribbled streaks down from the corners of her mouth. She added more blood to her chin, a drop or two on the top of her dress, and then, trying not to gag, hid the bucket behind an old watering can.

Then Mo realised, with horror, that her hand was coated in vampire blood. This was not good, not good at all. She was meant to have drunk the blood, not done a finger painting with it. She had to wipe her hand, but where? If she touched the shed floor or walls it would leave a clear print, like a prehistoric cave painting. She had no tissues, no cloth . . .

Then she realised the solution. She grabbed a handful of her long hair and, fighting back a whimper, wiped her bloody hand on it until it was clean. Done. She steadied her breath for one second, two seconds, then, reaching swiftly into her coat pocket, pulled out her gumshield and slipped it in.

'I've got this,' she told herself. 'I've got this.'

Then Mo sucked in a long breath and let out a huge roar and, as she roared, she spun around to face Bogdan, her eyes blazing, her fangs revealed.

Bogdan flinched. He actually flinched.

Yikes, Mo thought. Did I go too far?

Then Bogdan stood up slowly from the armchair, a smile of wonder spreading across his lips, like a child meeting a unicorn. He reached out with one finger towards Mo, fascinated by the blood trickling from her mouth, eager to touch it. Then he pulled his hand back and pivoted from the waist, folding into a bow. He stayed down for so long, Mo wondered if he'd put his back out.

'You have to tell him to rise, Your Majesty,' Luca whispered.

Mo nodded, raised both hands to her mouth and quickly whipped the gumshield out, then, in the deepest voice she could manage, she said: 'Rise, Bogdan.'

Up he came, still smiling, until he stood before Mo once more.

'My queen,' he breathed, gazing at her. 'You are more beautiful, more powerful, more awesome than I could have imagined. I am your humble servant.'

Mo nodded. Luca came and stood next to Bogdan.

'I, also, am your humble servant,' he said, bowing.

'Rise, my familiar,' Mo said, watching Luca closely, hoping for his full-beam smile. She searched Luca's face, but it was serious, not sunny, and he kept his eyes on the floor. The three of them stood there, Bogdan and Luca in reverential silence, Mo unsure what to do next. Eventually, unable to stand the quiet any more, she spoke.

'So,' she said, 'I guess that's that then?'

# 21

The candlelight flickered as a cold breeze blew under the shed door. Bogdan cleared his throat. 'Majesty, I ask that you release me now,' he said. 'My work here is done.'

'You may go,' said Mo, working the deep queenly voice again.

Bogdan nodded and then let out a 'whoop!' and skipped towards the door.

'Happy days are here again!' he said, in a sing-song voice. 'Luca, are you coming?'

'I work for the queen now,' said Luca, gesturing towards Mo.

'Of course, that was plenty silly of me,' said Bogdan. 'Also, this reminds me – my gift to you for your loyal service.'

He reached into his pocket and handed Luca a slim package. Luca opened it and smiled. It was a scarf, woven with silver thread. He wrapped it around his neck.

'It's finest cashmere, very delicate and expensive,' said Bogdan. 'So hand-wash only, please?'

'I promise,' Luca said.

Bogdan smiled. 'We had some times, eh?' he said.

'We sure did,' said Luca.

'Hug?' said Bogdan.

'Hug!' said Luca, and the two of them thumped into an embrace, back-patting each other and laughing.

'Enjoy your retirement,' Luca said.

'I will,' said Bogdan. 'I will write to the Vampire King, and to other vampires of Great Britain, and let them know triumphant news. The Vampire King will want to come and meet you, of course.'

'Will he?' Mo asked.

'But of course,' said Bogdan. 'To celebrate and feast with you. So I will stay in the area to greet him – don't worry, I'm on a diet, you won't know I'm here – and after that, Caribbean, here I'm coming! Take care of the queen, Luca. I worked hard for this one. What a way to end my career, but it was worth it. Mo, Your Majesty, you are spectacular. You will be great leader. I know this for true fact. Goodbye for now!'

Bogdan opened the shed door and reversed out of it, bowing to Mo and waving to Luca, and then was gone.

Mo let out a huge sigh and slumped down in the armchair, exhilarated but suddenly exhausted. She expected Luca to come over and full-beam smile at her, congratulate her, make a little joke. She hoped they might chat and laugh like they had in the charity shop. Or maybe even dance like they had in the market square.

But Luca didn't move. He stayed where he was, standing near the door, hands behind his back.

'Is there anything I can aid you with, Your Majesty?' he asked.

Mo frowned and searched Luca's face. Why was he being so formal? This wasn't how he spoke to her usually.

'No, thanks,' she said. 'Shall we just hang out here for a bit? That was quite something, wasn't it? Then I really should get to bed. Better blow out all these candles too. Fire risk!'

Confusion flickered across Luca's face and, with a sudden feeling of horror, Mo realised why. Vampire Queens didn't talk about getting to bed – certainly not in the middle of the night – and they didn't give a virgin's crucifix about fire risks.

'Interesting, I sounded like Mo then,' she said quickly, trying to cover her tracks. 'Perhaps the turning is not fully complete. Like when the Doctor regenerates, you know? No? You've never seen *Doctor Who*? Well, anyway, Bogdan said it takes a little while.'

'Indeed,' said Luca, looking puzzled but also curious.

'Anyway, I can tell I'm getting a headache, after all that excitement,' Mo said. 'Let's call it a day. A night, I mean.'

'Will you go back to the house? A vampire has to be invited in. Surely you won't wake your parents?'

Mo shook her head. 'No need. I'm sure I can still get inside, before the turning is fully complete,' she said, rushing for the door.

'I will be ready to serve you tomorrow, as soon as it gets dark. As your familiar,' Luca said, bowing again.

'Luca, you don't need to bow, even though I'm queen,' Mo said, searching for Luca's eyes, his warm treacle gaze, but he only nodded and looked down again.

'OK, well, see you tomorrow,' she said, and then ran through the darkness, back to the house.

Once upstairs, Mo slipped into the bathroom and turned the shower on. When the water was piping hot, she stood beneath it, watching Bogdan's blood run out of her hair and down the drain in red, snaking ribbons. She shampooed her hair twice, and scrubbed soap into her face, desperate to remove all traces of vampire blood from her mouth and lips. By the time she emerged, her face was rubbed pink as rhubarb.

'Bit late – or is it early? – for a shower,' her dad said, surprising her on the landing.

'Sorry, I couldn't sleep,' Mo spluttered.

'And you thought an invigorating, hot shower might help?' he asked, smiling at her kindly. 'Everything all right?'

Mo nodded. Her dad kissed her on the top of her wet head.

'Get some rest,' he said.

Back inside her bedroom, Mo hid her dress and coat at the back of the wardrobe, buried her fake fangs inside some old trainers and peeped out of the window. Had Luca left? Where would he live now that he was her familiar, now that he served her? Back at the Premier Inn? She hadn't thought to ask, and she couldn't find out now. The only thing that mattered was that she'd done it. She'd faked the turning. She'd pulled it off. She'd seized her destiny and was now, officially, the Vampire Queen of the whole of Great Britain!

Mo climbed into bed and pulled Mr Bakewell into her arms.

'I did it,' she whispered into his furry head. 'I actually, actually did it.'

# 22

'You look pretty cheerful for someone who couldn't sleep last night,' Mo's dad said to her next morning.

Mo was humming to herself as she made breakfast, her pale skin glowing with health. Last night's turning ceremony filled her mind. She pictured Bogdan bowing before her. She remembered her flashing fangs and regal roar. There was no question, she had smashed it. She'd pulled off the hoax of the century. Never mind debating society, I should join drama club, Mo thought. Wait, there isn't a drama club. I should *start* a drama club, join it and also become president. She choked back a delighted giggle.

I am now, Mo thought, on this Tuesday morning in November, Vampire Queen, but *at the same time* I am still Mo Merrydrew, buttering toast before a day at school. She had to cover her mouth with her hands to hide the huge smile that spread across it. She hummed with this knowledge like a pylon. And no one knew! Except, obviously, Mr Bakewell, but he would never blab.

When Mo sat down on the bus, Lou eyed her suspiciously.

'You look happy,' Lou said. 'Must have had a good time with your boyfriend last night.'

'Don't say it like that,' Mo said.

'Like what?' Lou shot back.

'Anyway, I keep telling you, he's not my boyfriend and we weren't on a date.'

'But I just heard Tracey Caldwell saying she saw you dancing with him in the market square yesterday,' said Lou. 'What were you doing? No one dances in the market square, except morris men and Peter the Drunk.'

Mo glanced over her shoulder. As usual, Tracey Caldwell was on the back seat, but the look she shot Mo felt different. It wasn't sneering. It seemed – what was it? – slightly hurt. Definitely suspicious.

'Don't let her look at you, Trace. She might attack,' Danny Harrington said.

Tracey quickly looked away. *She* looked away. That was new.

Mo quickly glanced at Jez Pocock. He smiled shyly at her, touched the back of his head and then gave her a little thumbs up. She took it to mean his head injury was mending. Mo flickered a tiny smile back at him.

'Have you kissed yet?'

'Kissed Jez Pocock?' Mo said, turning back to Lou.

'No – Luca! Or maybe Jez Pocock too. Is there something you're not telling me? Are you dating them both now? Wow, things are really moving fast for you, Mo.'

'Lou!' Mo shrieked.

'I dunno, do I?' Lou said, beginning to smile. 'I was talking about Luca though. What's the deal with him? Where's he actually from? How old is he? Does he go to school? Does he like Mini Battenbergs? He must do. End it immediately if he doesn't. Has he got a brother you can introduce me to? Is he still a vampire's fam-illy-blah thing?'

'Familiar,' Mo corrected her.

'Whatever,' said Lou. 'Tell me!'

'I don't know,' Mo protested. 'He's sixteen, but otherwise I don't know much about him yet. I'm hoping to find out.'

'Could be a new project for you,' Lou said. 'Replace The Plan, with The Man.'

'No way!' Mo said. 'No man is getting in the way of my Plan. That could never happen.'

'You're going to be busy though, with schoolwork and now a boyfriend.'

'He's *not* my boyfriend,' Mo said again, 'and it's OK, I can juggle it all.'

'If you say so, but don't forget about me, right? I am your oldest friend.'

'And best. I won't. I promise. Ever!' Mo laughed, throwing an arm around Lou's shoulder and hugging her. 'Friends forever.'

The bus pulled into school and Mo braced herself for an attack from Tracey Caldwell as she swept down the aisle, but none came. Tracey passed her without a word.

Inside school, Mo made her way to the maths classroom. Her first maths lesson of the week. She froze in the doorway when she saw . . . not Mr Chen, but a woman. A supply teacher. Of course. It could never be Mr Chen again. The shock thumped her in the chest. She had hoped to keep her vampire life and the 'people' in it confined to night-time, and her regular life neatly intact by day, but it was too late for that. The two had already slammed into each other, with fatal results.

Mo shoved her niggling worries into the box in her brain marked 'Unwanted Stuff', but the box must have had a faulty lid, because unwanted stuff carried on leaking out throughout the day. Mo kept imagining she saw Mr Chen, in the distance, or out of the corner of her eye. Was that him at the end of the corridor, in his favourite bruise-coloured jumper? No, it was just a poster about France. Was that his mustard tardigan lying on the sports field? No, just some spilled cheese puffs.

Mo was glad to get home, but she quickly realised she had no time to spare, not a moment. She had to do her homework because it was getting dark and Luca might be waiting for her. In fact, he might even be able to see her in the house, but she wasn't supposed to be in it. She was a vampire. They had to be invited in, but Mo's parents were both at work, so that didn't stand up. She flung herself to the floor, like she was under sniper fire, and commando-crawled from room to room, tugging the curtains closed.

Phew! she thought, springing upright when they were all shut. Note to self, close curtains as soon as I get home. I am not supposed to be in my house, or doing homework, or up during daylight hours or any of those things. No, no, no.

With each no she banged her forehead with the heel of her hand, hammering the message home. Then she peeped out at the shed where, very possibly, Luca was waiting for her. She felt excitement bubbling in her belly at the thought of him, a bubbling that turned to a fizz as she raced through some homework and bolted her dinner, like a dog at a steakhouse.

'Slow down,' her mum said, as Mo shovelled food into her mouth. 'I'm glad you've got a good appetite, but you'll give yourself indigestion.'

'Sorry, in a rush,' Mo explained. 'I'm going to study round at Lou's tonight, for our big science test on Monday. I won't be back too late. I'll get a lift with Lou's mum. I'm planning to do a lot of studying with Lou, from now on.'

Mo cleared her plate and headed for the front door. Her dad's request that she 'stay safe' was ringing in her ears as she grabbed her backpack and ran down the drive. As soon as she was out of sight, Mo dived behind a tree where she quickly took off her school uniform, shivering in the cold as she pulled the black dress and coat from her bag and bundled herself into them, before doubling back around, in the shadow of the hedge, towards the shed.

Once outside, Mo smoothed her hair and took a big, deep breath.

'My first night as Vampire Queen, with Luca as my familiar,' she whispered to herself. 'Be cool, be vampirey and definitely don't mess it up.'

# 23

When Mo opened the shed door, Luca was already there. He had tidied up. There was no trace of last night's turning ceremony. The candles were gone. Most importantly, the child's bucket containing the last oily drops of Bogdan's vampire blood had been rinsed out and put back with the other beach toys.

'Good evening, Your Majesty,' he said, bowing.

Mo frowned. 'No need to bow, remember?' she said, 'and let's not bother with *majesty* either. Bit old-fashioned. How about you call me Mo?'

'That's a little weird – like calling your parents by their first names,' Luca said.

'I'm not your parents,' Mo said.

'No, you're my master,' Luca said.

'Yeah, I'm not keen on master either,' Mo replied. 'It sounds very outdated and male. Let's aim for something more equal, more friendly. I prefer to think of us as co-workers. Colleagues. Work buddies. I do the ruling. You do the helping with the ruling.'

'OK, if that's what you want,' said Luca, frowning like a puppy who's been set some long division.

'I do,' Mo said crisply, wondering quickly whether she was being too Mo. Then she spotted a pile of presents piled up in the corner of the shed.

'What are those?' she said.

'Gifts from the other vampires in Britain, your loyal subjects,' Luca said, smiling, and, Mo noticed with relief, sounding friendly instead of formal. 'Bogdan put the word around that there's a new queen, and they sent them. They've been arriving by Express Bat delivery all afternoon.'

'Bats delivered all this?' Mo asked.

'Vampire bats,' said Luca. 'Working in teams, very strong wings.'

'I've never seen so much stuff,' Mo said. 'Should I open it?'

'No, I think you should look at it for a few days, then throw everything away,' said Luca.

'Really? OK,' said Mo, then she spotted his smile. 'Oh, I get it, you're joking! Ha! Of course. I *should* open everything. Makes sense.'

She picked up a package wrapped in gold paper and unwrapped it slowly, cautiously. Inside it was . . .

'A Vampire Beauty Box. Whatever that is . . .'

She opened the lid.

'There's a file for sharpening fangs, some vampire cleanser – "for tired and dry skin, gently removes even

172

the most stubborn bloodstains" – mouthwash and an eye mask for daytime sleeping. Cool.'

She read the label.

'From Natasha and "the girls" from Northampton. Shall I open another one?'

Luca nodded. Mo grinned and reached for a big parcel.

'I wonder what this can be?' she said, shaking it gently, smiling up at Luca. 'Feels heavy. The label says it's from Pat and Richard in Aberystwyth.'

Mo tore off the paper and then gasped. It was a polished wooden box containing beautiful writing paper, fountain pens and ink.

'Oh my god, luxury stationery! I love it so much! That is such a classy present. I've always wanted something like this. Wow, this is actually fun.'

Mo began to unwrap faster now, ripping off paper and squealing with delight as she discovered each offering was better than the last.

Embroidered gloves – 'Love these!'

Two pewter goblets – 'Very classy.'

A silk pillow – 'Feels gorgeous against my cheek.'

Golden bangles engraved with leaves – 'So beautiful.'

A hairslide with strings of gems hanging from it – 'This is so bling I can't believe I love it, but I absolutely love it.'

A black velvet robe dotted with tiny seed pearls, like constellations – 'it must have taken someone hours to stitch those on, and all for me!'

Mo beamed up at Luca. 'This is like Vampire Christmas,' she joked, beaming as she pulled off the wrapping from the last gift, a small one.

'Only without the turkey,' said Luca, but Mo didn't hear. She was gazing at a ring set with a huge red jewel.

'Is that a ruby? A real one?' she whispered.

'Of course it's real,' Luca said.

Mo slipped the ring on and waggled her finger. The giant stone sparkled in the light. Luca whistled approvingly.

'It's from . . . Derek in Newcastle,' Mo said, reading the card that came with it. 'He says, "A small gift for you, Your Majesty." I would not describe that rock as small, Derek, but hey, thanks a lot.'

Mo held the ring up to her eyes to examine it and caught sight of her reflection in the gem, her face lit up and excited. What am I doing? she wondered suddenly, dropping her hand. A strong, independent woman like me, losing it over a pile of luxury goods. That's not cool. Shame on you, Mo!

'It's too much,' she said abruptly. 'I can't accept all this stuff. I don't deserve it. I haven't done anything yet. I haven't proved I'm worthy. I'm going to send it all back. That's what I'm going to do.'

Luca stopped picking up the wrapping paper Mo had flung everywhere and stood up straight.

'You will offend the other vampires if you do that,' he said.

'But it's the right thing to do. These people, I mean, these creatures didn't elect me and they haven't met me yet and –'

'They are honouring the Chosen One,' Luca said. 'Do you want to deny them that?'

'Look, I don't want to upset anyone, so early in my reign. I don't want to be ungrateful or rude or –'

'So accept the gifts.'

'But –'

'Mo, accept the gifts, it's simple.'

Mo sighed, sat down heavily in the armchair and looked over the presents she had been sent, her fingers fluttering over delicate stitching and twinkling jewels.

'I mean, it *is* really nice stuff,' she said, her voice softening. 'I've never owned anything like this before. It's all so beautiful, like it was made just for me, like they know me.'

She stroked the silk pillow.

'Usually I get books for Christmas and my birthday, and maybe Dad recarpets my room, but not hand-crafted goblets and gems and luxury cushions.'

She pushed the golden bangles onto her wrist and then tucked the hairslide in above her ear and felt the gems trickle down over her shoulder.

'I had always imagined myself in a sharp suit, in the future, when I get a good job, but not jewels. I don't usually do jewellery, but these . . . These are really lovely.'

She shrugged on the velvet robe and glanced up to see Luca gazing at her.

'I look stupid, don't I?' she said, blushing. 'Sorry, yes. Getting totally carried away there. What an idiot.'

She yanked the robe off one shoulder, but he rested a hand on her arm.

'You look like a queen,' he said, softly.

Mo closed her eyes and took a deep breath. I look like a queen. That's good. I *need* to look like a queen, especially when I meet the Vampire King.

'Want to wear it all outside?' Luca said. 'A royal outing in all your fine gear?'

'Are you going to take me for a posh dinner?' Mo asked, surprised by how flirty she sounded, aware that it was not the most feminist tone to strike.

'I can find someone posh who could *be* your dinner, if you like,' he offered.

Mo laughed. 'No, thanks, I'm not hungry. Maybe just a walk. Let's go to the woods behind my house. I used to play there as a kid.'

Luca smiled and together they set off.

# 24

Mo and Luca walked quietly through the garden towards the woods, her robe brushing against the damp grass, its pearls glowing in the moonlight.

'There's an old oak tree with a big low branch which I loved sitting in when I was small,' Mo said as they arrived at by the trees. 'There!'

She ran towards it and climbed up onto the branch. Luca did the same, shuffling along to sit next to her. Then Mo remembered her conversation with Lou on the bus and realised again how little she knew about him.

'So,' she said, 'tell me all about your home, your village. Is it like Lower Donny?'

Luca laughed and explained that he came from a village tucked under the mountains, not surrounded by fields, where it was roasting hot in summer, not cool and damp. He told her about his parents, his two younger brothers and his dog, Chichu.

'Do you miss them?' Mo asked.

'Of course,' said Luca. 'But many young people leave their families to find work in cities, even though it means the village is slowly dying. Some go to other countries in Europe, in search of a new life, and then work really long hours to build their future.'

'Have your friends done this too?' Mo asked.

'Some have left the village, yes.'

'And your girlfriend?' Mo asked, braced for the answer.

'There's no girlfriend.'

She sagged a little, relieved.

'I've been waiting for the right one to come along,' he said.

'Luca's Chosen One,' Mo said, her heart twitching.

'I guess so,' Luca replied, smiling at her and then staring off into the night. 'Wow, I haven't spoken so much about me for a long time.'

And I've never spoken so much to a boy, ever, Mo thought. Check me out! She grinned inside and pulled her robe around her, feeling warm and happy.

'Once, me and Lou threw acorns at Danny Harrington from up here,' she said, memories from childhood flooding back. 'Then, for revenge, he climbed into the tree and tried to pee on Nipper on the ground.'

'In my country, we would never do that,' Luca said. 'We respect the forest. There is an old saying – it is better to scorn your grandmother than curse a tree.'

'It *was* slightly funny though,' Mo said, 'and Danny *was* just a kid.'

'In my country, we never disrespect dogs either,' Luca continued. 'There is another old saying – when dogs are lost to men, wolves sharpen their teeth.'

'I see,' said Mo. She didn't. 'What did you do for fun when you were small?'

'Tracked bears, painted cabbages, went bare-knuckle fishing, that kind of thing,' Luca said. 'We also played Throw the Cheese Down the Well and Tip the Goat.'

'Right,' said Mo. 'I've never played Tip the Goat.'

'Ah, you missed out,' Luca said. 'It's great fun.'

More fun than this? Mo wondered. Because this feels like fun, a fun I've never known before. Sitting in a tree, dressed in beautiful robes and jewels, chatting with a good-looking boy. Just days ago I could barely make eye contact with him . . .

Mo wanted to laugh, jump down from the tree and run around whooping and yelling and flinging leaves into the air. She felt light despite her heavy robes and threw her head back to gaze up at the stars.

'My hairslide!' she yelped, as it slid off.

Luca leaped to the ground and grabbed it. Mo landed alongside him and he tucked it gently back into place, arranging the strands of gems so they rested perfectly on her long black hair.

'Queen again,' he said.

'Thanks,' Mo said, sensing a blush rising in her cheeks and turning away.

They walked quietly home and Mo said goodnight to Luca at the edge of the garden. Feeling calm and content, she watched him disappear into the night, then went back to the shed, where she packed away her jewels and settled down in the armchair. She took a pen and paper from her new stationery box and carefully noted all the gifts and who had sent them. Then she studied the page.

That can't be more than twenty vampires, she realised. Not many. They all seem pretty nice, and excited to have me as queen, but it's not exactly ruling over a kingdom of vampire subjects, is it? There are hardly enough vampires to fill a minibus, let alone a whole country. How come there are so few? What are they all doing? No wonder Bogdan was keen for me to turn more humans.

Mo drummed the pen against her cheek, thinking.

Still, on the plus side, it makes ruling more manageable, I suppose. I think I'll start by taking a trip with Luca to meet everyone, maybe in the Christmas holidays. A royal tour that will go down in history as the start of a new era of good leadership and happy vampire citizens. They'll see me in my queenly gear, which Luca really liked, and they'll be impressed by it too. They'll cheer and think 'Here's a strong leader, dressed for the role,' and feel reassured that someone's in charge. That will give them all a boost, a fresh start, the confidence to go out there and be proud vampires of Great Britain. Then the Vampire King of the East will be satisfied that I'm doing a brilliant job and I can sit back for a bit and spend more time on my human life. This is going to be OK. It really is.

Humming to herself, Mo gathered up her gifts. So many beautiful things. Too many to carry, in fact. She carefully hid the stationery set behind a pile of old flower pots and, holding the rest of her presents, tiptoed back to the house. Her mum was snoozing in front of the TV and her dad was making tea in the kitchen, the kettle boiling noisily. Mo dashed upstairs and buried everything at the back of her wardrobe, then trotted back down.

'Night, guys,' she said, popping her head round the sitting-room door.

'You're back,' her mum said blearily. 'I didn't hear you come in. Did I nod off?'

'Yes, you did, like you do every evening at exactly 9.28 p.m.,' said her dad. 'Everything OK, Mo?'

'Great, thanks,' she said.

'Work going well?'

'Work is good. Under control,' she said, feeling the vinegar-sharp pleasure of knowing her dad was talking about schoolwork, while she meant secret vampire work, with its loyal subjects, luxurious gifts and Luca.

'Well done, love,' said her mum. 'Always on top of things. You're a star.'

Mo smiled and bounded back to her room, taking the stairs two at a time. A star, she thought. OK, I'll take that, but what you don't know, can't know, won't *ever* know, is that I'm much, much more . . . I'm the one and only Vampire Queen!

# 25

Mo cycled into school next day and didn't see Lou until lunchtime, when they bumped into each other in the corridor.

'Hey, been looking for you. You weren't on the bus this morning,' Lou said. 'Where are you going?'

'I need to go to the library, I have to catch up on some homework,' Mo said.

'But we always eat our sandwiches together on the field,' Lou said, a hurt look crumpling her cute round face. 'It's all because you've got a boyfriend, isn't it? I knew having a boyfriend and keeping up with school would be hard. I said, didn't I?'

'He's not my boyfriend,' Mo said. 'And it's fine. I'm fine. Look, I'm sorry, Lou – I just, you know, have to work . . .' Mo fidgeted from one foot to the other.

'You could come round tonight instead,' Lou said. 'Mini Battenbergs? I could do with some help revising for that science test.'

'I'd really like to, but . . .'

'You're not usually the sort of person who comes out with a but,' said Lou, with a nice dash of bitterness.

'Sorry. It's just . . . Can we do it at the weekend?' Mo asked.

'I might be busy at the weekend,' Lou replied. 'I'll have to check.'

'OK,' said Mo, a little surprised. 'You do that.'

'OK,' said Lou, a little offish. 'I will.'

Then she moved past Mo, leaving her standing alone.

Mo carried a guilty feeling with her to the library, but soon replaced it with anger. Hadn't Lou encouraged her to be with Luca, hadn't she said he was gorgeous? And now this – she was jealous and hurt. Great! Just what Mo needed, when she was busy trying to fulfil her Chosen One destiny. She could handle it all, sure she could – student by day, Vampire Queen by night – but Lou being needy? Well, that wasn't helpful *at all*. Couldn't she just be happy for her?

Mo didn't talk with Lou again in school. They were in different lessons, and when they passed in the corridor once, Mo said hi, but Lou didn't reply, didn't even look at her, just carried on walking. Confused and shocked, Mo hurried away in the opposite direction.

At the end of the day, Mo leaped on her bike and raced home. Once there, with the curtains drawn, she felt calmer, clearer. She put Lou ignoring her to one side and focused on the evening ahead. I was a great queen last night and I'm the Chosen One, she told herself. I've got this. She sat at her desk and worked with steely focus, sensing the countdown to seeing Luca ticking, feeling time speed up as she rattled through her last duties as a straight-up human – race through dinner, lie to parents, sneak out, change behind tree, rush to shed – and her transformation into Vampire Queen.

Luca was in the shed, waiting, when Mo arrived.

'Sorry I'm late,' Mo said, trying not to look him in the eye. She found it hard to look anyone in the eye when she was about to drop a big, fat lie. 'I've been out, you know, prowling around.'

'Of course,' said Luca. 'That is what vampires do.'

'That's *right*,' said Mo, eagerly. 'That's exactly what they – I mean, *we* – do. In the past, I would have been having dinner and doing homework. Well, not any more. Not now I'm queen. No way. Nope.'

She sat in the armchair and spotted her white school ankle socks. Gah, forgot to take them off. She quickly tucked her feet beneath her dress.

'Did any more gifts arrive?' Mo asked, then she hurriedly put her hand to her mouth. Too late – the burp that erupted was clearly audible. Luca's eyebrows twitched upwards.

'Sorry,' Mo muttered.

'Are you hungry?' he said. 'You didn't feed yesterday. Have you fed yet tonight? Can I help with that?'

'No, I absolutely have not eaten. Fed, I mean,' she said. 'I'm not very hungry this evening.'

Another tiny burp popped in the back of Mo's throat – she cursed herself for eating her dinner so quickly – but she was pretty sure Luca didn't hear that one. Which was good, because she was also pretty sure that real vampires didn't burp.

'It's no problem,' Luca continued. 'I can find a human and bring them here –'

'No!' Mo said, a little too forcefully. She took a breath, tried again, calmer now. 'No, thank you, don't do that. Actually, I have been thinking, Luca, that I might not want to eat human blood. It's so old-fashioned, don't you think? Like eating tripe, or Pop Tarts.'

'What are Pop Tarts?' he said.

Mo ignored this.

'As I mentioned, I want to do things my way,' she explained. 'That includes food. Let's find a diet suitable for a twenty-first-century Vampire Queen. So, no to human blood, but yes to . . .'

'Some other kind of blood?' Luca suggested.

'Yes, maybe,' Mo replied.

She tried to think of some animal that no one much cared about, but she'd been a vegetarian since she was eight and was struggling. It had to be something that wouldn't be missed if Luca bumped off a few and drained them. A rat maybe. Or a cockroach.

'Or a worm,' she said, out loud.

'A worm?' Luca asked.

'Worm's blood. Why not?' Mo snapped back. 'Delicious, and absolutely packed with protein too, I bet.'

'I don't think worms have blood,' Luca said.

'Well, maybe you can, I don't know, milk them?'

Luca's eyes grew wide.

'Or blend them up, in a blender?' Mo continued. (When you're in a hole, why stop digging?)

Luca nodded uncertainly. 'I mean, sure, if that's what you want,' he said.

'I do,' said Mo firmly. 'New ruler, new rules. I want worms and I want them blended. A delicious and nutritious worm-shake. For tea. Every day. That's my final worm on the matter. *Word* on the matter.'

'OK,' said Luca. 'I understand . . . I think. Would you like your blended worms today?'

Mo waved a hand impatiently. 'Tomorrow's fine,' she said. 'Right. I feel like doing some more prowling about, survey the land, the most local part of this great vampire realm I'm now boss of. Coming?'

'Of course,' Luca said. 'I go where you go. My role is to serve you.'

'I don't really need serving right now either,' Mo said, feeling irritated, and then surprised. How could she be irritated by Luca, she wondered? He smelled like a bakery, had a smile like sunlight on a calm sea and hair like a Greek god's.

'Remember what we said? We're colleagues, work buddies,' Mo added, in a softer voice.

Luca nodded. 'I can keep an eye out for some worms while we walk,' he said, a twinkle in his eye.

'Absolutely,' said Mo, trying not to smile. 'You do that.'

Mo and Luca walked along the lane and into the fields. It was very dark, only a sliver of moon to light the way, but Mo couldn't risk going into the village centre where there were street lights. She was supposed to be at Lou's, studying, after all.

It was also very cold. Mo pulled her long robe around her body and shivered a little. She felt Luca pause and look at her.

'Are you all right?' he asked. 'Vampires don't usually feel the cold.'

Oh great, Mo thought. First the burping, now the shivering. My body is letting me down, sending out the message that I am alive, human and not at all undead. I need to think fast.

'Luca, how many vampires have you met in your life?' Mo asked, reaching for a regal tone.

'Well, Bogdan of course,' he said. 'I served him for a year. Sometimes vampire messengers from the King of the East came by, but they didn't stay long.'

'Right, so you say, "Vampires don't usually feel the cold," when in fact you only know that Bogdan didn't feel the cold,' she said. Ha! Those years at the debating society were paying off.

'I suppose so,' he said.

'You then take that one example, Bogdan, and extrapolate it out to include all vampires,' Mo said.

'I don't know that word, *extrap-liate*,' he said.

'I am making the point that one vampire's behaviour – Bogdan's – cannot stand for all vampires' behaviour. As I have already explained this evening, I am not Bogdan. I'm the new Vampire Queen and I'm doing things my way. This vampire feels the cold, OK?'

'Absolutely, Your Maj . . .' Luca said.

Mo shot him a strong look.

'Absolutely, Mo,' he said, holding his hands up in submission.

They walked on in silence. Mo had just won an argument, usually one of her favourite things to do, but Luca's wounded expression troubled her. She longed for the comfortable sharing they had enjoyed just yesterday evening, sitting in the tree together. Tonight, though, she was slipping up, revealing her humanness and having to go full regal on Luca to convince him otherwise.

After a few minutes, Luca paused and frowned.

'Sorry, Mo,' he said. 'I think we're lost.'

Mo looked around.

'No, it's OK, I know where we are,' she said. 'Those sheep over there belong to Farmer Jameson, so we just need to cross the stile here and –'

'Sheep?' Luca said, sounding alarmed. 'I must get you away from them.'

'Why?'

'Sheep can smell vampires. From far off. In the olden times, people used sheep to track vampires. They're even more effective than dogs.'

'Sniffer sheep?' Mo said.

'Yes! Come quickly, this way. If they smell you, they might attack,' he said, putting his arm around Mo's shoulder and steering her back the way they had come.

They walked fast, until they were almost back at the lane leading to Mo's house.

'We should be safe here,' said Luca, peering over his shoulder anxiously.

'Safe from the deadly sniffer sheep,' Mo said, but Luca didn't laugh.

'OK, well, thanks for that. I would have walked right by those sheep otherwise. Lots to learn in this new job. Tiny bit overwhelming in fact. I think I'll go back to the shed and, you know, write up some Vampire Queen notes.'

'Whatever you desire,' Luca said.

Mo turned to walk home.

'You could try materialising,' Luca added. 'It would be faster, and it's good to practise.'

Mo tensed. Oh wonderful, she thought, only my second night as Vampire Queen and I have to disappear before his very eyes. How am I supposed to do that?

'Ah yes,' Mo said. 'Like when Bogdan appeared out of the hedge, that first time I met him. That kind of materialising, you mean.'

She edged slowly towards the hedge at the side of the lane.

'It was this exact hedge, I think,' she said, pointing at it. It looked pretty thick. Spiky, too. 'I will materialise right now, but, as it's my first time, I'd prefer if you don't look.'

Luca turned away. Mo reached her hands into the hedge, trying to make a Mo-sized gap that she could 'materialise' through.

'I'll see you tomorrow evening, at the shed,' Luca called over his shoulder.

'Yes, yes,' Mo snapped. 'Now, some privacy please. I'm going to materialise any second now. No peeking!'

Mo pulled a thick branch to one side and squeezed herself in. It was like wrestling with a hedgehog.

'I'm doing it,' Mo called from inside. She yelped – 'Ouch' – as a thorn scratched her cheek.

'It's a tiny bit painful,' Mo said, 'but here I go.'

She shoved her way forward and plunged out of the hedge on the other side, her long robes snagging on the spiky branches. She yanked herself free and crouched down silently. Had Luca gone? Had he bought her materialising routine? It was too dark and the hedge too thick to see if Luca was still there, but then Mo heard footsteps moving off across the field.

She stood up slowly. He'd gone.

'Thank god for that,' Mo muttered, pulling a twig out of her hair. She looked back at the hedge and pointed an angry finger at it. 'And as for you, hedge, thanks for nothing. Stupid, scratchy, nightmare twig thing.'

Then she turned and walked quickly towards home.

# 26

Next morning, a Thursday, Mo leaped onto the bus, keen to see Lou. Last night's burping, shivering and pretend-materialising had left her feeling a bit flat, a bit shaky about her new role as Vampire Queen. Seeing Lou and being in school would be a reassuring return to what she knew best; it would be like eating a simple slice of toast after a week of fancy continental breakfasts. She had a packet of Mini Battenbergs in her backpack which she planned to open right away and which she felt sure would reassure Lou of her love and loyalty. Only, Lou wasn't there.

Mo messaged her.

**You OK? Everything all right?**

Lou didn't reply. Mo looked for her in school, but she hadn't come in at all. Mo sent another message later in the day:

**I can come round later? Bring Mini Battenbergs?**

Still no reply so, after school, she took the bus home and then biked over to Lou's house.

'Oh, hi,' Lou said, when she opened the front door. She sounded surprised and also guarded.

'I said I could come round. You didn't reply, but anyway, here I am. And, I brought Mini Battenbergs. Ta-da!'

Lou took the box of cakes, but didn't move.

'Can I come in, or are you very, very infectious?' Mo asked, laughing. 'You don't look too bad. I mean, you look great in fact. I hope you feel great. Do you?'

'I have a headache, that's all,' Lou said quietly.

'Oh, have you taken paracetamol? Do you have any?'

Lou shook her head quickly.

'Let me go and get you some,' Mo offered. 'I can pop home and grab a couple. Would you like to borrow any books too? Or anything else at all, I could bring you –'

'I'm fine, really,' Lou interrupted.

'OK,' Mo said.

They were quiet for a few seconds, until Lou said, 'Actually, I'm kind of expecting someone. So I should probably go.'

'Oh,' said Mo, flushing a little. 'Yes, right. Sorry. I'll get going.'

She turned and walked down the path, blinking hard, and climbed clumsily onto her bike as Lou shut the door.

Who? Who was Lou expecting? Mo thought as she cycled home. Or was she making that up? Didn't really matter – the result was the same. She hadn't let Mo in, hadn't chatted, hadn't seemed pleased to see her.

Back at her desk, Mo struggled to concentrate on the science revision she was behind with, thinking only of Lou. Lou had never *not* let her in, never *not* shared Mini Battenbergs with her. What was going on?

Mo tossed her pencil across the desk, shoved her chair away and peered out of the window. It was almost dark; she would see Luca soon. His broad smile and silky voice would send all thoughts of Lou's odd behaviour skidding away, like a pebble on an icy pond. I'll wear my new robes, my ring, those lovely bangles, Mo told herself, feeling calmer. Maybe he'll have more presents for me.

He didn't.

Instead, once inside the shed again, Mo was confronted with a stack of letters.

'What's all this?' she asked.

'Correspondence, from the vampires of Great Britain,' said Luca.

Mo read one letter, then another and another, and sighed.

'They all sound miserable,' she said. 'Remember Pat, of Pat and Richard in Wales? She says Richard doesn't want to feed on humans any more and relies on draining the odd sheep now and then. He's lost all his confidence since the purges – whatever they are. Their social life is history, she's completely fed up and will I rip his head off, please?'

'Right,' said Luca.

'Then here's Natasha, from Northampton, saying the other "girls" aren't pulling their weight around the house. They keep leaving blood stains and corpses everywhere and can I come and talk to them about domestic hygiene, "or maybe just rip their heads off, please".'

She looked at Luca, with a 'can you believe this?' expression.

'She's even drawn a picture of me doing it, look,' she said, passing the letter to Luca.

'Proportions are all wrong,' he said, examining it, 'but nice use of shading around the fangs.'

'Oh yeah, that is good,' Mo said, looking at it again, 'but check out what I'm wearing. She's drawn me in some kind of catsuit and cape. I'm a vampire, not a superhero. Anyway, she goes on to say that they used to live each in their own homes, but since the purges they decided there was safety in numbers. The purges again. What are they?'

Luca shrugged and shook his head.

Mo picked up another letter. 'This one's from a group of Scottish vampires, calling themselves the Tartan Fangs. They say they're not keen on being ruled from "over the border" but do acknowledge they're not in a strong position since the purges by the –'

Mo gasped.

'By the vampire hunters!'

Mo looked up at Luca again, her eyes wide.

'So that's what the purges were. Vampire hunters, picking off most of the vampires. Not just the odd random attack, but a full-on purge. That must explain why there are so few left. Have you never heard of this? Did Bogdan or the Vampire King not know?'

'I don't think so,' said Luca. 'Bogdan never mentioned it.'

'I wonder when this happened. It seems that since then the surviving vampires have been hiding out, suffering in silence for years probably, on the edge of the vampire world, ignored and frightened and even turning on each other.'

She sighed deeply. 'Bogdan did say I'd have to pep things up a bit, but I didn't realise all the vampires would be so unhappy, so needy and scared. Can't they just be pleased that I'm ruling? Why do they have to bring me all their problems? I'm a queen, not a therapist.'

'Here, Mo, have something to eat. It will revive you,' Luca said, passing her a glass full to the brim with liquid. It was pinkish grey and horribly gelatinous. 'Blended worms, as you requested.'

'Yum!' she said, while every part of her was screaming, '*Gross!*' 'I'll go and enjoy these outside.'

She slipped out into the garden and tipped the shake into the bushes, watching it slither obscenely out of the glass, while silently apologising to all the worms who had given their lives for her. Then she froze. A sound in the darkness had caught her attention. Footsteps on wet grass, getting nearer. She dashed back into the shed.

'Someone's coming,' she whispered, eyes wide with alarm.

Then – a knock. She froze again, as Luca crept over to the door and opened it slightly. Then he stepped outside. Mo heard muffled voices, then Luca came back in.

'It's Derek's familiar,' he said.

'But Derek's up in Newcastle, isn't he? That's miles away. What is he doing here?' Mo said, in a whisper sent squeakily high by stress. 'He can't just show up out of the blue, giving away my location to anyone who's passing. What if my parents see?'

'He wants to speak to you,' Luca said.

'Really? All right, get him inside, quick.'

Mo gathered herself into her tallest, most regal pose as Luca pushed the door open and ushered the man in. While he slowly bowed, Mo took in his grey wiry hair, his corduroy jacket with patches on the elbows, his boring brown tie. The look was pure 'recently divorced geography teacher'.

'I come from Derek, my vampire lord and master,' he said in a shaky voice.

Mo said nothing, just fixed him with her steeliest gaze.

'He says,' the man went on, clearing his throat, 'he edges pallegiance. Sorry, he wishes to pledge his allegiance, his *devoted* allegiance. Sorry. Can I start again? I'm a bit nervous.'

'Take your time,' said Luca, but Mo said nothing, sticking with the silent regal treatment, which seemed to be working – the guy was now rubbing his sweaty palms on his thighs.

'He pledges his devoted allegiance to you,' he said, smiling quickly with relief, 'and begs a favour.'

Mo's eyebrows rose, slowly.

'He desires to serve you, as your deputy,' the familiar said. 'The ring he sent was a sign of his loyalty and commitment to you, dread Queen.'

The familiar bowed again quickly, and Mo glanced down at the glowing ruby ring on her finger, which suddenly seemed less beautiful. Quickly, she tore it off and dropped it on the floor in front of Derek's familiar.

'So what I took for a gift was in fact a bribe, was it not?' Mo hissed. She was angry now. How dare vampires wheedle for jobs and influence with fancy gifts, and how stupid of her to fall for it.

'You can tell your master that I have no need of a deputy. You can also tell him that I don't take kindly to bribery, I won't have favourites and I cannot be bought. Understand?'

The man nodded nervously.

'Now go,' she said.

He hastily bent to pick up the ring and then bobbed awkwardly in what looked like a curtsy, before fleeing from the shed.

Luca watched him go, sprinting across the grass surprisingly fast, and then shut the door firmly.

'Nice work, Your Maj,' he said, but Mo was too busy pacing crossly to hear.

'Such a cheek!' she said. 'Bribing me with pretty things. And me lapping it all up. What an idiot. You know what – I won't stand for this. I won't rule like some mafia boss running a racket. I never intended to rule with violence, like Bogdan recommended or like the Vampire King, but I cannot have the vampires of Great Britain bunging me backhanders or expecting me to settle their domestic disputes by ripping heads off. I don't care how hard they've had it, with the purges and all. There has to be a fairer way to rule, a stronger way, a more democratic, more –'

Mo stopped. There was another sound at the door. Not a knock this time, a scraping sound. Again Mo froze. Again Luca tiptoed to the door. He opened it a chink and peered out briefly, then pushed it wider, letting a huge bat fly in.

It swooped inside and began flapping around the small shed, skimming off the walls and butting against the roof. Mo shrieked and cowered in the corner, her hands protecting her face, a look of horror written there.

'It's just an Express Bat,' Luca said. 'Probably bringing more mail.'

'It's like a rat with wings!' Mo yelped.

It flapped towards her and she shrank lower.

'Get it away from me,' she squealed, too busy covering her face with her hands to catch Luca's confused expression. No use, the bat collided with Mo's head.

'Argghh, it's caught in my hair, it's attached!' she screeched, leaping up and batting her hands frantically around her head. The bat squealed and flapped, slapping

Mo's forehead with its big translucent wings until it finally wrenched its way free.

Mo stumbled back to the corner, panting. The bat settled on the armchair. Mo couldn't look away from its bulging black eyes, its flattened, crinkled nose that kept sniffing the air, its ears – hairless, ridged, pointed – that twitched constantly. She noticed two tiny fangs resting above its fat bottom lip, then watched as it nuzzled in the fur of its chest and pulled out a neat square of paper, which expanded to full size once it dropped to the floor.

'A letter, see?' Luca said, picking it up, but Mo raised her hand in an urgent stop.

'Someone's humming! Outside,' she whispered. 'I don't believe this. What *now*?'

Luca peeped out of the window.

'It's your dad and he's heading this way. Quick, behind the armchair!'

Mo flicked off the light, grabbed the vampire letters and dived behind the chair where Luca was already crouched, crushing herself against him. His cinnamon-meets-toast aroma filled her nose, his soft hair tickling her cheek.

'Wait, where's the bat?' she whispered.

Luca pointed at his chest, where it was wriggling beneath his sweatshirt.

'Oh gross,' Mo murmured, as the shed door flew open and the light clicked on.

'Now, where are they?' said Dad.

Mo tensed and held her breath. Was he looking for *them*? She looked at Luca, who winked. How come he was so confident? This was a nightmare. She was meant to be at Lou's, but was actually hiding behind an armchair pretending to be a vampire overlord, next to a boy who had a wriggling bat stuffed down his top, and her dad was right there – *right there!*

'Here, great, I knew it,' Dad muttered to himself, pulling a box out from under the workbench.

'*Woodworking Weekly* magazine, I've missed you,' he said. 'There must be thirty-plus editions here. Brilliant! Come to Daddy.'

Luca's eyebrows shot up with glee. Mo placed a finger across his lips to keep him quiet, but then felt the vampire bat's crinkled nose sniffing her wrist. She whipped her hand away, horrified, and Luca pushed the bat back down under his top. Then the shed went dark, as Mo's dad flicked off the light and kicked the door closed.

# 27

Mo leaped up and hurried to the far corner of the shed, desperate to get away from the bat. She tried to breathe deeply, but her body was quivering with adrenaline. They had come so close to being seen. So close!

Luca, on the other hand, had flopped backwards onto the shed floor, laughing.

'*Woodworking Weekly*, come to Daddy,' he hooted.

'That's my dad you're laughing at,' Mo snapped, amazed at how Luca could find all this so funny.

Luca carried on laughing, the bat squirming beneath his top.

'Luca, please. So what if he loves woodworking?' Mo said, surprised at how annoyed she felt. 'It's nice he's getting back into an old hobby. He hasn't done any woodworking for years.'

Luca slowly pulled himself together, sat up and scooped the bat out from inside his top. He held it in his hands as he stood up. Mo noticed how its head bobbed and its nose twitched. Did that thing never sit still?

'I don't know what's so funny anyway,' Mo said, sounding huffy. 'What if my dad had seen the bat, or us? He would have gone ballistic. I don't know what I would have said. How would I explain what I'm doing here?'

Luca let the bat out through the shed door and Mo sagged down into the armchair, chewing her lip.

'Why do you care?' he asked.

'What?' Mo looked up at him, hearing the suddenly serious tone in his voice and sensing danger.

'I mean, you don't need to care any more what that man thinks,' Luca said. 'He's not your dad. He was, but now he's just a human.'

Mo realised her mistake. 'Yes, you're right,' she said, then she gulped before making herself add, even though the words made her feel sick, 'I could kill him if I wanted to.'

Luca nodded and seemed reassured, but then added quietly, 'You didn't like that bat though, did you? Vampires often have them as pets, some like to change into them, but you really couldn't stand it . . .'

Mo felt the heat drain from her. Another trap, and she'd fallen right in. A vampire who was scared of bats . . .

'I told you before, Luca,' she said, trying to sound in control, trying to cover her tracks, 'I'm doing things my way. I'm not like all the other vampires. Do you have a problem with that?'

'No, I do not,' Luca replied, sounding a little tense. He held his hands up defensively.

'Good, because I bet I could find another familiar just like that.' Mo clicked her fingers. 'Someone just as efficient and good at blending worms and . . .' She trailed off. 'Understand?'

'Completely,' said Luca, allowing a second or two of silence to settle. 'You could ask Derek's familiar. Maybe he would do the job.'

What did that mean? Was he serious or joking? Had she hurt his feelings? Mo searched his face anxiously. He was looking at the floor, but when he finally met her gaze, a tiny smile curled at the corner of his mouth.

'I mean what I say,' Mo said, trying to sound stern but feeling relief flood her body. He *was* joking. 'I could easily replace you.'

'I know you could,' he said.

'Good,' said Mo, standing up. 'Now let's get out of here, before anyone else turns up. A quick walk to the oak tree and back; then I need to deal with these letters.'

Luca held the shed door open and Mo plunged out into the darkness, eager to walk off the tension that was gripping her body. It was a clear night, cold and frosty. An owl hooted in the distance. She suppressed a shiver. They walked to the oak tree and climbed onto its long, low bough, where Luca took a flask out of his backpack and poured a cup of hot chocolate. Mo inhaled its sweet milky scent, noticed the steam rising from the cup and watched as Luca gulped it back.

'That looks nice,' she said, without thinking.

'You can't have hot chocolate,' he said, his face concerned. 'You know it would make you sick, don't you?'

'I know,' Mo said, realising with a jolt she'd let her guard down again – vampires don't drink milky beverages – but feeling irritated too, because a hot chocolate right now would be really good. Her feet were freezing and her fingertips blue.

'Maybe your blended worms aren't enough for you to stay healthy,' Luca suggested. 'You should probably top up with real blood sometimes, you know.'

'Well, thanks a lot, Dr Luca, for your expert advice,' Mo said tartly. She hated thinking about vampires sucking blood. In her mind she saw Bogdan's 'feeding' face as he crouched over Jez, pictured Mr Chen under the willow tree, flinched from this world she had chosen to engage with.

'I'm just worried you may become weak,' Luca said.

Mo shook her head quickly. 'Worms are fine,' she said. 'I was just remembering hot chocolate from my human days, that's all. I used to love it. That and Mini Battenbergs.'

'What are they?' Luca asked. 'Are they like Tart Pops?'

'Pop Tarts,' Mo corrected him. 'And no.'

She looked away, thinking about giving the Mini Battenbergs to Lou earlier, and felt a powerful longing for her, like homesickness. It would feel so good to be up in Lou's room now, cosy and relaxed, maybe with Luca there too, instead of sitting in a tree in the dark in secret, pretending not to be cold, pretending not to want hot chocolate.

She pulled her phone out of her pocket and was about to click on her messages when she remembered – vampires can't use mobile phones. Gah! Another slip narrowly avoided. She passed it to Luca.

'Can you see if there's anything from Lou?'

He checked, shook his head. 'Nothing.'

Mo looked away, disappointed.

'Have you told her about your turning?' Luca asked.

'No, of course not,' Mo shot back hotly.

'She doesn't know? I thought you were really close,' Luca said.

'She wouldn't approve. She didn't want me to become a vampire,' said Mo. 'Maybe I've ruined our friendship.'

Had she? Ruined their friendship? Lou had said it would be hard to balance school and Luca, and so far in this new life of juggling, Lou was the ball Mo had dropped. I'm protecting her from the 'harm' the Vampire King of the East could bring, Mo told herself, but not from feeling ditched by her best friend.

She slid off the branch and thumped down heavily.

'Let's get back. I need to reply to those letters,' Mo said, actually thinking, I want to go home, pull on my pyjamas and sink into bed.

'You can ignore them if you want,' Luca said, jumping down next to her. 'You're queen. Do what you like. You don't have to reply.'

'I can't do that!' Mo said, shocked. 'Those creatures are my subjects. They deserve to be heard.'

Luca shrugged. They walked back to the garden, the silence heavy between them, and then Mo said goodnight. As Luca strolled away, she felt herself sagging like an old baguette. She was tired and cold. It was hard keeping up the vampire act – she'd slipped up so many times in the last few nights. Was Luca getting suspicious? And would she forever be having to go full queen, threatening him and speaking harshly to reassure him she was the real deal?

She plodded back to the shed, sighing heavily when she thought about the vampires she now ruled over – so unhappy, so demanding – and the way Derek's familiar had shown up, just like that. He could have so easily blown her cover.

Mo sat down heavily in the armchair. It felt cold in the shed and the lighting was rubbish. She opened the latest letter, just delivered by the bat. Another request to rip a vampire's head off. She sighed and stared into space for a few minutes, then shook herself.

'Just reply to the stupid letters, then you can get to bed,' she muttered, reaching for some familiar Merrydrew grit. She retrieved the stationery set from behind the flower pots, pulled out a pen and paper and then paused. What to say?

'Dear Natasha,' Mo wrote eventually. 'Thank you for your letter . . .'

She screwed up the paper angrily.

'Sounds like I'm writing to my gran after she's sent me a book token.'

She grabbed another sheet.

'Natasha, I hereby confirm receipt of your missive, and will consider in due course the contents therein . . .'

She crushed the paper into a ball and threw it across the shed.

'No, no, no!'

What did world leaders do? Mo wondered. She'd read about their lives, listened to their speeches, but now that it was her turn to govern, the words didn't come. She wished Luca were with her. She wanted his help and reassurance, but a real Vampire Queen wouldn't lean on her familiar like that, would she? No, and I mustn't either, Mo told herself. And I must stop eyeing up hot chocolate and cringing at the sight of bats, or he'll know I'm faking. And if I can't convince Luca, what hope do I have of convincing the Vampire King, when he arrives for our lovely Vampire Rulers summit meeting feast thing. Gah! Try harder, Mo, come on! Do better. You can't mess this up, or else . . . Or else . . . She didn't finish the thought.

Mo picked up her pen again. It hovered over the paper uselessly, wrote nothing. Then she heard the bells of Lower Donny church striking ten. She yawned and stood up, bundled the letters into her pocket and hid the stationery set again.

'Tomorrow,' she muttered, flicking off the shed light. 'I'll deal with all this tomorrow.'

## 28

Friday was not a good day. Mo still felt tired when she woke up. Unanswered vampire letters and unfinished schoolwork weighed on her mind, and the mistakes she'd made so far as a very human undead creature of the night were filling her with doubts. Lou wasn't in school again, but by the time Mo got the bus home that was just as well – she was too busy talking to herself, fast and feverishly, to have a conversation with her friend.

'That was a rubbish, rubbish day. Tracey Caldwell shouting at me on the bus in the morning, about me attacking Danny and had I actually lost it and did I really have a boyfriend? No Lou there to back me up either. She was off 'sick' again, only she didn't look sick when I saw her yesterday. Not sick enough to turn down those Mini Battenbergs, anyway. Bet she's managed to scoff them.'

She sighed.

'And how could I forget to do my maths homework? I can't believe it. That is totally unlike me. I *never* forget homework, definitely not maths, and that supply teacher – Mrs Singh – had a go at me, and I don't think I've ever had a teacher tell me off before, in my whole entire life. I hated it. It felt wrong, really wrong. *And* I got a rubbish mark for that English essay, and science revision . . . I've got *so much* science revision to do this weekend, for the test on Monday. It's going to take major cramming to get anywhere near the kind of mark I usually get, and if I mess up Mum and Dad will be all "what happened, this isn't like you, did you burn out?"'

She sighed again.

'I'm already behind as Vampire Queen too. I have a stack of vampire letters to reply to and all I've managed as queen so far is a bit of dressing up in fancy robes in the shed and cussing up Derek's familiar, which is probably not going to wow the Vampire King, and when is he coming over anyway? No word yet, but maybe soon. I don't even want to think about that. Will he be impressed by me? What if he guesses I haven't been turned, or just thinks I'm rubbish, a rubbish queen who hasn't ripped anyone's head off or eaten any teachers or turned innocent humans into bloodsucking vampires. He'll think I'm sleeping on the job. Am I sleeping on the job? I'm definitely not sleeping enough, that's for sure. I'm tired and I keep messing up. Luca might guess I'm faking, and I couldn't stand it if his deep, dark eyes were suddenly full of doubt and disappointment, because usually his eyes looking into mine feel all good and warm and safe and, no, that mustn't change, I can't handle that changing, ever.'

Mo sighed yet again and rubbed her forehead. The internal chatter rattled on.

'I feel like I'm getting a cold. Disaster. Vampires don't get colds, surely, but it's no wonder I'm getting ill, when I'm working so hard at being me *and* being queen. I definitely didn't catch it from Lou though, who doesn't seem ill at all, and isn't even spending time with me, wouldn't even let me in yesterday, just said she was busy, closed the door, that was it. Took the cakes and closed the door. Closed it. Just like that. Oh, here's my stop.'

Mo took her complicated mood with her to the shed that evening, along with the letters the vampires had written.

Luca was waiting for her, with a glass of blended worms. 'A few more letters arrived today,' he said.

'Oh brilliant,' Mo said, collapsing into the armchair like she'd fainted. 'More requests to rip off heads because someone didn't empty the dishwasher or remember to buy bin bags, I bet. More, "it hasn't been the same since the purges" misery. I haven't even replied to the others yet.'

'I thought you were doing those last night,' Luca said.

'I made a start,' Mo said, then didn't explain how hard she'd found it, how weary and distracted she'd felt, how lonely.

'Well, I can stick around while you work,' he said.

What's the point? Mo wondered miserably. I've got no time to chat with you, laugh with you, be human with you. It's be a vampire and work, work, work from now on.

Luca sat on the floor with his back against the shed wall and closed his eyes. Mo looked at him, his wavy hair flopping across his forehead, and felt her stomach unknot a little. Then she turned back to her task. She wanted to write something bold, powerful and inspiring, like all the best speeches, a sign of strong leadership, something that would be quoted for decades to come. Then she remembered how many letters she had to respond to, how tired she was, and simply wrote this:

*I have received your letter and am considering it. I will visit in the future. You should expect me then.*
*Yours, the Vampire Queen of Great Britain*

It was cold, firm, a bit vague. That'll do, Mo thought, and began writing it out again and again, so each vampire would get the same response. The shed was quiet and the garden too. No surprise visitors, no Express Bats with their hideous twitching noses. The only sound was Mo's pen nib scratching against the thick writing paper, and Luca's soft breathing. Finally Mo stuffed the last letter into an envelope, addressed it and slumped back in her chair.

'Done,' she said.

Luca opened his eyes blearily.

'Sorry, I dozed off,' he said.

'That's all right,' said Mo. 'I nearly did too. Writing to vampires isn't that exciting.'

'I'll send them tomorrow – Express Bat,' Luca said, taking them.

'But it's Saturday tomorrow. You get the weekend off. It's in your contract.'

'I'd forgotten,' Luca said. 'I haven't had a day off in a year. I won't know what to do.'

'I really recommend the Museum of Agricultural Machinery in Donny-on-the-Wold,' Mo said. 'The gift shop is overpriced but there are some fabulous exhibits, including an impressive seed drill from the eighteenth century.'

'Great tip,' Luca said.

'You're welcome,' said Mo, ignoring the twinkle in his eyes.

'What about food?' Luca asks. 'I can go out now and get some worms for you, to last over the weekend.'

'No, thanks. I'll be fine. I might even tuck into a real human,' she said, hoping to sound vampiric. 'Weekend treat.'

'Cool. Well, see you Monday then,' Luca said.

'See you Monday,' Mo replied, smiling despite a ripple of sadness inside, as Luca full-beamed her, opened the shed door and left.

# 29

Mo woke to see her mum's face looming over her.

'Oh, you are alive!' she said. 'You've been asleep so long, love, I thought you were ill.'

Mo sat up and peered at the clock. One in the afternoon. She had never slept in that late before. Ever.

'Get yourself showered and dressed, we're going into town,' Mo's mum said.

'We're what? I've got to study,' Mo protested.

'You've been studying late every evening at Lou's, so what you need today is a break,' said Mo's mum. 'Plus, I want your help choosing the new wallpaper for the downstairs loo.'

Mo appeared in the kitchen twenty minutes later wearing a hoodie and sunglasses. It was the closest she could get to a disguise, just in case Luca hadn't taken her advice and gone to the Museum of Agricultural Machinery – he'd be silly not to, but still – and was, in fact, in town, where he could see her, the Vampire Queen, wandering about in broad daylight, not being fried or melted or whatever was supposed to happen to vampires out during the day.

'Why the dark glasses, darling?' Mo's mum asked her in the car. The windscreen wipers were on, swooshing away the drizzle that was falling. 'It's not exactly dazzling sunlight out there.'

'My eyes are tired from studying,' she lied.

The sunglasses made it hard to really see the wallpaper samples.

'What about this one?' Mo suggested, pointing apathetically at a paisley pattern.

'That's so bright. It's like unicorn vomit,' her mum grumbled, before picking a simple dark navy with tasteful gold stars.

Back outside the DIY shop, they headed for the square, where the Saturday market was in full swing. Mo looked around anxiously. No sign of Luca. Her mum spent ages comparing potatoes and sniffing tomatoes. Mo drifted off to sit down on the steps by the clock tower, but just as she got there a hand grabbed her arm. A powerful hand. A hand that could strangle a squirrel or crush a melon. A hand with bright blue nails. This could only be Tracey Caldwell's hand. To verify, Mo moved her gaze from the hand to the arm and all the way up to the face. Yup, there she was. Tracey Caldwell.

'The Square, in the square,' Tracey said, eyeing Mo up and down.

Mo tried to yank her arm away, but Tracey's squirrel-strangling grip held firm.

'What are you doing here?' she said. 'Waiting for your boyfriend? The one that doesn't exist?'

'It's none of your business,' Mo said.

'Except it is my business, when you're hanging around in my market square, dancing to the Donnys Brass Band like the other night, reckoning you're queen of it all,' said Tracey.

Mo's eyes darted back to Tracey's face at the word 'queen'. Did she know something?

'My cousin Lenny plays the triangle in that band, you know. My granddad Percy founded that band. So that band is very personal to me, do you understand? You had no right to dance around with your so-called boyfriend like you were auditioning for *Strictly*.'

Mo said nothing.

'You think you're *it*, don't you?' Tracey continued, getting more worked up now, raising her voice. 'Want to know what I reckon?'

No, Mo said in her head.

'I reckon you're *not* it. I reckon you're a faker. I reckon you don't have a boyfriend at all.'

Mo remembered squeezing up against Luca when they hid from her dad, the warmth of his body against hers, the feel of his lips against her finger when she'd shushed him. She wanted to tell Tracey all that, but she kept quiet as she thundered on.

'I reckon that bloke was just someone you paid out of your pathetic pocket money to be seen with,' Tracey continued, 'because, where is he now? I don't see him – do you?'

She gestured around the market square with her strong arms, like she was singing opera onstage. Mo glanced nervously around. Peter the Drunk blew her a kiss from the bench where he was reclining like an artist's model, but there was no Luca.

There was, though, someone else, someone beautifully familiar, moving towards her. Mo's heart leaped like an excited gazelle when she saw her.

'Lou!' she shouted. 'Over here!'

Mo grinned uncontrollably as Lou walked towards her and Tracey Caldwell. She's coming to rescue me, Mo thought. Oh joy, deep joy! Kind Lou, loyal Lou, best friend Lou, with her big blue eyes and tiny hands like hamster's paws. Still there for me, despite this last week, despite me fearing that I'd ruined our friendship. Had there ever been a better friend?

Lou got nearer, but rather than smiling back, her face clouded with confusion.

'What are you doing here?' she asked Mo.

'I had to help my mum choose some new wallpaper for the downstairs loo,' Mo gabbled.

Tracey Caldwell snorted like a horse with a fly up its nostril. Lou said nothing. Awkwardness descended like fog.

'What about you?' Mo asked.

Lou gestured quickly at Tracey Caldwell.

'Tracey invited me to go to The Diner with her,' Lou said.

'Oh,' was all Mo managed. She took a small step back, as if Lou's words had shunted her. Lou and Tracey Caldwell, going to The Diner together. What? How? *Why?* She couldn't take it in, this, this . . . *betrayal* – that's what it was! She could only feel it, like a punch to the gut.

'Hi, girls,' said a familiar voice.

'Hello, Mrs Merrydrew,' said Lou.

Mo's mum beamed at the three of them.

'So nice to see you, Lou,' she said. 'I gather you two have been studying hard for the science test. Amazing effort. Please say thanks to your mum for dropping Mo home each evening.'

Lou glanced at Mo, who shook her head, just a fraction, just the teeniest pinch. Did Lou understand her signal, her pleading expression behind the sunglasses?

'That's OK,' Lou muttered.

Mo exhaled silently. She'd been holding her breath.

'It's good you're taking a break today though,' Mum went on. 'Mo, are you going to hang out with your friends? I can come and pick you up later.'

Mo shook her head.

'No, I should go,' she said, turning and walking off towards the car park.

She heard her mum talking a little more to Lou, and then saying goodbye. She heard her footsteps as she jogged to catch up.

'Everything all right, love?' she asked. 'Didn't you want to be with Lou?'

'Yes! But also no. It's complicated,' Mo said.

'Complicated? She's your oldest friend.'

'Please, Mum, no more questions. Can we just go home?'

'Sometimes friendships hit rough patches, rocky times, but you have to stick with them until things settle again,' Mum said.

'I don't need a speech about friendships, Mum,' Mo said.

'It's like that in every relationship,' her mum went on. 'Me and your dad, we've had some tricky times, when the joy seemed to go out of –'

'Oh my god, Mum, not again!' Mo shouted. 'I don't want to hear about your relationship with dad, especially not now, but basically not ever, not in the kind of detail you seem to really like telling me.'

'Just trying to help,' Mum replied, looking shocked. 'It's important to talk, that's all.'

# 30

Mo and her mum didn't speak on the drive home. Mo was bathed in anger – How could Lou go to The Diner with Tracey Caldwell? – but also regrets. I haven't been around for Lou, she admitted to herself. I haven't told her the truth about my life. She thinks I've dumped her for a boy, but it's not like that, not that simple at all . . .

Rinsed with misery, Mo jumped out of the car the second it stopped on the drive and ran towards the house, eager to flee to her room and wallow about in all her complex feelings, like a Labrador in a stinky puddle. She pushed the front door open and was racing for the stairs when she glanced quickly into the kitchen. And froze. Jez Pocock was there.

'Er . . .' Mo managed.

'No need to look so surprised,' Mo's dad said. 'Jez and I are whittling.'

On the kitchen table in front of them were some wooden poles a bit skinnier than a chair leg and various tools – chisels, files, sheets of sandpaper.

'See?' said Dad. He held up a pole with a spiralling line carved around it.

It was pretty underwhelming.

'I don't understand . . .' Mo spluttered.

'It's very simple,' he said. 'You take this carving chisel and then you carefully press it against the wooden pole and . . .'

'No, I don't understand why Jez is here,' Mo said.

'That's simple too,' said Dad. 'Jez came round to thank us for taking him to hospital after he fell over in the lane. He saw my magazines, we got talking and we quickly realised that we share a love of whittling. So, here we are, whittling away. Right, Jez?'

'Yup.'

Jez's green eyes flickered up to Mo's and away again. He looked embarrassed, which seemed fair. He had been caught whittling, and the person he was whittling with was the dad of his sometimes-girlfriend's most-picked-on person. It didn't make sense. How could Jez Pocock, he of the cool stare, also be into woodcarving? Surely her dad had got the wrong end of the stick. Or pole.

Mo ran up to her room. Things were getting too weird. First Lou was out with Tracey Caldwell, now Jez Pocock was in her kitchen. Maybe Luca was at the Museum of Agricultural Machinery in Donny-on-the-Wold. Actually, that would be great, Mo thought. She felt sure he'd love it there. Especially the seed drill. But the rest? It was all seriously nuts.

A knock at her bedroom door, then Jez edged into her room.

'Sorry about down there,' he said. 'I didn't mean to invade your space.'

'No, it's fine,' said Mo. 'When you've got to whittle, you've got to whittle.'

Jez laughed and sat down awkwardly on the end of Mo's bed. She pulled her long legs into her chest, barely able to comprehend that Jez Pocock was *in her bedroom*. If Tracey Caldwell knew, she'd break furniture.

'It wasn't quite how your dad described it,' Jez explained, rubbing his close-cropped hair with the knuckles of one hand. 'I came round to thank *you*, actually, for helping me when I fell. I don't know how you dragged me here afterwards. You must be stronger than you look. Or maybe you had help?'

Was he fishing for intel on Luca? Him too? First Tracey, now Jez.

'I'm quite strong,' Mo muttered.

'Cool. How are you doing anyway? Tracey said she saw you dancing with some bloke in the market square earlier in the week,' Jez continued.

He *was* fishing for intel!

'Not you as well!' Mo snapped. 'Why is everyone suddenly so interested in that? I go for years trying to be invisible, trying not to be noticed, just getting on with my life, and now all anyone can talk about is me doing one little thing in public. Just because I was with a boy – is that it? Suddenly I'm interesting. I thought I was pretty interesting before. I mean, I've got my whole life and career planned out and it's totally crammed with interesting stuff, but no one took any notice then, except to bully me.'

'You're right, I'm sorry,' said Jez.

'What I do in the market square, what I do anywhere, with anyone, is my business,' said Mo. 'Understand?'

'Yes,' said Jez, flinching backwards a little. 'Wow, you're quite full on when you're angry. I've never seen this side of you before.'

'I just told your girlfriend the same thing, half an hour ago,' Mo continued.

'Tracey? She's not my girlfriend,' said Jez. 'We just hang out together sometimes.'

'Well, she hangs out with Lou now too,' said Mo.

'Your best mate Lou?' Jez asked.

'Ex-best mate, apparently,' said Mo. And then, damn it, a tear escaped from the corner of her eye and skidded down her pale cheek.

Mo swiped it away quickly, but Jez saw.

'It's OK, Mo,' he said, in a voice so full of kindness it barely resembled his usual Jez-on-the-bus deep grunt.

'It's really not,' Mo said, more tears escaping and splashing onto her lap. 'I've been so busy lately and I've let her down, but now she's hanging out with Tracey Caldwell. I just didn't see that coming. Tracey freakin' Caldwell! Our enemy. Our tormentor. Sorry, no offence.'

Jez shrugged. He plucked a tissue from the box on the desk and handed it to her.

'Don't let Tracey get to you,' Jez said. 'She's not worth it. Just be yourself and ignore her.'

But who am I? Mo wondered. Not a brilliant student, not a loyal friend, not a proper vampire, not a real girlfriend.

'I should get back to my whittling,' Jez said, making for the door. 'Take care of yourself, Mo. See you on Monday. Stay safe.'

Mo heard him running down the stairs, then heard her mum complaining about the mess in the kitchen. Couldn't they whittle somewhere else?

Mo watched through her window as her dad and Jez carried their wooden poles and tools out to the shed. Oh great, she thought. What if Dad's whittling spreads into the evenings? Luca and I won't be able to use the shed at all. It felt like the final straw.

She slumped on her bed and clutched Mr Bakewell to her chest.

'Life never used to be this complicated before, did it?' she muttered to him.

Mr Bakewell didn't reply.

# 31

Mo's dad's woodworking obsession continued throughout Sunday. He whittled all day in the shed, headphones on, his enthusiasm in huge contrast to Mo's lack of it. She flicked through her science textbooks, painfully aware that the test was tomorrow and that she hadn't revised enough, but she just couldn't concentrate. Her mind kept returning to Lou and Tracey hanging out together at The Diner. It was like being stabbed in the heart. Painful. Really painful.

Mo picked up her phone every five minutes to check for messages. None. She texted Lou, asked how she was, sent her a funny clip of a man playing saxophone to a squirrel, of a dog vomiting up spaghetti, of a toddler with a cheese slice on his head. No reply. Nothing.

At least I will see her on the bus tomorrow, Mo thought. I'll apologise for being distant over the last few days and she'll apologise for hanging out with Tracey Caldwell. Maybe we'll eat some Mini Battenbergs together. Things will go back to normal, or some version of it at least.

Unfortunately, when Mo climbed onto the bus on Monday morning and headed for the seat Lou always occupied, Lou wasn't there.

'Lost something?' came Tracey Caldwell's voice.

Mo looked towards the back. Tracey was grinning triumphantly because there, sitting next to her, was Lou. Her big manga eyes caught Mo's stunned gaze for a second, then skidded away.

Mo thudded down into her usual seat. She felt sick and faint. Her face burned but her hands were cold and clammy. She wanted to sob, but also to scream. Her best friend, who disliked Tracey as much as she did, was sitting with her, along with Danny Harrington and Jez Pocock. Jez! He'd told her on Saturday to ignore Tracey. Fine, but Mo could not ignore Lou when she'd gone over to the dark side. How could she?

The science test was first period. Mo stared at the questions, trying to focus, but hot tears made the writing swirl and swim. Get a grip, she urged herself. You're a strong, independent . . . But when she wiped her eyes and refocused on the page, her mind was a blank. This had never happened before, this emptiness, this nothingness. She scribbled a few answers but, realising they were wrong, despair bloomed inside her, taking over like a virus. She felt paralysed, made dumb and weak by misery. She could hear the steady writing of the students around her, but couldn't find the strength to pick up her pen again.

At lunchtime, Mo sat at the bottom of the field in shock. Doing tests usually filled her with confidence and energy, as she powered through the questions, filling the pages with all her solid, smart learning. Not today. It had been as if another Mo sat in that exam hall. The test had been a tear-stained disaster. This wasn't in The Plan, any plan. Losing Lou and failing tests? Mo hadn't predicted this.

She chewed her sandwich miserably, barely tasting it, and briefly caught sight of Lou, again with Tracey, sprawling about by the bike sheds. When the bell rang at the end of the day, Mo hurried for the bus and huddled down into her seat, making herself as small and invisible as possible.

No use. Tracey Caldwell blustered on a few minutes later and, rather than her usual slow, commanding walk, she stormed towards Mo like a charging baboon.

'What the hell do you think you're doing, Square?' she yelled. 'Jez just told me he was round your house on Saturday afternoon, when I was in The Diner with Lou.'

Mo was mute with shock. Tracey looked so angry Mo thought she might start ripping up bus seats and hurling them out the window.

'I thought you paid that hot bloke to be with you and dance with you, but now I know the truth,' said Tracey. 'You put a spell on him and then you put a spell on Jez. You're a witch!'

This was new. Hang on, no, this was *stupid*. A witch? Was Tracey serious? Mo wanted to laugh. I'm a vampire, Tracey, not a witch. Like, duh!

'Tracey, calm down.'

It was Jez. He had appeared behind her and laid a hand on her arm.

'Get lost, Jez,' Tracey said, flicking it off angrily. 'Merrydrew is out of control again. I always said there was something not right about her. Look at her. Now I get it – she's a witch, and she put you under her power and that's how you ended up in her house.'

'That's not what happened at all,' Jez protested.

'It is. She magicked you and you were under her evil power and didn't have a clue what you were doing.'

'She didn't "magic" me,' Jez said.

'Don't do air quotes at me,' Tracey thundered. 'She did work some spooky, freaky magic on you. I don't understand why you're not angrier about it. Putting a spell on you, it's against your human rights, you know.'

Wow, thought Mo, Tracey Caldwell talking about human rights. That's a first.

'That's how she pinned Danny to the hot-dog van at Halloween too. Using her freaky powers,' Tracey went on. 'It's so obvious she's a witch. Look at her hair. Totally witch hair. It's not normal.'

'Come on, Trace, let's go and sit down,' said Jez wearily.

'Yeah, fine, before she does another spell with her nasty witchy-witch mind.'

Jez escorted Tracey to the back of the bus. Mo didn't move. She stayed as still as she could, until the bus pulled up at her stop and then walked slowly home. As she stepped onto the drive, she noticed that the lights were on in the shed. Dad must have got back early from work and was in there. Mo headed upstairs and crawled into bed.

She lay there for what seemed like hours, neither awake nor asleep. What has happened to my life? she wondered. The Plan seemed like a childish doodle from a lifetime ago. The Plan Part Two: Having It All wasn't working either. Pretending to be a vampire was hard – so much lying, so many blended worms, so many unhappy vampires wanting her to rip heads off – and her best friend had ditched her for Tracey Caldwell, who was now accusing her of being a witch. She'd had no time to study and had just massively flunked an important test, and she was tired too. Really tired.

At least Luca was still in her life.

Luca! Mo sat up in bed. He would arrive soon and go straight to the shed, but her dad was in there. She had to intercept him. Dad hadn't exactly warmed to him when they'd met briefly, the night Bogdan attacked Jez. Mo couldn't risk Luca blundering into the shed and finding him there.

With weary limbs, she pulled on her Vampire Queen outfit, snuck out of the house and ran towards the lane. She crouched by the side of the hedge as the light faded to wait for Luca. This was exactly where Bogdan had first appeared, Mo realised. This was where it all started.

'Mo, are you OK? What are you doing here?'

Mo jumped. She hadn't heard Luca approach.

'Thank god you're here,' she gasped. 'My dad is in the shed. He's whittling.'

'What is whittling? Is it a kind of fish?'

'A kind of woodcarving. Must have seen it in *Woodworking Weekly* magazine. Anyway, we can't go there.' She sneezed.

'Are you ill?' Luca asked.

'Just a bit stressed. Tracey Caldwell – remember her from The Diner? Big hair, powerful arms? – said I was a witch. I mean, I'm a vampire, right?'

'The Vampire Queen in fact,' said Luca.

'Exactly,' said Mo. '*Not* a witch.'

'No, but you do have a certain bewitching quality,' Luca said, smiling. Then he quickly glanced past Mo, up the lane.

'What?' she said.

'A car, I think, coming this way,' said Luca.

They crouched at the side of the lane in the thick wet grass, the hedge prickling their backs.

'I'm sorry, I spoke out of turn just then,' said Luca. 'I am your familiar. I should know my place.'

'No, I mean, yes, but also, it's fine,' said Mo, flustered.

No one had ever called her bewitching before. She wanted to grab Luca's shoulders and tell him to say it again. She wanted to be back in the full beam of his smile and his golden-syrup gaze, away from friendship worries, science-test disasters, Vampire Queen politics. Instead she kept quiet, shrinking down further as the headlights swung into view and the car drove slowly past.

'Isn't that your car? The one that Bogdan got off Clive Bunsworth?' Mo asked.

'Yes, and that was Bogdan driving it,' Luca said, jumping up. 'He's heading for your house.'

'I thought he said he'd stay out of the way for now. Why is he back? Is he looking for me, for us?' said Mo, her voice breathy with stress. 'He'll go straight to the shed, but my dad's in there . . .'

'Whittling!' they both said at once.

'Quickly, Luca,' Mo gasped, 'we have to stop him!'

# 32

Mo and Luca raced down the lane, pausing only to check that the car, pulled in at a layby halfway along, was empty. It was. Bogdan had continued on foot.

The two of them dashed across the gravel drive of Mo's home and spotted a figure at the far end of the garden.

'Bogdan! Over there!' Luca shouted.

'Go after him, find out what he wants,' Mo said. 'Do not let him into the shed.'

Luca sprinted off into the darkness, but Mo stood still. She had picked up a sound coming from the side of the house. A dog barking.

'Nipper?'

Mo ran past the front door and the kitchen window, turned the corner and almost crashed straight into Lou. She was struggling to control Nipper, who was leaping around on his leash, barking and snarling in the direction that Bogdan, and now Luca, had run off in.

'Lou! What are you doing here?' Mo panted.

Before Lou could answer, someone else appeared alongside her from the shadows. Tracey Caldwell.

Mo stared, speechless, for a second. 'Why is she here? What's going on?'

'Tracey wanted to check something,' Lou said.

'Check something? I don't understand,' Mo said, trying to control the trembling in her voice. 'In my garden? What are you on about?'

'We came from the woods, behind,' Lou said. 'Where we used to play, remember? Tracey didn't want us to use the lane in case we were seen.'

'What?' Mo said, shaking her head. None of this was making sense.

'We were trying to spy on you,' said Lou.

'Don't tell her that, Townsend,' Tracey Caldwell snapped, punching Lou's arm sharply.

Lou didn't seem to notice. Nipper was still lunging and barking, nearly ripping the lead from her hand.

'Spy on me?' Mo said.

'Yeah, that's right,' said Lou. 'Tracey wanted to see if you were with Luca. She wants to know if he's really your boyfriend. She also thought she might spot you mixing up spells.'

'That's right, witch, over your cauldron or something,' said Tracey.

'God, Tracey, I'm not a witch!' Mo said, flinging her arms out, exasperated. 'How can you think that? It's just so . . . Stupid!'

'Are you calling me stupid?' Tracey Caldwell spat back.

'Yes,' said Mo, looking plainly at her. 'That's exactly what I'm calling you. Creeping around my garden in the dark, trying to see me being a witch. Like, hello? It's totally stupid. You're totally stupid, and a bully, and a massive, huge, nasty . . .'

'Oh, shut up, both of you,' Lou yelled over Nipper's barking. 'I can't stand it. Tracey, Mo isn't a witch – of course she's not. I don't know how you could even think that. It's so dumb. I don't know how you managed to persuade me to come with you tonight either. This is a total joke. I'm done with it.'

Tracey looked shocked. The Square and now the Spare had talked back to her. Mo, on the other hand, looked delighted.

'Don't look so pleased, Mo,' Lou went on. 'Don't smile at me and make out we're a team, that we're best friends. We're not. I'm not your friend, Tracey, and I'm not yours either, Mo. Since you got with Luca you've abandoned me, abandoned everything. If you cared about me, you'd make time for me. You've totally changed. The old Mo would never have done this.'

'But I'm still Mo. I'm still here, your oldest friend,' said Mo, reaching out to her. 'It's me.'

Mo looked deep into Lou's eyes, but there was no recognition there, only tears. Then Nipper lunged again and this time yanked the lead clean out of Lou's hand

and ran off, speeding across the garden, following the scent of a six-hundred-year-old vampire.

'Go after him. He's getting away,' Mo shrieked, but Lou just stared into the darkness, tears pouring down her cheeks.

'Come on, I'll help you, we can find him together,' Mo pleaded, grabbing Lou's arm, but Lou shook her head quickly and broke free.

'Where are you going?' Mo called after her.

'I've had enough. I've had enough of both of you. I'm going home.' And she dashed away.

Mo was about to run after her, but Tracey Caldwell's words stopped her.

'Now, can you see what you've done?' she said. 'I bet you put a spell on that dog and–'

Mo wheeled round and almost flew the two steps it took to stand in front of Tracey and push her face right into hers.

'Shut it,' Mo growled. 'Shut. Your. Mouth. Now.'

Tracey Caldwell's eyes expanded to pizza size. Her jaw dropped open, but nothing came out. Then Mo spun on her heel and raced off to find Lou.

She had made it across the gravel driveway and was almost at the start of the lane when a sound reached her from up ahead in the darkness. Tyres screeching on tarmac, a scream, a horrible thump.

Mo stopped in her tracks. Mo knew that scream, that voice, the second she heard it.

'Lou!' she breathed, her heart stopping.

Then Mo began running again, fiercely now, tearing up the lane like a cheetah, a single word falling from her lips as a chant:

'No, no, no, no, no . . .'

She spotted the red rear lights of a car up ahead. It was moving. The car hadn't stopped. It was driving away, driving fast, engine roaring and tyres once again screeching on the road. Bogdan – it was Bogdan!

Then, in the red glow of those receding lights, Mo spotted a shape at the side of the road.

Lou.

Mo fled to her friend's side, flinging herself on top of her, smothering her.

'Lou, Lou, Lou,' she pleaded, 'don't be dead, don't be dead, please don't be dead.'

'I'm not dead,' Lou said, her voice muffled.

'You mustn't be dead,' Mo continued. 'You must not be dead.'

'Yeah, I'm not,' Lou mumbled, 'and, actually, can you get off me, please?'

'You're alive!' Mo said, sitting up suddenly. 'Oh, Lou, I'm so sorry! Are you OK? Are you hurt?'

'I'm all right,' Lou said, struggling to sit up. 'I bounced off really. My leg feels a bit weird, but I'm OK.'

Mo glanced down and then away. The shin of Lou's left leg was bent at an unnatural angle. Quickly she pulled off her coat and draped it gently over her friend, and then sat behind her, cradling her into her body.

'Lean on me, Lou,' she said. 'I've got you.'

Lou relaxed into her friend's arms, her body becoming weak, her breathing shallow. Tracey Caldwell thudded up alongside and crouched in the grass next to them.

'What's happened?' she asked.

'Call an ambulance, Tracey,' Mo said, in a voice filled with authority and urgency. 'Now!'

Tracey jumped up and reached for her phone. Punched in the number. Spoke.

'A car accident, I think . . . Yes, Lower Donny . . . Thank you.'

Lou was Mo's only focus. She barely heard Tracey Caldwell. She stroked Lou's head and kissed her hair and told her it would be OK, OK, OK until a siren shattered the night air and blue lights licked through the darkness of the lane.

Mo held Lou's hand as she was helped onto a stretcher and lifted into the ambulance.

'We'll take her from here, love,' said the paramedic. 'You can let go of her now.'

Reluctantly Mo loosened her grip, and as she did, the tears came, tumbling down her cheeks, racing each other to the bottom. Lou managed a little wave as the paramedic shut the rear doors, and then, the ambulance drove off up the lane.

# 33

Mo collapsed into a ball on the tarmac, her body rocking with sobs, her long black hair tumbling around her like a veil. She was barely aware of footsteps running up behind her, of a strong hand on her back. It was Luca.

'What's happened?' he asked.

Mo gulped and gasped. Her voice was so clotted and choked she couldn't speak.

'Mo, please,' he said, crouching next to her, parting her hair gently to see her face.

'Bogdan ran Lou over,' Mo eventually managed, in a twisted, high-pitched voice nothing like her own. Then she dissolved into sobs again, her hands across her face.

Luca helped her to her feet and then held her in his arms. Mo sobbed into his shoulder, her body shaking against his, lost in misery, unaware of anything – including Tracey Caldwell, watching from a distance.

Eventually Mo pulled out of the hug, her face blotchy and soaked. She rubbed her hands across her drenched cheeks a few times. She looked about her blearily, like someone waking from a deep sleep, and spotted Tracey Caldwell.

'Why are you still here?' Mo asked, in a voice croaky with crying.

'I think you should go now,' Luca said.

'It wasn't my fault,' Tracey spluttered. For someone who said she never got scared, she was doing a good impression now. 'None of this was my fault.'

'Just go,' Luca repeated firmly.

Tracey hovered for a few seconds, then walked quickly away.

Mo turned to Luca, an urgent look in her eyes.

'I thought you were going to catch up with Bogdan,' she said. 'I thought you were going to stop him.'

'I did, but then that little dog came at us and Bogdan panicked and materialised. It was hopeless,' said Luca. 'I looked for him in the fields nearby, but he was gone. Then I got trapped by those sheep we saw the other night. They must have smelt Bogdan. They pinned me to the fence!'

Mo shook her head, miserable, inconsolable.

'Lou's leg is broken,' Mo said. 'She bounced off the bonnet of the car and Bogdan didn't stop. *He didn't stop!* It was a hit-and-run, Luca.'

'Well, that's always been his style. Remember how he attacked Jez Pocock, right about here in fact.'

Mo turned away angrily and began marching back to the house.

'Hey, what's the matter?' Luca said, catching up with her, laying a hand on her arm, turning her towards him.

'Bogdan's just run over my friend, and all you can say is, "Yeah, that's his style." Like I'm supposed to be OK with this. He hits a girl in the road and just drives away.'

'What did you expect?' Luca said.

'That he'd stop and help, that he'd care, that he'd –'

'He's a vampire, Mo,' Luca interrupted, exasperation crackling in his voice. 'That's how they are. I thought you, of all people, would understand.'

Mo closed her eyes for a few seconds, realising her error. She was, yet again, being too human. When she opened them again, she saw that Luca's expression had hardened. She turned and began walking towards home.

'Mo?' Luca said, his voice sounding oddly flat and serious. 'Is there something you want to tell me?'

She stopped.

'Is there something you want to say?' he asked.

Mo turned, slowly, to face him. She held his gaze for longer than she ever had before. She felt tears prick her eyes again, but her voice, when it came, was calm and steady.

'I'm not a vampire, Luca,' she said.

Luca tilted his head to the right and frowned. 'What?' he said.

'I faked the turning.'

'Excuse me?'

'I'm a human, like you,' Mo said. 'I'm sorry.'

Luca didn't react at first. He seemed frozen, but then slowly, slowly his face stiffened into a glare. He sucked in his breath, crossed his arms over his chest and turned away.

'I can explain,' Mo said, talking to his back, his rigid shoulders. 'I didn't want to let Bogdan down, or get anyone in trouble with the Vampire King, but I really didn't want to be a vampire either.'

Luca didn't move.

'I thought I could convince you and Bogdan and the Vampire King, when he comes, that I was the real thing, and then just get on with my life too,' she went on, 'but it's been so hard.'

She twisted her fingers into knots, waiting for Luca to respond.

'Luca? Say something, please.'

He turned around slowly.

'What were you thinking? What on earth did you imagine you were doing?' he said, his voice quiet but lit up with anger. Mo felt herself flinching. 'A spoilt kid messing with centuries-old vampires?'

'I wasn't messing,' Mo protested. 'Bogdan said if I refused to be turned, the Vampire King of the East would hurt Lou and my family and hurt Bogdan too, and –'

'Yes, but you can't play at being a vampire,' Luca said. 'You are, or you're not.'

'I just, I just –'

'You just made a huge mistake,' he said. 'The Vampire King will come over soon, to meet you, the so-called Vampire Queen. That's probably why Bogdan was here tonight, to tell you to get ready.'

'I can still convince him I'm a vampire though, can't I?' Mo said. 'Derek's familiar believed I was. Bogdan did.'

'But he's the most ruthless vampire leader of all. You're playing with fire. Serious, deadly vampire fire.'

Mo gulped hard and went to speak, but no words came.

Luca pushed his hands through his hair and looked up at the stars. 'Oh, Mo, what have you done?' he murmured.

'I didn't mean any harm,' Mo pleaded. 'I was trying to *stop* harm. I thought I could protect everyone this way, keep the humans safe and the vampires happy. Keep you happy too. You wanted that promotion after all, to serve the queen.'

'To serve the *real* queen,' Luca said, the words exploding out of him. 'Not a fake.'

'Please don't be angry with me, please don't look at me like that,' Mo said, reaching a hand out to him, then pulling it back to her side.

'You have lied to me this whole time, Mo,' he said. 'I thought we were getting to know each other, building our bond, our trust, but it was all a fake. What have you been honest about? Anything? Anything at all? How can I trust you ever?'

'I'm being honest now. This is me, Mo Merrydrew, no fake fangs, nothing,' Mo said. 'Give me a chance to put things right. I'll be straight with you from here on in, I promise. Don't shake your head, Luca! Please.'

'I only serve the real Vampire Queen, not a faker,' he said bitterly. 'Sorry, Mo, you're on your own with this one. Goodbye, and good luck. You're going to need it.'

'You're not going, are you? Luca? Luca!' Mo said, her voice becoming shrill. 'You can't just abandon me. You're my familiar. You're my . . . I thought we were friends.'

But Luca was walking away now. 'This is all too much,' he said, beating the air angrily with one hand. 'I can't . . . I can't do this.'

Then he was gone.

## 34

Mo didn't remember finding her way back to the house, pulling on her pyjamas and hiding in bed. She had no sense of what time it was when her mum came in, concerned about Lou – news travelled fast in the Donnys – and worried about her too.

'You look terrible, Mo, so pale, and your eyes are all puffy and red,' she said. 'Such a shock. I found out while I was at work and rushed home. Dad didn't even realise. Whittling with his headphones on and missed it all, didn't hear a thing!'

She stroked Mo's face.

'Are you all right? Lou is going to be OK, you know. She's got a broken leg, apparently, and bruises. They're keeping her in for now. The police are out searching for whoever did this to her. Dad's gone to help too. They'll find them, don't you worry.'

Mo refused dinner, wouldn't speak, barely moved. She drifted in and out of sleep, her mind like a jigsaw puzzle that's been overturned and all the pieces scattered. She heard Luca's angry voice in her ears, calling her spoilt, calling her a faker. She saw him turning his back on her, walking away. She heard Lou saying they weren't friends any more. She saw her lying on the ground, her leg broken. She felt Lou's wounded body resting against her. She saw ambulances and stretchers. She pictured Bogdan flitting through the night. She imagined flocks of angry sniffer sheep tearing after him, with Nipper flying beside them – actually flying – barking and urging them on.

Eventually Mo woke. She squinted at the clock. It was 10 a.m. Tuesday morning. The terrible facts of the previous day thumped into her exhausted brain. Lou was in hospital, Luca was gone. All because of her.

'I'm an idiot,' she muttered to Mr Bakewell. 'I deserve to be miserable. I deserve to be alone. I deserve to have no friends. It's not Tracey Caldwell who's stupid, it's me. Actually, she is pretty stupid, but so am I. I am as stupid as Tracey Caldwell. Probably more stupid in fact, as I should know better. I have brought harm to my lovely friend Lou. The Vampire King of the East didn't do it – I did! It's my fault she's in hospital. It's my fault she hates me. Does she hate me? I don't know, but I deserve it if she does.'

Quickly Mo texted Lou, asking how she was, telling her she loved her. Then the terrible thoughts streamed back.

'What about Luca?' she mumbled, rolling onto her side and curling up into a ball. 'I knew I didn't deserve to even look at him, to even be near him, to sniff his delicious cake-shop aroma. I should have stayed hiding behind the fridge door, where I was the first time he walked into my life. It would have been better. It's right that he hates me. I lied to him. No, worse than that, I *was* a lie, a great big lie, dressed up in silly clothes and fake fangs.'

She texted Luca too, apologising, begging him not to tell Bogdan what she'd done, asking to see him. Then she dragged herself out of bed. Her legs felt weak and her head felt heavy. She stubbed her toe on a chest of drawers. I deserve that, she thought. She got shampoo in her eye in the shower, which stung. I deserve that, she thought. She knocked her elbow on the kitchen door frame. I deserve that. She opened a cupboard and a bag of muesli fell on her head. I deserve that. She burned the toast. I deserve that. Dropped a bottle of milk on the floor. I deserve that. Stepped in it and slipped. I definitely deserve that.

Eventually Mo gave up on making breakfast and slumped at the kitchen table with a packet of biscuits. When she remembered her first meeting with Luca, and how he'd eaten biscuits then, tears tumbled down her cheeks. She made no effort to wipe them away. I don't deserve a proper breakfast, I deserve biscuits soaked in tears, she thought. I certainly don't deserve Mini Battenbergs. I will never eat them again, ever.'

She checked her phone. Nothing from Lou or Luca. Then she spotted a note on the kitchen table from her mum, saying she'd be back around three and would take Mo to visit Lou in hospital then.

The words 'Lou' and 'hospital' made Mo cry even more. When she'd finally finished crying and eating biscuits and eating biscuits while crying, she heaved her coat on over her pyjamas and trudged outside, heading for the woods, avoiding the lane where only bad things happened.

Mo swung herself up into the oak tree and watched the rain tumbling from the grey sky. Few drops found her here, nestled in against the trunk. Even the rain doesn't want to be around me, Mo thought, letting her tears fall.

After she'd been sitting there for minutes, hours maybe, Mo's weary brain began turning over the same question. What should she do now? Maybe it was time to tell her parents everything – how she'd faked becoming a vampire – and then go to the police. Get Bogdan arrested for killing Mr Chen and Clive Bunsworth, and for running over Lou.

It was tempting, but when she'd confessed to Luca, it hadn't solved a thing. She had hoped it might bring them closer, but in fact it had driven him away. If she told anyone else, would they even believe her? It was such a crazy story . . . And even if the police actually took her seriously, there were the practical issues. Arresting and detaining Bogdan, a six-hundred-year-old vampire, who could materialise in seconds and who ate humans faster than you could shout, 'Do you want chips with that?' It just wouldn't work.

Then there was the Vampire King of the East, due to arrive to meet her. How was she going to stand up to him without a familiar to back her up, with her confidence shredded like cabbage in a wood chipper?

Mo trudged home. Back in her garden, she headed to the shed. Her dad's whittling had been tidied to one side of the workbench. Otherwise, the place looked as it always had. She sat in the armchair. The turning ceremony danced before her eyes like an out-of-body experience. Mo could see herself crouched in the corner then spinning around, scary gumshield in, blood around her mouth, roaring and making Bogdan quake with fear and joy.

Mo couldn't recognise that crazily courageous version of herself, that girl who believed she could fake it, have it all, student by day and Vampire Queen by night. Now, on this dreary Tuesday, she felt weary, alone and suddenly much older. Luca was right. She'd landed herself in a huge, very dangerous mess. She'd tried to play around with vampires, dip in and out of their world. What did she think this was? The hokey-cokey?

When Mo walked into the kitchen, her mum was hovering nervously.

'I've just heard from Peg, Lou's mum,' she said. 'Lou's doing OK, only she needs to rest. She's been through a lot, and Peg said she's still upset about Nipper. They haven't found him. So unfortunately we can't go and see her this afternoon.'

Mo sat down. She was quiet for a few moments, staring at her hands on the table in front of her.

'She's not resting, Mum,' Mo said eventually. 'She doesn't want to see me.'

'Of course she does,' Mum protested. 'It's just that she needs to take it easy.'

'It's my fault she got hit by the car,' Mo said. 'We argued, and she ran off.'

'No, that's not right,' Mo's mum said, sitting down next to her, urgently grabbing her hands and staring into her eyes. 'You mustn't think that. It was an accident.'

'All this is my fault,' Mo said, her mouth beginning to tremble.

'All what?' her mum asked. 'What do you mean, Mo?'

Mo shook her head, pulled her hands away and ran up to her room. She peered out of the window, towards the shed, in case Luca was there waiting for her. Of course he wasn't. He was probably enjoying his new life, in which he would never have to see her again. He was probably dancing around, smashing plates and teapots, totally ecstatic about being free of Mo forever. Fair enough, Mo thought miserably.

Mo's mum knocked softly on the door and came in.

'I don't want you blaming yourself, Mo,' she said. 'Accidents happen – it's part of life. Would it reassure you if I told you about the time Dad got his trouser zip stuck –'

Mo shot her a look of such fury and horror that she stopped mid-sentence.

'OK, sorry, but I'm just saying, bad things happen to good people all the time – it's life, and no one's to blame. I'll be downstairs if you need me.'

The door clicked shut and Mo sat down at her desk. She tidied some pencils with all the enthusiasm of a toddler eating spinach, then stacked up some textbooks. That's when she found it. There, under a pile of books, a sheet of paper and written on it:

### The Plan - Part Two: HAVING IT ALL!

Mo stared at the words for a second or two, as if they were written in Egyptian hieroglyphs. Then, with a grunt that got higher at the end, like the sound an outraged weasel might make, she ripped it up, gasping and growling, and hurled the pieces at the wall.

Mo watched as they fluttered prettily to the floor – 'Gah! I can't even throw things right!'– and then she flung herself onto her bed and screamed into her pillow. This was better. This was good. This was letting something out. Mr Bakewell tumbled to the floor, landing face down, as if he couldn't stand to watch.

The scream slowly turned into a howl, then a piggy snort and then stopped altogether. Mo sat up, blinking and panting.

'I need to *do* something,' she said. 'I can't just sit here. What do I normally do when I'm feeling complicated? Good question. I don't normally feel complicated. What do I normally do, just, anyway?'

Suddenly Mo knew. She pulled on some jeans but left her pyjama top on, and ran downstairs.

'Where are you going?' her mum asked, as Mo grabbed her coat.

'To the library.'

'Really? But it's getting dark, and you're tired, aren't you?'

'I want to pick up some books, do some studying. You know, that stuff I do,' Mo said.

'Wait, don't rush off, I want to talk to you,' her mum said. 'Your science teacher called me today. I wasn't going to mention it, because of Lou, but Mo, you only got fifteen per cent in your test yesterday. I thought you'd worked hard for that, with Lou. What's going on?'

'Nothing,' Mo said. 'I need to go.'

'Wait, please. I also got an email from your new maths teacher, Mrs Singh, saying you keep missing homework,' her mum went on. 'It's not like you at all. What's going on, love? You're obviously not really OK.'

'I'm fine. Everything is fine, and normal, apart from Lou getting run over. And that nice guy. Luca? Do you remember him?'

'Yes, of course, but I wasn't sure you two were, you know, together.'

'We're not,' said Mo rapidly. 'Never have been, never will be, the end, over, forget it, goodbye. All my fault as well. Totally my fault. I tried to sort of "keep him around", but that didn't work and now he's not. Around, that is. But that's fine. Back to business as usual. Which is why I'm off to the library. Nothing can go wrong there, can it?'

'Mo?' her mum said. 'You're worrying me now.'

'Mum, I just need to get back to my books,' said Mo, pointing towards the front door. "I have been neglecting my schoolwork but I'm going to jump back on it right now. Right this minute. OK?'

Her mum looked keenly at her, trying to read her daughter's expression, then nodded. 'All right,' she said, 'but don't be long. You need to rest too.'

# 35

The librarian greeted Mo like a long-lost friend.

'Mo! Haven't seen you in a while,' he said. 'I've got a new book about American Civil War politics for you, and one on . . . Mo? Are you OK?'

Mo had drifted away and plonked herself down in her favourite booth. The librarian brought over her books. Mo mumbled her thanks, but didn't open them. She still could not stop thinking about Lou, in a hospital bed, and Luca, who knew where. Had he gone home to his parents? Had he told Bogdan she had faked the turning? Was he still smashing plates or was he done with that? The bike ride hadn't driven these two from her mind. The library didn't either.

Mo took out her phone. She never normally used it in the library. It felt wrong and disrespectful. Today was different though.

She texted Lou again:

**How are you? I'm sorry.**

Then she texted Luca again:

**How are you? I'm sorry.**

Then she stared at her phone for about ten minutes, hoping for a response. None came.

'Hey, Mo, your books . . .' the librarian called after her as she left.

Mo didn't turn around. She leaped back on her bike and pedalled fast towards home, her legs pumping, hair flying out behind her. All she could think about was Lou and Luca. Luca and Lou. Her mind going from one to the other like a spectator at a tennis match. As she neared her lane she reached for the phone in her coat pocket. The screen lit up, she peered down, still cycling hard, but nothing. No replies.

Then Mo glanced up again and . . .

'Aarrgghh!'

Something had stepped out in front of her. Stepped out? Appeared, more like, as if from nowhere (or perhaps the hedge). Mo dropped her phone. It clattered against the tarmac. She squeezed the brakes hard and stopped just in time.

'Baaaa,' said the something.

A sheep. In the road. What was it doing there? Mo stared at it, panting hard, her heart racing like a sewing machine. She got off her bike, scrambled in the road for her phone. The screen was shattered. Lou was always telling her not to cycle and use her phone at the same time. Lou was right; it *was* dangerous.

The sheep blinked at her then wandered over to the verge to nibble some grass. Mo watched it for a few moments and then picked up her bike, climbed back on and started pedalling again, not towards home this time, but in the opposite direction. As her legs drove the pedals, they seemed to power her brain. It began to turn, to whirr, to spin into life. She picked up speed, going faster and faster, the dull fog of despair burning off in the blazing sun of action. Finally, suddenly, she knew what she had to do.

I need to visit Lou and tell her I'm sorry. I need to admit what I've done. I need to ask her for help. Then, Luca.

Pedal, pedal, pedal.

Luca, Luca, Luca.

Pedal, pedal, pedal.

I need to find him. I need to speak to him. What will I say? The same, I suppose. I'm sorry I messed up. I need your help.

Pedal, pedal, pedal.

Mo was back in the heart of Lower Donny now.

She leaped off her bike and ran into the local shop.

Is that all I want to say to Luca? she wondered, as she grabbed a packet of dog treats, then a box of Mini Battenbergs, and went over to the checkout.

There was something else coming up, some other message floating to the top of her mind like a slow-motion bubble. Something bigger, more truthful. Honesty, she told herself, that's what matters. No more lies. Luca, I need your help, she said again in her mind and then, there it was, a bright and shining truth that must be spoken.

'I need you,' she said out loud, thinking of Luca's smile, his cinnamon-toast aroma, his twinkling brown eyes, his excellent hair . . .

'Do you, dear?' said Mrs Spreadbury, behind the counter.

Mo blinked hard, focused. 'No, sorry, not you,' she said, blushing. 'I was thinking of something, someone, that I need, very much.'

'What, like a plumber? My Jack's quite handy with a spanner and he's got a full set of rodding poles if your drains are blocked.'

'No, thank you, my drains are fine,' Mo said, taking her things and leaving the shop. They've never been better in fact, she thought, as she climbed back on her bike. And I'm fine too. I'm here, I'm alive and I know what I have to do. I'm going to apologise to Lou. I'm going to tell Luca I need him. First, though, I'm going to find Nipper.

Mo must have cycled three or four miles looking for Nipper. She checked the playing fields and around the bins at the back of the Drowned Rat pub. She even sneaked into Lou's garden and looked in the shed. No luck. She tried to get inside the brain of Nipper which, admittedly, was pretty small and filled with sausage dreams. Having chased a six-hundred-year-old vampire in the dark, where might a small terrier go? Perhaps he wouldn't try to get home, but simply to a safe space.

'Of course,' Mo said out loud. 'He'll be in the woods near home! He knows those woods, where we used to play as kids. That's where he'll be.'

She cycled hard to the edge of the woods, leaped off her bike and, using the torch on her phone, ran towards the oak tree, calling Nipper's name and rustling the packet of dog treats.

Silence.

Mo ventured deeper into the trees, but all was quiet. Doubts trickled in. After all, Mo had been here just this afternoon and seen no sign of him. Perhaps she'd got this wrong.

'Nipper?' Mo called again, casting the beam around, hoping to see the reflective gleam of doggy eyes shining back. Still nothing. Only an owl, hooting mournfully. Mo tramped about, calling and calling, and was losing hope when she heard a rustle. She turned to face it, and suddenly – whoosh! – there he was, bombing towards her like a streak of furry white lightning.

'Nipper!' Mo roared. She dropped to her knees, her arms outstretched, laughing as the little terrier hurled himself at her, clambering over her lap, licking her face, barking excitedly. His white fur was smudged with mud, his lead had come off and he was hungry too. He guzzled the palmfuls of treats Mo offered him, his tail beating hard against her body.

Once Nipper had calmed down, Mo popped him into her backpack, his head poking out of the top and cycled to Middle Donny Cottage Hospital. Outside, she locked up her bike and then, apologising to Nipper, closed the backpack zip over his head, to hide him. The front doors swished open and Mo followed the signs to the children's ward.

She didn't have to ask where Lou Townsend was. A door to one of the small rooms opened, a nurse emerged and, through a chink in the blue curtains, Mo spotted two pink feet at the end of the bed. Mo would know those feet anywhere. She ducked into the room and locked the door behind her.

'I don't want any pudding,' Lou murmured from behind the curtains.

Mo quickly unzipped her bag and pulled Nipper out.

'Really?' Mo said. 'Not even a Mini Battenberg? Or perhaps a face lick?'

She poked Nipper's face through the crack in the curtains. Lou gasped, roared his name. Mo felt him squirming to get at her. She put him down and he raced forward and sprang up onto the bed.

'Oh Nipper, Nipper, Nipper,' Lou said, as Nipper yelped with joy. 'I've missed you, where have you been, how did you get here?'

Slowly, Mo moved the curtain aside, just a slither, with the tip of one finger.

'It was me,' Mo said, smiling shyly. 'I brought him in.'

# 36

Mo approached the bed, then spoke quickly and urgently.

'Before you kick me out, I have to talk to you, please. I came to say I'm sorry. Sorry that I abandoned you. Sorry I got caught up in my own stuff. Sorry we fought and you ran off and got hit by a car.'

'Yeah, that hurt,' Lou said sulkily. 'Like, a lot. Broken leg. Bruises all over the place. I'm the colour of a plum under these pyjamas. You should have a look.'

'I don't want to see your bruises. Actually, I do a bit, but maybe later,' Mo said. 'Mostly, I want to apologise and beg you to please, *please* be my friend again. I don't want to lose you, Lou. You're the best person in the world, the best friend I've ever had and will ever have. And, well, that's it, actually. That's what I came to say.'

Lou blinked hard, like an owl with hay fever. 'You basically dumped me,' she said.

'I know,' said Mo.

'And that's after you had promised me you'd never forget about me, even if you did replace The Plan with The Man.'

'I know that too, but it wasn't exactly because of Luca,' Mo said. 'It's complicated.'

'It didn't feel complicated to me. It felt pants,' Lou said. 'I'm used to you studying so hard you don't have much time for me, but abandoning me just like that, completely, almost overnight, for a boy. That was rubbish.'

'I know, and I'm sorry,' Mo said. 'I've been an idiot.'

'A big idiot?'

'Yes, a really big idiot,' Mo said. 'The kind of massive, humongous idiot that thinks they can fake being Vampire Queen.'

Lou gasped. Her mouth fell open like a trapdoor.

'Yup, I pretended to be turned into a vampire,' Mo went on, 'so I could do the whole Chosen One thing, but also just be me, with my Plan – The Plan.'

'You never! How did you pull that off? What about fangs?'

'I painted teeth on Tracey Caldwell's gumshield,' said Mo.

'No way!' laughed Lou. 'You Caldwelled Caldwell's gumshield.'

'Kind of,' said Mo. 'I'll show you them one day.'

'Yes, please,' said Lou.

'I also bought a long dress . . .'

'The one you were wearing last night, in your garden? That was nice, that.'

'Yes, and I sort of acted all regal and fierce, and Bogdan believed it and I thought I'd be fine, but it was just so hard. I had to be with Luca each evening, which was really great, but as a vampire, so that meant pretending to drink blended worms and avoiding sheep, and not burping in front of him or using my phone or shivering, because vampires don't do any of those things. Plus I had to lie constantly – to him, to you, to Mum and Dad.'

'You could have told me, your oldest friend,' Lou said, a tiny pout forming on her lips.

'I couldn't,' Mo said. 'I wanted to, but it felt too dangerous. Anyway, I'm telling you the truth now, all of it. No more secrets. No more lies. The only thing that matters is us being friends again. Please. Can we?'

Lou gazed at her in silence for a moment.

'I cannot believe you did that, Mo,' she said eventually. 'You utter numpty. I bet you reckoned, with your big brain, that you could think your way through this, outsmart the vampires, stay on top.'

'It wasn't quite like that,' said Mo.

'But it was a *bit* like that, wasn't it?' Lou said, enjoying herself now. 'And instead, you did something really stupid.'

'Well, OK, but I had my reasons,' Mo replied.

'Like Danny Harrington levels of daft.'

'OK, yes, fine,' said Mo, a little flustered, 'but the point is, do you forgive me? Can we be friends again?'

'Oh yeah, that,' Lou said. She looked at Mo, standing there, sorry and stressed and so very Mo-ish. Her mouth stretched into a grin, her eyes sparkled and she threw her arms wide.

'Of course, you big loser,' she said. 'Come here.'

Mo tumbled gratefully into the hug, making Lou laugh and yelp – 'I've got bruises, remember?' – then she scooted into the bed beside Lou, with Nipper in the middle, and passed her a Mini Battenberg.

'Cheers,' said Mo, tapping her cake against Lou's.

'Cheers,' said Lou, taking a bite. 'Just like old times.'

'Except this is a hospital bed,' said Mo.

'Yeah, and except you've morphed into the kind of wild woman who thinks she can fake being a vampire and has fallen hard for a boy.'

'And who gets fifteen per cent in a science test,' Mo added.

'Shut. Your. Mouth!' Lou shouted, staring at Mo.

'You shut yours,' Mo laughed back. 'I can see all the cake in your teeth, it's totally gross.'

'Fifteen per cent! That's unheard of for you.'

'I was too busy thinking about you, and how you'd gone off with Tracey Caldwell,' Mo said.

'Really?' Lou said.

'Yeah, I was hurt. I felt abandoned too.'

'You started it,' said Lou.

'I know,' said Mo, then she pointed at Lou's broken leg. 'I see Tracey's signed your cast already. Are you still friends? Will you go off with her again?'

'No!' said Lou. 'I didn't know she was coming. She just showed up. Basically, she was really worried I'd think the accident was her fault, because it was her idea to go and spy on you. She didn't really care about me – she just wanted to know if she was in trouble.'

Mo nodded, blinking back a few tears, the shock and pain of the last few days surging through her like a current.

'Look, let's not talk about Tracey flippin' Caldwell – she's so not worth it,' Lou said.

'You're right. Sorry,' said Mo, wiping her tears hurriedly and passing Lou another Mini Battenberg.

'I wonder if they'll ever catch the guy who hit me,' Lou said.

Mo felt her stomach drop. 'You didn't see him?'

'No, it was just headlights in my eyes and then . . . *boom!*' said Lou.

'Oh god, Lou. It was Bogdan,' Mo said quietly. 'I'm so sorry. That's my fault too. He's here because of me.'

Lou blinked hard as she processed this new piece of news, and then squeezed Mo's hand. 'He's here because you're the Chosen One,' she said, looking at her friend steadily. 'You can't help that.'

Mo smiled sadly and blinked back more tears.

'At least you've still got Luca, right?' said Lou.

Mo shook her head. 'After you went off in the ambulance, I told him the truth about faking being a vampire and he stormed off. He said he can't trust me.'

'Oh,' said Lou. 'Oh, that sucks. I'm sorry. What are you going to do?'

'Same as I did for you,' Mo said. 'Find him and apologise. I don't think it will work, but it's all I've got. I have to try.'

A sharp knock at the door grabbed their attention.

'Quick, hide Nipper – put your blanket over him,' Mo said, hopping up and opening the door.

'You shouldn't really lock the door to a patient's room,' the nurse said to Mo, just as the sound of Nipper's tail thumping against the bed and making the blanket bounce caught her attention.

'Is there a dog in here? This is a hospital – dogs aren't allowed.'

'He's an assistance dog,' said Mo, leaning over the bed to pick Nipper up. 'Good dog, you've done some lovely assisting this evening, now it's time to take you home. Lou, I'm sure you feel very assisted, don't you?'

'I really do,' she said, grinning and nodding.

'Wonderful,' said Mo, then she waggled Nipper's paw goodbye. 'Our work here is done.'

# 37

Mo cycled back to Lou's house. Nipper was so happy to be home he did an ecstatic wee on the hall carpet, and Mrs Townsend hugged Mo so hard she wondered if she had bruises now too.

Then Mo jumped back on her bike, and pedalled for . . .

Where? Where would Luca be? Was he around still? Could he have left, just like that, in the space of a day? Mo then realised again, with a thud, that she wasn't sure where he'd been staying. She called the Premier Inn in North Nollerton. A receptionist – Kimberly? – chirped a greeting.

'Do you have a guest staying with you by the name of Luca?' Mo asked.

'Luca what?' the receptionist replied.

'Luca, umm . . .' Mo realised with a shock that she didn't even know his last name. 'Idiot,' she muttered, furious with herself.

'Luca Idiot?' the receptionist asked. 'I don't appreciate prank calls. Good evening.'

The line went dead.

There was nothing else for it – Mo would have to go there. It was a long ride, and it started to rain soon after she set off. By the time Mo turned her bike into the Premier Inn car park, her hair looked like rats' tails and her wet jeans were clinging to her legs.

She decided asking which room Luca Idiot was in, while dripping all over the floor, wasn't a great plan. Instead she dialled the hotel one more time and watched as the receptionist – yes, it was Kimberly – picked up.

'Hello, I was just walking my dog behind your hotel and I saw someone near the kitchen doing weird stuff,' Mo said.

'What kind of weird stuff?' Kimberly asked.

Mo, hiding behind a car, peered in through the big glass windows and could see her troubled expression.

'I'm not sure, but you should check it out. It was weird and suspicious, maybe a bit witchy? Bye.'

Mo hung up. She saw Kimberly hurry down the corridor towards the back of the building and grabbed her chance. She raced in through the lobby and up the stairs. She was trying to remember which room Bogdan was in before. Third floor, yes, but as Mo began walking down the corridor, she felt a flicker of panic. The doors all looked the same. She couldn't remember which one they had knocked at when Luca had brought her here, all those days ago. 302? 305? 309?

The panic surged into her legs now and she began running, hoping for a sign, maybe a whiff of cinnamon and toast escaping from under one of the doors. Nothing. It was like one of those nightmares when the corridor gets longer and longer as you run, you can never get to the end, it just stretches off in front of you, forever and ever and . . .

'Luca!' Mo yelled suddenly. 'Luca, please. If you're here. Come out.'

Silence.

'Luca, I'm sorry, please let me see you. I'm so sorry,' Mo shouted, feeling angry, desperate, lonely, very embarrassed.

Movement behind a door. Room 306 opened, just a chink. A bald man stuck his head out.

'Keep it down, love, I'm trying to watch *Bake Off*,' he said.

Mo blushed, dropped her head, began retreating backwards, eyes on the carpet. Then . . . *thud*. She reversed into something solid and warm. She turned.

'Luca!'

Mo smiled up at him – sweet sunbeams of heaven, it felt good to see him – but her smile quickly faded. Luca's face was flat and expressionless.

'What do you want?' he asked.

She shook her head, trying to gather herself. Her wet hair whipped her cold, rain-flushed cheeks.

'Can we talk inside?' she said. 'That man is trying to watch *Bake Off*.'

'What is *Bake Off*?' Luca asked, squinting at the man, who glowered at them and then slammed his door shut.

'Competitive cake making,' Mo said. 'Although they sometimes do pies too. Or biscuits.'

'Sounds really thrilling,' Luca said flatly.

'Please can I come inside?' Mo asked, twisting her hands into knots, peeping nervously at him.

Slowly, reluctantly, Luca pushed the door of his room open and went in, holding it for Mo.

'I guess I don't have to invite you in,' he said, 'seeing as you're not a real vampire.'

That blow landed. Mo felt it wind her.

'That's what I wanted to talk to you about,' she said. 'No, not talk about, apologise for. You're right. I was a faker. I was stupid. I know that now, but I also know . . .'

She hesitated.

'What?' he asked.

Mo took a deep breath.

'That a part of why I faked being queen, actually a really big part, was to keep you around, with me, near me,' Mo said, looking at the floor, blinking fast and talking faster. 'I was frightened of the Vampire King hurting Lou and my family and me, like Bogdan said, but I was also frightened of losing you. I can see that now. I couldn't see it then.'

'OK,' said Luca.

'It's fine that you don't like me, in that way, or at all. Especially now, after I've lied to you for so long and pretended to be something I'm not,' Mo said. 'I just needed to be honest with you, properly, finally, before you go.'

She glanced over to a suitcase on the floor, stuffed with his clothes.

'You're all packed,' Mo said.

'Yes, but with nowhere to go,' Luca said. 'I can't go back home. I won't know how to explain to my parents that I'm out of a job. They were so proud of me.'

'Then stay here with me,' Mo said, her voice urgent, pleading. She longed to reach out to him, touch his sleeve, feel the warmth of his hand, but she didn't move.

'Stay with you how? As your familiar?' Luca snapped.

'No, just as you,' Mo said. 'And me just as me. The new me, if you're OK with that. Not the Mo you first met in my kitchen, the one with The Plan for her life. Not the fake vampire either. This me, wearing wet jeans, who's just cycled five miles in the rain to apologise to you, who's made a mess of everything and is quite scared and would really like your help.'

Mo had never made a speech like this before. At debating society she argued a side, took a position, made three carefully prepared points. This, though, was something true, unplanned, felt. It poured out of her, like good clean water from a mountain spring.

Luca said nothing, but slowly his mouth bent into a smile. Not his full-beam smile, something quieter, smaller, shyer.

'You know what I think?' he said.

Mo shook her head nervously.

'I think you need a hot chocolate.'

# 38

Mo slumped down in an armchair while Luca mixed her a hot chocolate, using the tiny hotel kettle on the tiny hotel tray on the also tiny hotel desk. She felt suddenly exhausted, but in a good way. The big-scale, peaceful fatigue that washes over you when you've spoken your truth and can't do any more.

Luca passed her the drink and then sat in the chair opposite. Mo cradled the warm cup in her hands and sipped it gratefully.

'Better than blended worms?' he asked.

She nodded.

'I never drank them, by the way,' she said. 'I just tipped them in the bushes.'

'I know,' Luca said.

'What do you mean, you know?'

'I mean, I suspected,' Luca replied, 'that you weren't quite the full vampire.'

Mo stared hard at Luca.

'Feeling the cold, not materialising very well through that hedge, frightened of bats, burping . . .' He counted her failures off on his fingers.

'I knew it! I knew vampires weren't supposed to burp!' Mo said.

'They're not supposed to only stay up until ten either, or get colds, or eat worms or live in sheds.'

'So why did you go along with it?' Mo asked, her cheeks flushing with a blend of anger and embarrassment. Who had been fooling who exactly? 'If you guessed I was faking, why were you so furious with me last night?'

'It's complicated,' said Luca.

'That's my line!' said Mo angrily, sloshing hot chocolate on her lap. 'You don't get to say, "It's complicated." I'm the one who's been dealing with "it's complicated" for days now. Not you.'

'All right, sorry,' Luca said, holding his hands up. 'It wasn't easy for me either – is that better? I wasn't sure whether you were a vampire or not. You seemed pretty human to me, but Bogdan believed you were turned, and then you silenced Derek's familiar just like that. So, I thought, maybe I'm missing something. You're weren't quite like a regular vampire, but then again, you've never been quite like a regular human either.'

Mo frowned.

'That's a compliment, Mo,' Luca added.

'Is it?'

'Anyway, when you confessed you had faked it, it was my worst fears confirmed,' Luca said. 'I was angry and worried for you. You're in big trouble – you know that, don't you? But I was also disappointed.'

'Disappointed?' Mo said.

'Because that meant the end, right? I can't be your familiar any more. We can't hang out in the oak tree. I can't talk to you every evening. I was . . .'

'Yes . . . ?' Mo said.

'I . . .'

A knock at the door. Three hard bangs from a fist.

'Ignore that, they'll leave, probably just that *Bake Off* guy,' Mo said quickly. 'Carry on – what were you saying?'

*BANG! BANG! BANG!*

Louder this time.

'I should check who it is,' Luca said.

'Finish your sentence. You were something. What was it?'

No good, Luca had run to the door. He peered through the spyhole and turned back to Mo, his face suddenly pale.

'It's Bogdan!' he whispered. 'Quickly, you must hide.'

'Why?' said Mo, jumping up. 'I can see him. It's OK.'

'But look at you! You're not dressed like a queen. You've got jeans and a . . . what is that?'

'Pyjama top,' Mo said.

'You've got jeans and a pyjama top on. You're shivering and wet. You've just had a hot chocolate. He might suspect.'

'But I want to hear him apologise for running over Lou. I want justice for that!'

'Vampires don't apologise!' Luca said. 'Now quickly, in here.'

He slid the wardrobe door open and, before Mo could protest, he shoved her inside and rolled it shut. Mo blinked in the darkness and listened hard as Luca opened the room door.

'Bogdan, sir, good to see you,' Luca said.

'Invite me in, and make it quick sharp – there's a bald guy here looking plenty furious,' Bogdan muttered. 'If he stares at me much longer, I might have to eat him.'

'You are most welcome inside,' Luca said.

Mo heard Bogdan stride into the room and Luca shut the door.

'How may I assist you?' he said.

'Where is Mo?' Bogdan asked. 'I can't find her anywhere and there is much to discuss.'

'I don't know,' Luca said. 'Probably out feeding.'

'Why are you not with her?' Bogdan asked. 'Familiar must always stay with his master.'

'She likes to eat alone, remember?' said Luca.

'Well, when will she be back?' Bogdan asked.

'Later?' Luca suggested.

*PING.*

Mo fumbled, as quietly and quickly as she could, for the phone in her pocket, now lit up with a text from her mum.

Where are you? Come home soon, please, it's dark and I'm worried about you. What do you fancy for dinner? Quiche or veggie chilli?

'What was that?' Bogdan asked.

'The microwave,' said Luca.

'In the wardrobe?'

'Yes, keeps the cooking smells inside.'

Silence. Maybe Bogdan was considering the benefits of putting a microwave in a wardrobe. Then . . .

'Achoo!'

Mo sneezed.

'And that?' Bogdan asked. 'I may be ancient vampire, but I know microwave cannot sneeze. What's going on in this damn stupid cupboard.'

Mo heard his footsteps getting nearer. She shrank into the corner, trying to become tiny.

'There's nothing there, really,' Mo heard Luca saying. Too late. Light spilled into the dark interior and Mo, blinking, looked up to see Bogdan staring down at her.

'What in the name of all that is unholy . . .'

'Hi,' said Mo, with a small wave. 'Looking for the minibar?'

Bogdan said nothing. His eyes narrowed with questions and Mo thought she detected a slight curl to his lip as she unfolded her long legs from beneath her and stepped out of the wardrobe. Finally, once she was upright, smoothing down her rumpled and still wet clothes, he bowed quickly.

'Your Majesty,' he said. 'Unusual place to sit.'

'I was hiding,' said Mo, squeezing past him. 'I was going to jump out on Luca. He had no idea I was in there. It would have been a really funny prank, but you ruined it unfortunately. Never mind. Shall we sit?'

Mo sat down and Bogdan took the armchair opposite. He pulled a letter, written in familiar jagged red ink, from his coat pocket and was about to read it, when an irritated tut escaped his lips.

'Before I begin, may I ask why you are wearing this top, these jeans?' he said, his forefinger waggling up and down. 'Forgive me, my queen, but it's not very special on you. Denim is so everyday, you know?'

'You can talk,' said Mo. 'May I ask why you're wearing a shirt with pineapples and palm trees on it? Bit jolly for a vampire, isn't it?'

'Ah yes,' he said, 'it's my new holiday shirt, for when I retire to Caribbean. You not like? It's nice, made from linen which is natural fibre, not like your shirt.'

He leaned across and rubbed the material of her pyjama top between finger and thumb, then pulled his hand back sharply like he'd touched something you should wipe up with disinfectant.

'What is this – some kind of flannel? Bah! And the pattern, little animals?'

'Woodland creatures,' Mo said.

'But this is penguin right next to deer,' Bogdan said. 'Funny kind of woodland. No, no, no. Not fitting for Vampire Queen. Luca, take Mo shopping before Wednesday.'

'What's happening Wednesday?' Mo asked.

'This is my big news,' said Bogdan, fluttering the letter. 'He is coming. At last. Like mighty wind across all Europe. The Vampire King of East. To meet you, Vampire Queen of these lands. I hardly can believe it!'

Bogdan's eyes were gleaming, like a child seeing the tree lit up on Christmas morning.

'What do you say?' he added. 'It's pretty cool smart, no?'

Mo glanced at Luca, then took a deep breath.

'It is very cool smart, and we will look forward to greeting him,' she replied. 'Hang on – did you say Wednesday? That's tomorrow!'

'No, day after tomorrow,' said Bogdan.

'No, today is Tuesday. Wednesday is tomorrow,' said Luca.

'Ah yes, I lost track of time. It happens, when you're over six hundred years old,' Bogdan said, smiling. 'Wonderful. The better the sooner. He's coming tomorrow!'

'What time?' Mo asked.

Bogdan reread the letter quickly.

'His boat docks at 5 p.m. sharp. Vampire King of East is always punctual. I will collect him in car so should be here by seven.'

'That's only twenty-four hours away,' Mo said. 'Almost no time at all.'

'My advice?' Bogdan said. 'Make a big fuss and bother of him. Then he will be so happy and go home content. Then I'm off to Caribbean and we live happily always after, yes?'

Bogdan grinned, but then suddenly his smile slipped, his eyes narrowed, his nose wrinkled. He sniffed the air like a meerkat on sentry duty.

'There is strong scent in here,' he said. 'Familiar scent. I know it, but it can't be.'

He picked up Mo's cup and sniffed it, his face darkening.

'It's the smell of a human,' he said.

'It must be Luca,' said Mo quickly. 'He is very fragrant, isn't he? Like toast and spices and baked goods. Quite overpowering.'

Luca opened the window, muttering, 'Sorry for my smell.'

Bogdan ignored Luca. He was staring at Mo. He stood up, leaned towards her, his nose twitching, sucking in the scent of her like a dog at a lamp post.

'Gah!' he said, recoiling. 'It's you! *You* stink like a human. The same smell you had before you were turned. Mo, how can this be?'

'No idea what you're talking about,' Mo said, hopping over to the other side of the room.

Bogdan wheeled around to face her, his eyes now terrifying black coals. His lips parted in a sneer. Mo gasped. There, gleaming white and sharp as razors, were his fangs, fully descended.

'Mo, what is the meaning of this?' he asked, his voice deep and slow now. 'Answer me, vampire to vampire. Show me your fangs. Now!'

Mo patted her pocket hopelessly, knowing already that her gumshield fangs were at home.

Bogdan edged towards her.

'Please step away from the queen,' Luca said, rushing forward and standing in front of Mo, his arms thrown out wide.

'Move, Luca!' Bogdan hissed.

'I cannot do that, sir,' Luca replied, edging Mo backwards into the corner, where she cowered, trembling.

'Luca . . .' Bogdan threatened. He seemed to grow taller and wider as he stepped slowly towards them. What if he hurts Luca? Mo thought quickly. Luca, who's defending me, but this is my fault, my mess.

Then she saw it, on the bedside table. A pencil, lying next to a little hotel notepad. Would that work as a stake? Could she drive it through Bogdan's heart if he attacked? Would it penetrate his shirt, his skin, his chest wall? Would it snap on a rib? Did she even have the courage to do it? No answers came, but Mo grabbed the pencil anyway and, clenching it in her fist like a tiny spear, she pushed Luca firmly to one side and stepped forward.

'Back off, fang-face,' she said, 'or I'll drive this stake right through your heart.'

Bogdan hissed and dropped backwards, raising one arm defensively.

'You'd deserve it, too, for running over my friend,' Mo continued, anger flickering inside.

'You're lucky I didn't stop the car and eat her,' Bogdan spat back, flashing his fangs.

'That's my best friend you're talking about, you bloodsucking pig!' Mo shrieked, furious now.

She jabbed the pencil towards him, her face set hard, her body tense.

Bogdan flinched and hissed again. 'I'm no pig,' he said. 'I am a vampire.'

He spread his arms wide, then caught sight of his pineapple shirt, and folded them back in.

'Well, I'm not,' Mo shouted. 'Never have been, never will be. You guessed right, Bogdan. You smelled the truth. I'm still a human. One hundred per cent living. Now you can deal with that or you can get staked through the heart with this very sharp HB pencil. What's it going to be?'

# 39

Bogdan stared at Mo, silenced by her fury, by the power in her voice, appalled by what she'd told him. She hoped he couldn't detect that her hand was shaking, that the pencil wasn't actually that sharp. The silence stretched on for seconds, but finally Bogdan turned away and retreated to the armchair, where he sat down heavily, shaking his head, rubbing his eyebrows.

'Mo, Mo, Mo,' he muttered, his hissing replaced by a tone of weary regret. 'What have you done? Did you think you could mess with the Vampire King of the East?'

'That's what I said,' Luca muttered. Mo stepped hard on his foot.

'This is bad. This is plenty, extra bad,' said Bogdan.

'I was trying to keep you happy. Protect my family and Lou from his anger. Protect you too. I don't know why I bothered. No one – literally no one – is grateful. Besides, it was you who harmed Lou anyway, when you ran her over,' she said, jabbing the pencil at him again.

'She was in the way,' Bogdan shot back in a 'what did you expect' voice. 'People should take care on dark lanes at night.'

'You could have killed her,' Mo shouted, gripping the pencil so hard her knuckles went white.

'I could have killed anyone, I'm a vampire. It's what we do,' said Bogdan. 'Well, we real vampires, that is.'

Mo took a breath, trying to calm herself. Luca shifted uneasily.

'Look, I did what I did, and now the question is, what do I do next?' Mo said. 'The Vampire King of the East is on his way. I'm not a real vampire. He might find out. Those are the facts. So –'

'It's not too late to turn you,' Bogdan interrupted, looking at Mo with narrowed eyes.

Mo raised the pencil higher. 'Don't even think about it,' she snarled.

'We could do it right now,' Bogdan said.

'No, Bogdan. I refuse to be a vampire,' Mo shouted. 'Understand?'

Bogdan glared at her, silent.

'Do. You. Understand?' Mo roared.

'OK, I get it,' Bogdan said, sounding sulky.

'Good,' said Mo.

She lowered the pencil and let her breathing slow down a little before speaking again.

'I need to convince the Vampire King of the East that all is well. Then he'll go away, no one gets eaten and you get to retire to a nice quiet island where there are no young people for you to drive into. Right?'

Bogdan's face flickered with irritation, but he said nothing.

'I'm sorry I faked being turned,' Mo added. 'I owe you that apology.'

'I'm sorry too, because now you have much trouble coming your way,' Bogdan said. 'We all do.'

'But you believed I was the Vampire Queen at the turning ceremony, remember?' Mo said. 'Surely I can convince the Vampire King that I am, one more time, just for a short visit.'

Bogdan made a dismissive 'pffftt' noise with his lips. 'You need to stop smelling so like a human, for startings,' he said.

'That's a great tip,' said Mo. 'I need more advice like that. I need your vampire expertise, your years of knowledge. You're the only one who's met the Vampire King. You know how he operates. I have Luca on my team, but I need you too.'

'I trusted you, Mo, and you tricked me. You lied to me,' he said. 'Why should I do anything for you again?'

'Because I'm being completely honest with you now,' said Mo, 'and also because your undead life depends on it. You said yourself, he could execute you if he discovers you haven't created a proper queen. Just think, so close to retirement, six hundred years of being a vampire, and –

Mo clicked her fingers. 'Finished off, just as you are about to taste freedom.'

Bogdan glowered at Mo. 'I could get out of here now, go into hiding somewhere, leave you alone to face him,' he said.

'The Vampire King would find you,' Mo said. 'He'd track you down, wherever you go.'

'He would pardon me. I have been his loyal subject since he became king,' Bogdan protested.

'Really? Sure about that?' Mo said. 'He's ruthless, remember? He hates betrayal. You told me that yourself.'

'All right, stop saying words,' Bogdan snapped. 'You always did like to talk.'

Mo sensed her advantage and pressed on.

'Look, we all lose if the Vampire King of the East works out I'm not the real deal,' she said. 'So it's either carry on faking, for just a bit longer, or feel his fury.'

'Like a mighty wind,' Luca said.

'Yes, precisely,' said Mo.

Bogdan stood up and began pacing the room. 'I still can't believe this,' he fumed. 'I don't know how I got it wrong. I thought you were Chosen One. I was so sure.'

'Master, she is,' Luca said.

'Rubbish!' Bogdan stormed. 'Chosen One would be out draining blood from tasty humans in cool, excellent outfit right now. Not wearing terrible, nasty pyjamas and drinking hot chocolate.'

'Think about how she's behaved though,' Luca persisted. 'Pretending to be a vampire took courage. She just stood up to you too. That's brave. She's quick-thinking and focused, and she also knows when to apologise. That's what you'd expect from a queen, isn't it? From the Chosen One?'

Mo felt heat rising in her cheeks. Wow! Luca thinks all that about *me*!

'This is sign of nice leader, true, but without the violence that's usual in a ruler,' Bogdan replied. 'You know, having pleasant chat and then, *bosh!* Someone's head comes off and is rolling across floor.'

Bogdan was quiet for a few moments, perhaps picturing all those wonderful times when a Vampire Ruler had decapitated an innocent human, *bosh!* Just like that.

'It's risky,' Bogdan said finally. 'Faking being Vampire Queen in front of Vampire King . . . very risky. Plenty risky. Extra plenty risky.'

'I know,' said Mo.

'Even if we work together, it's still super-much risky,' Bogdan said.

'It's risky, agreed. I got that,' Mo said.

'Risky, risky, risky,' Bogdan muttered. 'I just hope Luca is right. I hope I was right, too, about you, Mo. That you are Chosen One, in some deeply-down way. Little bit special, yes?'

Then he smiled faintly at Luca.

'I see she's got, how you say? Inside your skin, eh, boy?'

Luca blushed and looked at the floor, but Mo continued to watch Bogdan.

'So you'll do it?' she said. 'You'll help me prepare to meet the Vampire King, help me convince him I'm the real thing?'

'Do I have a choice?' he huffed.

'No,' said Mo.

Bogdan sighed theatrically and threw up his hands. 'All right, all right, I'll do it,' he said.

Mo whooped and Luca let out a huge 'yes', but Bogdan silenced them with a stern look.

'But –' he raised a finger in warning – 'but this will be much work, so no messing, OK? The stakes are high – and you know how much I hate stakes. We start planning tonight. Right now. This instant. There is no times to lose.'

# 40

Mo grabbed the pencil that just seconds ago she'd wielded like a stake, and the notepad.

'Love making plans,' she said, grinning. 'I've been doing this all my life, but first I need to text my mum, tell her I'm OK. I can't be back too late or she'll kill me.'

'Oh my stars,' Bogdan said. 'The Vampire Queen, worried about her mum killing her. The world has gone plenty silly.'

'Veg chilli, please,' Mo muttered, quickly finishing off her text, then putting her phone away. 'Right. The way I see it, we need to minimise the Vampire King of the East's time with me. Build up the idea that I'm very busy dealing with the other vampires of Great Britain, my time is precious and I don't have long, even with him. It's the kind of thing a big star or a world leader does.'

'Go on,' said Bogdan.

'So, a greeting, pleased to meet you, welcome to England, did you have a nice journey, how was the weather, etc. Then a brief chat and we're done. Then get him out. Short but sweet, and no attempt to make being here look appealing. He needs to think it's rubbish and be happy to leave me to rule and never come back.'

'Yes, this can perhaps work,' said Bogdan. 'I certainly want never to be coming back here. Very sad, damp, tragic little place.'

'Bogdan, you can then drive him away in the car,' said Mo. 'I want him far from the Donnys as soon as possible.'

'Same old story, vampires never welcome anywhere,' Bogdan sighed.

'Well, if you stopped eating people, you might find the red carpet getting rolled out a bit more often,' Mo said tartly. 'Now, how should I address him?'

'His real name is Matislav Rosstistavich,' Bogdan said.

'Ros-stitch-a-vich?' Mo tried.

'No, it is *stist* sound,' said Bogdan. 'You put your tongue on roof of mouth. Stist, stist . . . Try it.'

'Ros*stist*avich,' Mo said awkwardly.

'Hmm, you sound like snake with lisp. Try again,' Bogdan huffed.

'Ros*stist*avich,' Mo said.

'Again!' Bogdan ordered.

'Ros*stist*avich. Ros*stist*avich. Ros*stist*avich!'

'Not bad,' he said, 'but a still a little harsh on the ear. Also, you look like you might tiny bit spit on him as you say it. Probably best if you stick to Your Majesty.'

Mo sighed. 'Fine,' she said. 'Next we need a suitable location for the meeting, and *not* my dad's shed.'

'A castle,' Bogdan said. 'A bit ruined, for atmosphere, you know? Not too neat and human. Shabby chic, yes?'

'There are no castles around here,' Mo said.

'Manor house?'

'There's Donny Under Oak Manor – they hire it out for weddings and functions,' Mo said.

'Bodily functions?' Bogdan asked.

'No, conferences and big meetings,' Mo explained.

'Sounds terrible,' Bogdan said. 'Very human and boring. What about a great hall?'

'None of those nearby either,' Mo said, 'unless you mean a village hall.'

'Great hall, village hall, same thing,' said Bogdan.

'*Almost* the same thing,' said Mo.

'It's hall, yes?'

'I suppose,' said Mo, thinking of Lower Donny's village hall, not much bigger than a garage, with a tiny stage at one end and a single loo.

'Good,' said Bogdan. 'Get me this hall. Then we need a big fuss for him. When Vampire King of East visited Vampire Duke of Malprattia in 1790, they fired thirty canons, burned a whole village down and cooked three hundred peacocks in his honour.'

'Surely he couldn't eat the peacocks,' Mo said.

'It's the thought that counts.' Bogdan shrugged. 'Then there was music and juggling dogs.'

'I didn't know dogs could juggle,' Mo said.

'Juggling *with* dogs. Little ones – I don't know, chihuahuas or something. And yes! Decorations!' Bogdan shouted. 'We must decorate the great hall, fit for the Vampire King. He is very snappy dresser, cares about appearances, you know? Decorations essential.'

'Lou has bunting,' Mo said.

'Made from human tongues?' Bogdan asked.

'No, fabric. Floral mostly, some gingham.'

'I suppose that will do,' Bogdan shrugged. 'In seventeenth century we used tongues, but they can attract flies a little bit. Thrones! That's another. Need one for you and one for him. Can't do special nice meeting standing up.'

'They have stacking chairs at the hall,' Mo said. 'OK, let's see . . . We have venue, thrones, decorations. It's coming together nicely. What else. A gift, maybe?'

'A couple of female virgins is a nice, traditional gift for a vampire king,' Bogdan said.

Mo slammed her pencil down against her notepad. 'No way. We're not doing that old-skool stuff on my watch, got it?'

Bogdan raised his eyebrows in surprise, but didn't say anything.

'I was thinking more a commemorative plate or maybe some bath products,' Mo said. 'Leave that with me. Then, when we're done – fifteen minutes tops – you drive him away. Anything else?'

'Oh my coffins. Food!' Bogdan shrieked. 'We forgot about food.'

'No food,' Mo said firmly. 'It was in my original contract, remember? Banquets are off! I forbid it.'

Bogdan sucked in his breath slowly, like a builder working out how much to charge for knocking through your living room. 'That is dangerous,' he said. 'What kind of state visit doesn't include banquet, with selection of local delicacies?'

'Maybe some alternative blood,' she said, thinking of the blended worms. 'I'll tell him it's what vampires eat here, a regional thing. He'll hate it but have to respect it. What does he know, he's never been to England before? Plus, then he'll be even more glad to leave. OK, this is taking shape. We can do this, right? We totally can. Anything else I've missed?'

'You need to be careful about how you present yourself, Mo,' said Luca. 'Hide your humanness. That means don't burp, yawn, shiver, sneeze, drink hot chocolate, say you don't like bats or pretend to materialise, or he'll guess immediately that you're faking.'

'Yes, definitely don't burp,' said Bogdan. 'Whoever heard of a vampire burping? No way! And please hide your smelly human smell.'

'That's quite a lot to remember, but I can do it,' Mo said, chewing the pencil, reading through the list.

'Alternatively,' said Luca, 'and this is just a suggestion, we could simply kill him.'

'What?!' Bogdan screamed, pinging out of his chair like he'd sat on a wasp. 'Have you lost your thinking brain? Are you drunk? Kill Vampire King? And bring all the vampires of Europe down on this tiny village, looking for revenge? Luca, really. What a stupid suggestion.'

'Sorry,' Luca mumbled.

'*Stupid*, stupid suggestion. The stupidest thing I ever heard,' Bogdan said. 'Plenty super stupid.'

'Let's stay on track, both of you,' Mo interrupted, pointing her pencil at Luca and then Bogdan. 'There will be no killing, of vampires or humans. We will achieve success by commitment, excellent preparation and tight execution on the night.'

'Execution?' said Bogdan, his eyes suddenly sparkling. 'I thought you said no killing.'

'Execution of the *plan*,' said Mo. 'Agreed? I need you both backing me up to pull this off.'

'I will be your faithful familiar,' Luca said, bowing. 'I'll call you Majesty and Queen, and be on my best familiar behaviour.'

'I will bring king to hall, and get him out quick sharp,' said Bogdan.

'Great. That's it then. We have a plan,' said Mo, smiling at Bogdan and Luca.

'Yes, we have a plan,' Bogdan said, 'but still this won't be easy. You must convince him you are queen. Only you can do that, Mo. It won't be a nice walk around park, you understand? Vampire King trusts no one, and he can sniff out a human like a pig finds truffles. You must give the performance of your *life*! Good luck, and don't mess it up.'

# *41*

Wednesday. The day after Tuesday. The day the Vampire King of the East, powerful vampire leader and renowned violent despot, would arrive in Lower Donny to meet his appointed queen.

Wednesday, about 11.30 a.m., and the aforementioned appointed queen had told her mum she felt ill, wasn't in school and was, instead, leaning over a bowl in the kitchen sink, whisking rapidly.

'Add more carpet cleaner,' Mo said. 'It needs to have a real kick, you know?'

Luca, standing next to her, poured in some blue liquid from a huge plastic bottle. Mo stirred again, and then they both bent over it, sniffing.

'It's very . . .' Luca said, rubbing his nose, trying not to sneeze.

'Chemical? Aggressive? Painful to inhale?' Mo suggested. 'I'm not getting the bubble bath coming through though. Maybe a bit more of that.'

Luca drizzled some in. Mo whisked. They both took another deep sniff.

'Better,' Luca said. 'Not nice, but better.'

'Will it mask my human smell?' Mo asked. 'What was it Bogdan said? The Vampire King can sniff out a human like a dog sniffs bacon?'

'A pig smells truffles,' said Luca, doing his best Bogdan impression.

Mo laughed, a little hysterically. 'Why am I laughing? I've got to stand up to a notorious vampire lord in about eight hours' time. He's coming for me.'

'Like a mighty wind,' Luca said.

'Yes, like a mighty wind that's also really violent,' Mo said, biting her lip. 'I'm so jittery this morning. It's nerves. Focus, Mo!'

She began pouring the homemade perfume into a small scent bottle, her hands shaking slightly.

'I never realised I had a smell until Bogdan said.'

'Oh yeah, you smell kind of like fresh laundry and orange zest and, hang on . . .' Luca leaned in close and sniffed her neck. It made Mo's hands wobble even more and she sloshed some of the perfume on the draining board.

'There's a note of wet dog in there too,' he said.

'Hey!' Mo said. 'You can talk. At least I don't smell like overpriced flapjacks.'

She put the stopper in the bottle and held it up to the light.

'This should mask my human whiff,' Mo said, 'and also make the perfect gift for a Vampire King.'

'The second perfect gift,' Luca said. 'He really would prefer a couple of virgins, like Bogdan said.'

'Well, that's never going to happen. Patriarchal pig!' Mo huffed. 'When are vampires going to move into the twenty-first century and start eating a more balanced, diverse diet? Now, what else is there to do? Think, think, think. I've texted about booking the village hall. The manager hasn't replied yet, but I'm sure it's fine. Nothing goes on in there anyway. My dress has just had a wash. My velvet robe, bangles and hair slide are in a bag by the front door, ready. Oh, did you do the worms yet?'

'Done,' said Luca, pulling a glass bottle filled with grey liquid out of his backpack.

'Nice decanter,' said Mo.

'I borrowed it from the kitchen at the Premier Inn.'

'Perfect,' Mo said. 'It's all coming together.'

She began putting everything into a box, ready for the evening, then paused and looked up.

Luca was smiling at her.

'What?' she said.

'You look nice with your hair tied up like that,' he said. 'I can see your face.'

Mo touched her long ponytail, blushed a little and felt suddenly self-conscious, her focus shattering like a wine glass on concrete.

'I just need to throw my dress in the tumble dryer and then we can go round to Lou's to collect the bunting, OK? She messaged to say she got out of hospital first thing this morning. I can't wait to see her back at home.'

When Mo and Luca arrived at Lou's house, Mrs Townsend hugged them on the doorstep, while Nipper pinged vertically up and down like he was on springs.

They went upstairs.

'I don't want any more porridge,' Lou moaned, after Mo tapped on the door.

'No porridge – just me and a surprise visitor,' she said.

Lou was lying slumped against her pillows, her leg with its heavy cast flat out across the duvet. Mo moved into the room and Luca followed. His arrival acted like an electric shock on Lou, who shot upwards, simultaneously tousling her wavy hair, straightening her pyjamas, scowling at Mo and also smiling at Luca.

'I didn't know you two were coming over,' she said, then whispered to Mo. 'You made up then?'

Mo nodded quickly.

'How are you feeling?' Luca asked, beaming at Lou. 'Sorry about Bogdan – he's never been the best driver. They didn't have cars when he was a human, six hundred years ago.'

Lou laughed, loud and hard.

'We came to borrow your bunting, if that's OK,' Mo said. 'I need to decorate the village hall. We've got a special visitor arriving tonight.'

'Like a mighty wind,' Luca said.

'Who is it?' Lou asked.

Mo glanced at Luca, unsure whether to let Lou in on the details.

'Mo . . .' Lou said, stretching her name out like it was elastic, 'when you came to see me in hospital, you said you'd be honest with me from now on. No more secrets, remember?'

'I did say that, yes, annoyingly I did,' said Mo. 'OK, look, it's the Vampire King of the East. He's the head vampire, Bogdan's boss, and I'm supposed to be his queen, ruling things over here in Great Britain, but obviously I'm not a real vampire and he totally is, complete with a violent streak a mile wide.'

'What kind of violent?' Lou asked.

'Ha ha, where to begin?' Luca mumbled.

'Like, Tracey Caldwell levels of horribleness?'

'If only,' said Mo. 'You know how Caldwell can rip an apple in half with her bare hands? Yeah, well, the Vampire King does that to human heads, apparently.'

'Oh, Mo,' said Lou, her hand flying up to her mouth. 'He sounds so scary. Do you have to do this?'

'I do, but it's going to be OK,' Mo said. 'I have a plan, and this time I've got Luca and Bogdan on my side.'

'But it sounds risky,' Lou said, grabbing her hand. 'You look nervous – I can see it in your eyes. Maybe I can help you. I could come along too, to back you up.'

'No. It's not safe,' Mo said.

'But I could hide out of the way and then attack him with my crutches if he gets out of hand,' Lou said. 'Anyway, I'd quite like to get a look at this Vampire King. He sounds sort of terrifying but also, you know, amazing. What does he look like?'

'No idea,' said Mo. 'This is all new to me, but I think I'm ready. We've planned out every detail of the meeting. We'll keep it short and then Bogdan will drive him away.'

'And bunting is part of that plan?' Lou asked, a little uncertainly.

'Yes, and these,' said Mo, quickly slipping her gumshield fangs into her mouth and hissing at Lou.

Lou shrieked. 'God, Mo, you scared me,' she said.

Mo laughed and tossed the fangs at her friend.

'Well, that's the idea,' she said. 'I am the Vampire Queen, after all.'

# 42

The overhead strip lights in Lower Donny village hall blinked into life and flickered uncertainly for a few seconds. Mo and Luca stepped inside. Luca put up a folding table in the centre of the room and Mo dumped the box full of props and bunting on it. Then she glanced at the large clock on the wall.

'Six o'clock,' she said. 'We've got one hour before he gets here.'

'Maybe you should eat something?' Luca suggested.

'No, I can't think about food right now. This energy drink is enough,' she said, swigging some from a can.

'Have you turned your phone off too?' Luca said. 'Don't want your mum texting you halfway through meeting the Vampire King, asking what you want for dinner.'

'I told her I'm at Lou's, but good point,' Mo said, fumbling for her phone and switching it off. Then she surveyed the space.

'Right, we need thrones,' she said.

Luca placed two brown stacking chairs either side of the table.

'Great. Can you draw the curtains – we mustn't let anyone look in – and I'll unpack the rest of the stuff and set it all up on the table,' said Mo. 'Blended worms in Premier Inn decanter –check. Two glasses – check. Gift of hideous perfume in presentation bottle – check. Hang on, what's this?'

Mo's fingers found a box in among the bunting. She pulled it out. Mini Battenbergs, hidden there by Lou, with 'Good Luck' written in marker pen on the packet. Mo smiled and put them on the table too. It would feel good to have a bit of Lou with her.

'Let's get some of this bunting up then,' said Luca.

In silence, they draped a few lengths around the hall's walls. Mo thought it looked a little sad, hanging limply in the harsh overhead lighting. Then she looked at the table with all the meeting's props arranged on them and felt a geyser of doubt erupt inside her. Why had they thought this would be enough? Some bunting and blended worms, a rubbish gift of reeking perfume, and not a roasted peacock in sight. Sure, the Vampire King might decide 'these islands' were sad and tragic, as Mo hoped – prayed – and race back to the East, but then again, he might be outraged by this lame DIY reception and, and . . .

Mo thumped down hard on one of the thrones. The plastic seat creaked against its metal legs.

'Oh, Luca, is this enough? Is this going to work?' she said.

'Sure, why not? It's not all this he's come for anyway,' Luca said, indicating the odd selection of props on the folding table. 'It's you.'

'I know, that's what I'm worried about,' she said, her voice sounding childlike and tearful. 'I'm just me, a geeky schoolgirl from the English countryside. How did I get mixed up in all this? I can't convince a homicidal vampire lord that I'm anything else. I can't do it. It's all a big fat mistake.' Mo spread her hands across her face.

Luca crouched next to her and unpeeled her fingers one by one. 'I don't think it's a mistake,' he said calmly. 'I think you are the Chosen One. One way or another, it's you. Bogdan got it right. He saw something, I see something. You need to see it too. You can do this.'

Mo sucked in a huge breath and sighed it out, trying to compose herself.

'Remember how you stood up to Bogdan, with only a Premier Inn pencil to defend yourself?' Luca added.

Mo nodded shakily and smiled a wobbly smile.

'See? You can do this.'

'I hope so,' she said in a tiny voice, her eyes searching Luca's. 'I hope you're right. It's too late now anyway, isn't it? He's probably just a few miles away.'

Mo glanced at the door nervously. Luca's voice brought her back.

'I'm here for you,' he said. 'Bogdan will back you up too. It will be over quickly and then . . .'

'What?' Mo asked him.

Luca continued to stare up at her but said nothing. Seconds stretched into more seconds. Mo found her head dropping down towards his. She was dimly aware of his face rising to meet hers. She sensed her eyes closing, her lips tingling and then . . .

'Oh hello!' said a voice. 'Did we interrupt something?'

Mo's eyes snapped open. She shot to her feet. Around fifteen women were spilling into the hall, carrying cakes and bags stuffed with wool.

'This is our crochet club night, isn't it, ladies?' said the woman, stepping forward. Mo recognised her. Mrs Spreadbury from the village shop. Lower Donny resident for over fifty years and, apparently, keen crocheter. 'The youth club is on Fridays.'

'But I booked the hall,' Mo spluttered. 'I have a very important meeting happening here in about –' she glanced at the clock above the door – 'ten minutes,' she said. 'You can't be here. Trust me, you really cannot be here.'

Mo pictured the Vampire King of the East blasting into the hall, seeing the women gathered there, his eyes lighting up, assuming this was the catering. How many senior citizens could one vampire overlord eat in a single night? Oh god, Mo thought, it was like the first line of a really bad joke.

'Well, my dear,' said Mrs Spreadbury, 'I think there's room for all of us. Perhaps you could have your meeting up this end and we could do our crochet down near the back?'

Luca stepped forward, urgency toughening his voice. 'I am very sorry but that won't work,' he said. 'You must go, at once. Now.'

'It's just a double booking – I'm sure we can work something out.' Mrs Spreadbury sounded offended.

Luca advanced towards the women, his arms outstretched like he was herding a group of jittery alpacas into their pen. 'Please, take it from me, you do not want to be here this evening,' he said.

The crochet club members looked at one another, confused, but then Luca smiled at them, his richest toffee and liquid amber smile. It was like the sun coming out. Vampires could hypnotise their victims, but here was Luca, a regular human, hypnotising a group of Donny pensioners with a single flash of his perfect white teeth.

'Where do you suggest we go?' Mrs Spreadbury asked.

'How about the pub?' Luca suggested.

'Only if you take us there,' came another voice, from the back. Giggles.

'Yes, why don't you come with us? I'll buy you a drink,' said another woman. More giggles.

Luca looked back at Mo.

'Go on, Luca,' said Mo. 'Take them. I'm OK.'

He frowned hard, made a frustrated growling sound, didn't move.

'Please, Luca. Get them away,' Mo said urgently. 'To safety.'

He remained still a second longer, staring at Mo, then spoke hurriedly.

'All right. I'll come back as soon as I can. You'll be OK. The queen can't invite him in anyway – a human has to do it, remember? Just don't move until I get back.'

Mo nodded quickly and Luca turned and began shepherding the women towards the door. They wouldn't be rushed. They were too busy clucking and asking Luca his name and offering him cake and patting his arms. Mo watched, motionless, until finally she heard the hall's heavy front door thud shut. Her eyes darted to the clock. Five minutes to seven. Five minutes! She swayed a little, and tiny bright stars flickered at the corners of her vision.

'Breathe, breathe,' she murmured. 'I can do this. I have to do this.'

Then she glanced down at herself.

'Oh god, I need to change, put my fangs in, slap on some of that perfume. Quickly. Come on, Mo, keep it together. You've got this. Dress, robes, fangs, scent . . .'

She rushed over to the box and scrabbled in it for her dress. She pulled it out, shook it sharply and held it up.

'What?!' she squeaked, feeling her stomach trampoline. 'It can't have shrunk in the dryer. Oh god, it *did* shrink in the dryer.'

She held her formerly long, elegant dress against her tall frame. It was now, at best, a crop top. She hurled it to one side.

'At least I've got my robe and jewellery,' she said, looking for the bag she'd put them in, the bag she'd left ready by the front door. The bag they'd walked straight past on their way out. It wasn't here.

Mo gasped and flung her hand over her mouth, her eyes flickering left to right, unable to focus.

'It's OK, it's all right, I can do this. Jeans and a T-shirt are OK,' she muttered. 'I've got my fangs anyway.'

She returned to the box, still full of bunting, and pawed at it, like a wombat digging a hole, waiting to feel cool gumshield plastic against her hand. Nothing. She tipped the box upside down. A pastel avalanche of bunting tumbled to the floor, but no fake fangs.

'Where are they? Where are they?' she squeaked.

Her brain cycled back through the last few hours. She had had them at home. She had taken them to Lou's. She had thrown them at Lou after scaring her with them. She had FORGOTTEN TO PICK THEM UP OFF THE FLOOR OF LOU'S ROOM. No, no, no, no, no!

Mo groaned and sank down onto her knees. She'd left her robes and jewels by the front door, shrunk her majestic dress to the size of a teabag, forgotten her fangs, watched as Luca left with a bunch of senior crochet fanatics, and now, *now*, the Vampire King would be here any moment. Mo checked the clock again. It was two minutes to seven.

*Literally* any moment! He's always punctual, Bogdan had said.

'He can't come inside. He has to be invited in and I won't do that,' Mo said, pacing. 'Luca has to do it, when he gets back. I've got time, time to calm down, maybe wash the sweat off my palms.'

She rubbed her hands together and felt how they trembled. Then she froze. A noise. The heavy iron door handle twisting. Mo squeaked in terror. Was the Vampire King here, already? Not just punctual, but early?

Slowly, as if her head were made of lead, Mo turned towards the door, her breath frozen in her chest. The door swung open, painfully slowly, and the overhead light picked out a stooped figure, limping out of the night-time darkness . . .

'Lou!' Mo shrieked.

Lou hobbled to meet her. Her crutches thumped out a lopsided rhythm against the wooden floor of the hall, her broken leg and its heavy cast hovered off the ground awkwardly.

'I told you not to come!' said Mo, hardly recognising her own voice. It was shrill with stress.

'I know, I know, but you left your fangs at my house, I just found them,' said Lou. 'I thought you'd definitely need them. They're in my bag.'

'No, no, no,' said Mo. 'Go, get out, he'll be here any second. He could kill you.'

'Am I late?' Lou said, glancing at the clock. 'I would have got here earlier but these crutches slow me down.'

The big hand of the hall clock jolted one minute on. One minute until seven.

'Oh, Lou, what have you done?' said Mo. 'You can't be here. It's too dangerous.'

'It's OK, there's time, I'll leave right now,' said Lou.

'No, wait. Listen!' said Mo. 'I can hear footsteps.'

They stood still. Mo was right. Someone was striding across the gravel outside.

'Is that him?' Lou whispered.

'It has to be,' Mo whispered back, 'but there's no time for you to leave. He'll catch you at the front door. He'll kill you! Quick, hide in the loo. Don't make a sound.'

Lou, her hands juddering on her crutches, began speed-limping towards the back of the hall.

'Faster, Lou,' Mo squeaked. 'He's opening the front door.'

Lou's crutches sped up, sounding like a hysterical metronome.

'What about your fangs?' she called over her shoulder.

'No time,' said Mo, then she turned to face the door, her thoughts spooling out at a hundred miles an hour. I'm not ready – no fangs, no dress, no Luca. And now Lou's here and . . . He's turning the door handle, but he can't get in, he can't walk inside. Someone has to invite him in . . . Except, oh no, the door is opening . . . Cold air rushing in against my ankles. It's wide open now, I can see a silhouette, someone's there. It's him, it has to be him. He's coming inside. But he can't, can he? Impossible. Oh god, oh help me, how can this be happening? I'm alone, I'm not prepared, I'm –

The terrified commentary in Mo's brain stopped abruptly as a figure stepped into the light and stood motionless, like a statue.

Mo gasped, rocked on her feet just a little, and steadied herself. Then, summoning every last scrap of courage, she spoke: 'Good evening, Great King, I have been waiting for you.'

# 43

As Mo uttered those ten shaky words her eyes flickered across the Vampire King, taking in every detail, all the details – and there were a lot. He was wearing tight high-waisted trousers in some sort of gold brocade fabric, with tassels on the sides. His white shirt had a frilly collar and cuffs and he wore it open, all the better to show off the clutch of medallions and chains draped over his hairless chest. A purple jacket that trailed almost to the floor completed the look, its left shoulder embroidered with a cascade of jewels, like a bling waterfall. Oh, and heels. He was wearing black leather boots with heels. He must have been handsome once, Mo realised, a golden boy, but now his long blond hair was dull and his skin had the same pale, papery appearance as Bogdan's.

'Mo, I presume,' he said, walking slowly towards her.

Mo nodded, her head trembling like a newborn lamb's.

'I am the Vampire King of the East, mighty and feared leader. My name is Matislav Rosstistavich,' he said. 'But you can call me . . . Steve.'

He stretched the Steve out like a cat purring.

'Welcome . . . Steve,' Mo said, handling the name tentatively, like a fragile bird's egg. 'You didn't need to be invited in then.'

'Nah, I'm the king of vampires, I do what I like. Normal rules do not apply.'

He smiled lazily and Mo clocked his fangs. Normal rules did not apply to them either, it seemed. Weren't fangs only meant to come down when a vampire was feeding?

'Good journey?' Mo asked, clasping her sweaty hands tightly in front of her and wondering when Bogdan would appear. 'The traffic can be bad at this time of night.'

'Traffic? It was the police that were the damn problem,' the Vampire King said, running both hands through his lank blond hair. 'They pulled us over and arrested Bogdan. Something about theft of a vehicle and the disappearance of some tedious human. Cliff Jobsworth?'

'Clive Bunsworth,' Mo murmured, trying to process the fact that first Luca and now Bogdan were not here. This was not in the plan!

'Whatever,' said the king. 'I had to jump out of the car and walk the rest of the way. It was extremely boring.'

'Oh, I'm sorry,' said Mo. 'Couldn't you materialise?'

'I wanted to conserve my energy for our meeting,' said the king. 'Even for a great powerful lord like me, materialising can be tiring. Now, here we are at last. A little delayed, admittedly, thanks to the vampires of the damn Real East.'

He spat on the floor. Mo flinched.

'Always the same. Bickering over territory and resources,' said the king. 'I have the best land, the tastiest humans . . . It's very boring. You shut everyone up for a while then some other upstart little vampire organisation decides to try their luck. Pah! Someone is always coming for you, Mo, when you're in power. Always.'

He ran his fingers through his hair again and closed his eyes briefly, then snapped them open and looked Mo up and down. She tried not to shrink. While Luca's gaze seemed to warm her, being looked over by the Vampire King felt like being tasered.

'You're younger than I expected,' he said. 'How old?'

'Fifteen,' Mo replied.

'Huh,' he said, and then picked his fang with a long fingernail before casually examining the debris underneath.

'I'm two hundred and seventy, but I was nineteen when I was turned,' he said. 'In the prime of life. About to marry the most beautiful girl in town, destined for a career in politics, leadership, government, you know?'

'Yes,' said Mo, feeling a flicker of hope. She had things in common with this guy. Similar age (before he was turned anyway), eager to work in politics . . . Maybe they could get along.

'Then I was chosen, like you,' the Vampire King continued. 'At first I despaired. I wanted to go back to my old, human life. I missed bacon so much. I didn't want to be some Vampire King's deputy, but then it came to me. In a vision.'

As he drawled out the word vision, he drew a rainbow shape in the air.

'I have visions. It's my gift,' he added conspiratorially. 'Anyway, the vision showed me I should kill the old, boring Vampire King, and do the job myself. Inject some life into the role, some new ambition. Plus what a bonus – you get all this strength, once you're turned, don't you? All this physical power. Shame to waste it. So I ripped his head off. Pop!'

Mo nodded and gulped.

'The other vampires were all . . .' he put on a whiny voice, '*Oh no, you can't do that, a vampire killing the king is against the rules*. I was like, "Boring!"'

He pronounced the last word in a loud sing-song, like a vampire doorbell.

'So the other vampires whined a bit, but they got the message. This guy is ruthless! Then I continued to be ruthless, I didn't stop being ruthless, I was ruthless 24/7. I grabbed more land, I crushed more vampire uprisings, I ate record numbers of humans. Cool stuff. You see, Mo, here's the thing. I'll let you in on a secret. It's amazing what effect violence has. It's brought me total domination. Everyone fears me. Vampire and human alike. That's my tip for you, Mo. Make . . . them . . . fear . . . you.'

Mo barely moved as his final four words hissed out into the room, like a sinister slow puncture.

'The only downside,' the Vampire King continued, 'is that everyone fearing you can get irritating. A lot of bowing and averting eyes, even from the big vampires out there. I'm, like, come on, guys, that's boring too! It's just little old King Stevie.'

He threw his arms wide and laughed a high-pitched, aggressive sort of laugh. It made his medallions jangle. Then he sighed like a deflated balloon and looked suddenly irritable.

Mo sensed the dangerous change of pace and moved over to the table.

'I have a gift for you, to welcome you to England,' she said.

'Ah, about time!' the king said, cheering up. 'Presents!'

Mo picked up the bottle of homemade perfume and held it out. 'It's a bespoke scent,' she said.

Then, with a jolt of panic, she remembered she hadn't yet put any on herself to mask her human aroma, and quickly snatched it back. The Vampire King's eyes narrowed with suspicion as Mo nervously yanked the stopper out and sloshed a palmful over her neck.

'Mmmm, smells so good,' she said.

The king approached, sniffed tentatively.

'What's in it?' he asked.

'It's a secret recipe,' Mo lied.

His nostrils flickered.

'I'm getting roses, maybe a little lavender,' he said, slowly, 'but I'm picking up something else fragrant and delicious too. What is that?'

Please don't let it be me, please don't let it be me, Mo chanted in her head, quickly ducking away from him and walking over to one of the plastic chairs.

'Would you like to sit down, on this, erm, throne?' she said.

The Vampire King's lip began to curl, revealing the tip of his fang. 'The Duke of Malprattia had thrones encrusted with real *teeth*,' he growled.

Where's Luca? Where's Luca? Mo thought, her eyes flicking nervously to the door.

'Sounds lovely!' said Mo. 'Well, I might sit down anyway.'

She perched nervously on one of the brown chairs, and instantly regretted it. The Vampire King of the East was now looking down on her.

'You're not what I expected, Mo,' he said. 'Is this how you dress to greet a king? Where are your fine robes?'

'In the wash,' Mo said. 'They were totally covered in blood! It does stain, doesn't it? Anyway, I like wearing jeans. More practical.'

The Vampire King sniffed dismissively.

Luca, Luca, Luca, hurry up, hurry up, hurry up, Mo thought.

'Also, I was expecting a banquet,' the Vampire King added. 'Bogdan said we don't have long, so let's bring out the food, yes? I haven't eaten for a day. I could drain a whole choir.'

'I thought you might like to try a nice drink I created, especially for you,' Mo said, reaching for the decanter with a trembling hand. 'It's blended worms.'

The Vampire King folded his arms across his chest and stared grimly at the grey liquid.

'I found a diet exclusively of blood is a bit monotonous, and draining humans can take effort, plus it's so messy, all that blood spraying everywhere,' Mo said, starting to babble but unable to stop. 'Whereas worms are, you know, widely available and easy to catch. Cheap too. Kind to your digestion. What's not to like?'

What am I talking about, she asked herself, and where the absolute hell is Luca? And Bogdan? One at the pub and the other detained by the police – this was *not* in the plan. I'm not supposed to be doing this alone, dressed in jeans, without my fangs, with my best friend hiding in the loo . . .

The Vampire King remained silent, stony-faced. Mo felt sweat prickle on her top lip. She became aware of her heart rate galloping. She breathed in tiny sips. Then it happened. A twist in her belly, a bubble of fizzy energy drink rising up through her body, rumbling in her throat, puffing her cheeks out faintly. Her hand flew up to her mouth.

'What was that?' said the Vampire King.

A disaster, Mo thought, that's what that was. I'm burping and sweating. Vampires don't burp, they probably don't sweat. Do they cry? she wondered, blinking hard, trying to head off the panicky tears that threatened to well in her eyes. Luca! Bogdan! *Where are you?*

'I drank some blended worms just before you got here,' Mo muttered. 'They must have upset my belly.'

'You said blended worms were easy on your *gut*,' the Vampire King replied, hurling out the word like he wanted to launch it into space.

The plastic chair creaked under Mo as she shifted nervously. She glanced towards the door yet again. She wanted to flee, to run for her life, but what about Lou, hidden in the hall toilet behind her? She couldn't abandon her.

'What is it about you?' the Vampire King asked. 'I sense something unusual, Queen Mo.'

Mo stayed still, dared not move as he walked slowly around her, sniffing and scanning her, his heels clacking on the wooden floor.

'Yes, what is it about you?' he repeated, his lips twisting and twitching.

'I'm the Chosen One,' Mo said, in voice that was pathetically small. 'Bogdan found me, he spotted me.'

'Bogdan, yes. Maybe his judgement is a little off. He's so damn ancient. Going a bit soft in his old age,' the king said. 'Perhaps he made a mistake.'

'No mistake,' Mo replied.

'Yet you're not like other vampires I know,' he said, leaning in, bending over her, his face hovering close to Mo's, so close she could spot stubble on his top lip, smell his breath – metallic and pond-like.

'It's beginning to worry me, Mo,' he said, his voice gaining force. 'Which is a pity. I don't want worries, Mo. I've enough worries with the damn Vampires of the Real East.'

He spat on the floor again.

'I'm really, really bored of vampires who don't behave like I want them to. Do you understand me, Mo? Do you?'

Mo blinked rapidly, desperate to leap out from under his towering body, his angry, cold breath, his piercing gaze. Her muscles tensed, her hands squeezed into balls in her lap, her breathing sped up further and then . . .

The door handle turned with a piercing squeak. The Vampire King wheeled around, his long purple coat flying out like a cape, his fangs exposed with a rasping hiss.

'Who is there?' he roared.

The door opened and, panting hard, Luca burst into the room. Mo let out a little gasp of relief.

'It is a great honour to meet you, mighty lord,' Luca puffed, bowing deeply.

'Who is this?'

'My familiar,' Mo said, standing up slowly on shaky legs. 'It's Luca. He's my familiar.'

# 44

The Vampire King stared coolly at Luca for a few seconds, until another sound rumbled into the hall. A car pulling up outside, then someone tapping at the window. Luca peeped behind the curtain.

'Bogdan is here, great one – I will invite him in,' he said, rushing for the door.

A second later, Bogdan strode into the hall. 'Sorry for delay,' he said. 'The stupid police put me in a cell. Of course I simply materialised out of it, grabbed the car keys and here I am. Anyway, lord, you have met the queen, very nice, and now I can take you to your lodgings. Shall we go?'

Mo held her breath. Please go, please go, please . . .

The Vampire King of the East, using only his eyes and a flick of his wrist, slammed the door shut.

What was that? Mo thought. How did he do that? He's got weird powers, hasn't he? Oh, great . . .

'I don't want to go,' he said. 'Not just yet. First I have some questions.'

The four of them stood in tense silence for a second, and then Bogdan cleared his throat.

'What kind of questions, great master?' he asked.

'No, actually, when I say questions, I mean concerns . . .' the Vampire King replied, chewing the last word like it was gristle. 'Please, Mo, take a seat again.'

He laid a pale hand on her shoulder and gently but forcefully pushed her back down onto one of the plastic chairs.

'My concerns are these. Everything feels a bit . . . what's the word? Rubbish!'

'Majesty?' Bogdan interrupted.

'Silence, old fool,' snapped the king. 'Yes, rubbish. You bring me here to this sad, damp, tragic little place, to this tiny damn hall, with pathetic bunting and disgusting drink. No food, no peacocks, no juggling with dogs. Where are the fireworks? I'm wondering. Do these folk not know who I am? Do they not care? You call these thrones? At the Duke of Malprattia's we had golden thrones encrusted with human teeth! Remember? I told you about those. Real teeth. Real! So, my concern is, what the damn hell is going on?'

'We didn't have long to prepare for your visit, master,' Bogdan said, stepping towards him anxiously.

'I said, "Shut it, grandad!"' the Vampire King shouted, holding up his hand, stopping Bogdan in his tracks.

'Mo, I repeat my question. I don't want to have to repeat my question, but here goes. What. The. Damn. Hell. Is. Going. On?'

Mo shook her head quickly.

'Oh, she doesn't know!' the Vampire King roared, throwing out his hands like a footballer appealing a yellow card. 'The queen doesn't know what the damn hell is happening here. Oh, that's not good. That's not cool. Somehow, though, I'm not surprised, because to me, Mo, you seem . . . weak.'

'I'm not weak,' said Mo, sounding weak.

'You seem . . . not very majestic,' he went on. 'You seem . . . I'm searching for a word? A word I hate? It's on the tip of my tongue . . . Ah yes, *kind*.'

Mo felt her body shrink. She knew this feeling, this sensation of trying to be physically small, of trying to disappear. The way he leaned over her, invading her space, crushing her with his presence. It was all familiar. Of course it was. It was what Tracey Caldwell did, looming over her on the bus every morning, insulting her, intimidating her.

Suddenly it all made sense. She saw everything with sharp clarity, saw how stupid she'd been, to think she could fool the Vampire King, how utterly deluded. Mo felt herself submit to this understanding, to this old familiar fate of being prey, to Tracey once and now, quite literally, to the Vampire King of the East. He is onto me, she thought. He has sniffed out my humanness, and now, surely, he will –

A loud rumble shattered the silence, popping Mo's dazed, defeated thoughts like a needle in a balloon.

'Damn!' the Vampire King shouted. 'That's my belly. I'm starving. I need to eat.'

With the word 'eat', his hands became expressive upturned claws. His mouth contorted into an angry sneer. His bejewelled jacket sparkled menacingly.

'Come, Mo, let us feed together, and maybe I can overlook all this,' he said, waving his hand limply at the bunting and the blended worms and the thrones that were not encrusted with human teeth.

'A human meal?' Mo spluttered. 'I haven't arranged any catering –'

'What are you talking about?' the Vampire King said, pointing at Luca. 'This guy will do nicely. Look at him. So pretty. Yum, yum, yum. I cannot wait to taste him.'

'But he's my familiar – you can't eat him,' Mo said, rising to her feet.

'I've eaten plenty of familiars before,' said the king. 'There's always another stupid damn human queuing up to work for a mighty vampire. You can get a replacement easy as malaria.'

He marched up to Luca and stared at him.

Mo noticed Luca's eyes becoming watery and out of focus. 'What are you doing to him?' she gasped.

'Hypnotising him and, wow, he's *very* receptive. He loves it! Look how he's grinning and flopping about. Fantastic! I love it when this happens.'

'Can I get a selfie with you before you drain me?' Luca asked, smiling woozily, his voice thick with sleep.

'I don't think we have time for that, my friend,' said the Vampire King, sounding suddenly businesslike as he grabbed Luca roughly by his collar and lifted him high off the floor. Mo watched as the king swept Luca through the air, like he was no heavier than a coat, and hurled him down onto a chair. Luca barely seemed to notice. He was as floppy as out-of-date lettuce.

Shakes rippled through Mo's body now, uncontrollable. She could only stand, rooted to the spot, her mind struggling to take in what she was seeing. Things were spiralling out of control. This was not in the plan. No one had mentioned the risk of Luca being eaten. Why didn't Bogdan do something, say something? But Bogdan looked oddly calm, curious even; perhaps the prospect of spilled human blood, even if it were Luca's, was too appealing.

The Vampire King of the East was easing Luca's floppy head over to one side now, stroking his exposed neck, licking his fangs. Mo was screaming 'No, no, no' in her head, but no words came out. Her eyes were wide, and she was blinking back tears of pure liquid terror as the Vampire King leaned in towards Luca and then –

They all heard it. A sneeze, coming from the back of the hall.

'Someone is there,' the Vampire King shouted. 'Bogdan, go check.'

Finally the words came. 'Stop!' Mo squealed, but Bogdan had already sped over to the hall loo and smashed the door down with one thump of his ancient vampire shoulder. Mo heard sounds of a struggle and then he reappeared, holding Lou tightly around the waist as he carried her off the floor.

'Found this one hiding in the toilet,' he shouted, over Lou's yelps. 'Her name's Lou. Used to be friend of queen's.'

'Get off me. No! No!' Lou screamed, trying to hit Bogdan with her crutches. Mo watched, mouth open, as Bogdan marched the wriggling Lou over to the other chair and dropped her onto it. Then he snatched away her crutches and threw them against the wall.

'Wonderful,' said the Vampire King, rubbing his hands together and licking both fangs. 'Now we have dessert.'

When things are going wrong, so wrong that everything you care about most in the world is in terrible jeopardy and everything you thought you knew is just a puddle on the floor, time seems to both speed up and slow down. That's what Mo discovered. She felt she was flying through her own life, powerless and paralysed, as terrifying event after terrifying event flickered wickedly into life and played out like a high-speed nightmare around her. And yet she noticed tiny details too, in luxurious slow motion. A curl of hair on Luca's neck. The two freckles on Lou's nose that were shaped like New Zealand. Bogdan's teeth.

Bogdan's teeth! Or, more precisely, his fangs. They had descended. He must be preparing to feed, Mo thought.

He's supposed to be on Team Mo tonight, but at the first chance of a blood meal, he goes full vampire again.

Mo tore her gaze away from Bogdan's glinting fangs and looked at Luca, slumped and unconscious, completely defenceless. Then she looked at Lou, marooned in her chair by her broken leg, shaking with fear, her eyes pleading for help and begging for forgiveness. Suddenly something ignited inside her. A spark, that built to a flame, that grew to a fire. A fire that burned through her powerlessness and fear, scorching them to ashes, and blazed through every particle of her body.

I'm not going to let Lou be hurt again, or Luca be hurt ever, Mo found herself thinking. I'm not that girl who Tracey Caldwell bullied on the bus. That was the old me, from a lifetime ago. How could I forget that I did stand up to her, outside my house, the night Lou was run over. That I stood up to Bogdan too, in the Premier Inn. That I flattened Danny Harrington against a hot-dog van. There *is* something in me, some strength, something Bogdan spotted, something Luca sees, some force *I* don't even understand. I'm the Chosen One after all. I. Am. The. Chosen. One. And I say . . .

'Enough!'

Mo's voice exploded out of her, at least an octave lower than normal, and as she roared her hand reached for the decanter of blended worms. It gripped the neck. It lifted it high. With a rush of superhuman power, it hurled it downwards, smashing it against the floor, shattering the glass into a million pieces and splattering slimy grey liquid everywhere.

'Bogdan, put your fangs away! You will *not* eat Lou. Understand?'

Bogdan shook his head, emerging from his pre-feeding haze, and his fangs slid back up. The Vampire King of the East watched Mo with curiosity and then laid a skinny hand on her arm.

'Mo? So angry. What has come over you?' he said. 'I'm all for a bit of rage. Very fitting in a vampire, but don't be a party pooper. The feast is just getting started. We have a delicious young girl to enjoy, so succulent, *mmm* . . . but first the meaty, macho main course.'

He whirled round towards Luca, his medallions tinkling, and ran a long fingernail down Luca's throat.

'Here is the vein, all ready and waiting,' he said, licking his lips. 'Looks delicious, doesn't it? See how it's pulsating. I love it when they pulsate. Come to Stevie –'

'Leave him alone!' Mo said, her voice still a deep, authoritative growl.

'Mo, you're being boring,' the Vampire King snapped impatiently. 'Don't be boring.'

He glanced angrily at her and then turned back to Luca, which is why he didn't notice Mo, both hands out in front of her, launching herself at him. She hit him hard, much harder than she expected. She thumped both palms powerfully into his side, catching him completely off guard.

The Vampire King toppled on his heels, staggered backwards, slipped in the worm puddle and landed on his back on the hall floor. Bogdan rushed to his aid, but the king angrily batted him away, a torrent of vampire expletives tumbling from his furious lips. Then he pinged to his feet in a single move, his eyes smouldering with rage.

'How dare you . . .' he said, rushing at Mo, his fangs bared.

Bogdan leaped in front of him. 'Master, please, calm down,' he said. 'It was accident. The queen is not herself tonight.'

The Vampire King tossed Bogdan to one side with a flick of his hand, sending him flying across the hall to land like a sack of spanners by the door. Then he strode up to Mo.

This time, though, Mo didn't flinch or shrink. She was no longer shaking or struck dumb. She pushed her shoulders back. She lifted her chin. She held his gaze.

'How dare you push me!' he roared, right in her face.

Still Mo didn't move. She calmly stared into the Vampire King's eyes.

'What do you say?' he bellowed.

Mo let his words settle, barely blinking, before she spoke in a voice as quiet as it was controlled.

'You don't eat Luca. You don't eat Lou. All right, Steve? If you've really got a problem with that, if you really want to eat someone, you know what you can do?'

She yanked at the neck of her T-shirt, revealing her pale white throat.

'Bite me!'

# 45

The hall was totally silent now. Nobody moved. Inviting the Vampire King to bite her was not in any plan, but Mo was done with plans. She was running on instinct now, running on blood and adrenaline and emotions, all the things that made her real and human and honest. No more lies! It was time to come clean, with everyone, and that included the Vampire King of the East.

'What are you doing?' he said, his face appalled. 'A vampire cannot feast on another vampire. They must suck the blood of living things.'

'I'm alive,' Mo said. 'Never felt more alive in fact.'

'What are you saying?'

'I think you know,' said Mo. 'I'm flesh and blood, Steve. Human.'

The Vampire King narrowed his eyes. 'I don't believe this. You are messing with me, Mo . . .' he said. 'You look like a vampire. The clothes are pathetic, but that pale skin, that hair . . . Maybe the ponytail is a little young, but otherwise –'

'No fangs though. Look,' Mo said, baring her teeth.

'Well, you're not feeding right now,' he said.

'I can eat food too,' she said. 'See this? This is a Mini Battenberg.'

She ripped open the box that Lou had smuggled in, pulled one out and waved it under the Vampire King's nose.

'Smells good, doesn't it? Sugar, sponge, marzipan. Tasty. When did you last eat food? Real food you can chew? Must have been a while ago. Let me guess? The 1760s?'

The Vampire King shrugged.

'Want me to take a bite?' Mo said.

She raised the tiny pink-and-yellow cake to her mouth, opened her lips, was about to sink her teeth into it when –

'No!'

The Vampire King swatted it out of her hand and sent it flying across the hall.

'Eat that and you will be sick for hours, spraying it all up the walls,' he said. 'I didn't come all this way to see that.'

'Suit yourself,' Mo said.

Silence again. The Vampire King of the East eyed Mo closely. Mo was dimly aware of Lou and Bogdan staring at her, and sensed Luca was watching too, emerging from his hypnotised state. She could feel them all silently screaming at her – 'What are you doing?' – but she ignored the question.

'You are definitely messing with me, Mo, I feel it somehow in my *guts*,' he said, slapping the high waistband of his golden trousers. Then he hissed with frustration, so loud the windows rattled.

Mo stayed right where she was. 'Maybe *you're* messing with *me*,' she said. 'How do I even know you're the Vampire King of the East.'

Lou, Bogdan and Luca all gasped at once.

The Vampire King of the East pulled an incredulous expression. 'Are you out of your mind?' he asked, horrified. 'Questioning me?'

'You turn up alone and on foot, with no familiar and no staff. It's not very regal,' Mo said.

'My people got held up at the border, something about not having the right visas,' he snapped. 'Ridiculous. Visas to get into this sad, isolated little island. No wonder I've never been before.'

'You can't just come and go as you please,' Mo replied. 'We're not in the EU any more. Everyone knows that.'

'I don't know what the EU is, and I don't care,' he shouted back, like a furious child.

'You've got an eye infection too,' Mo said, pointing at his right eye. 'A stye, there.'

The Vampire King hissed again, even louder. His face seemed to stretch in all directions at the same time, like cheese on a radiator. 'What is a stye?' he asked, spitting the question out between clenched teeth.

'A small lump on your eyelid, caused by an infection,' Mo said.

His fingers wandered over to the lid and he winced. 'It is a bit sore, yes,' he said. 'I can't check in the mirror though. So boring. I miss seeing my reflection. I was so damn handsome.'

'I didn't know vampires could get styes,' Mo pressed on. 'Let's see now . . . No familiar, no staff, a stye, didn't need to be invited in. All a bit suspect, I'd say. I'm not sure you're a real vampire at all. Can I seem some ID, please?'

For the first time, Mo saw a flicker of confusion in the Vampire King's face. He stepped away from her, turned his back and walked slowly over to the far side of the hall as if lost in thought. She watched him, her body tense. Hold your nerve, she told herself. Don't move.

Then, with his back to Mo, the Vampire King let out a terrible scream. Lou yelped while Mo's hands flew up to her ears and then she watched as he came at her, fast – part running, part flying, part shape-shifting through the air and then arrived, suddenly, right in front of her, his fangs bared, his lips pulled back, like a snarling dog . . .

Mo's eyes bore into his. 'Go on, do it,' she said calmly, exposing her neck again. 'I dare you. Bite me!'

The king snarled again and a growl rumbled in his throat. His lips twitched, he leaned in and Mo swayed just a little, just the tiniest amount, feeling his breath on her neck for one second, two seconds, three . . . Then suddenly he twisted away.

'All right!' he roared. 'All right. Nice game, Mo. That was pretty good. Well done.'

Lou whimpered a bit, Luca exhaled loudly. Still Mo didn't move.

The Vampire King paced the hall a little, then turned back to Mo.

'This has been kind of fun,' he said, laughing a little uncertainly and scraping his fingers through his hair. 'First I'm not sure you're a very good Vampire Queen. Then you say you're actually a human and tell me to bite you! Finally – what a finale, so dramatic – you accuse *me* of not being a vampire!'

He started clapping, slowly.

'Very good, Mo. Quite a ride, and definitely not boring. Double points for that. It worked too,' he said, slowly walking towards her. 'I am satisfied at last. No human would stand up to the Vampire King like this. No human would offer their neck. No human would look me in the eyes like you did. You're strong and a bit weird too. I like it.'

He eyed her for a few seconds, then flung his coat out behind him and bowed deeply.

'Congratulations, Mo. You are an excellent Vampire Queen.'

Once again silence descended on the hall like snow at midnight. Mo didn't bow back. She didn't move. She made sure her face was impassive, she kept her eyes fixed onto the Vampire King's. Don't mess up now, she told herself. Don't relax even a pinch until he's well and truly gone.

'Luca,' Mo said, still looking calmly at the Vampire King, 'please return those crutches to Lou and escort her to the back of the hall.'

'Your Majesty,' he said, rushing to collect the crutches from where Bogdan had flung them.

'Still think it's a shame to waste such a delicious meal,' the Vampire King muttered, watching Lou hobble away, 'but what the queen wants, she gets, right?'

Mo nodded silently.

'Hey, I've got a cool idea,' said the Vampire King, suddenly grinning. 'Why don't we get married and rule together. We could be unstoppable! And, with a little of my personal styling, you could be quite, you know, attractive.'

Mo felt his eyes slide up and down her body and suppressed a shudder.

'Thank you for the offer, Mighty Steve,' Mo said, 'but I don't need a husband. I'm the strong and independent type. I can rule alone, with a little help from my familiar, of course.'

'Oh yes, him,' the Vampire King said, looking over at Luca. 'That's another delicious meal wasted. He was A-negative, too. I could smell it. My favourite blood group. Full-bodied, notes of ripe cherry and chocolate, long on the palette. Argh! Look at me, I'm practically drooling.'

Bogdan approached. 'Master, if you'll come with me, we can leave Lower Donny. It's pretty sad and damp after all.'

'It really is,' said the Vampire King.

'I have arranged accommodation near the ferry port. You can sleep tomorrow and then sail back in the evening. We can travel there now, and enjoy a bite to eat on the way.'

'Very well,' said the king. 'If we can't eat these two humans, let's go find some people we can drain. Lots of them. I'm famished.'

Bogdan led the Vampire King towards the door, where they both paused.

'Farewell, Queen Mo, it has been interesting meeting you,' said the king. 'A bit odd, at times, and I would have preferred thrones encrusted with real teeth, but anyway . . . I leave Great Britain in your capable hands. I don't imagine I'll need to come back for another couple of hundred years. Transform these lands into a vampire stronghold. Rule with power and energy. Be ruthless. Make them fear you, remember. You certainly put the willies up me a bit, with your "I'm a human – bite me" routine, and that doesn't happen often. Congratulations and goodbye.'

Bogdan held the door open for the king and, as he strode through, Bogdan looked back at Mo quickly and gave her one brief nod. Then the door swung shut.

'Oh . . . My . . .' Lou gasped, but Mo quickly shook her head at Lou, holding up a finger and staring fiercely. The message was clear. Wait, wait . . . Lou slapped her hand over her mouth and the three of them remained silent while they listened to Bogdan and the Vampire King crunching over the gravel to the car.

'I have beautiful rooms arranged for you, Noble Majesty,' they heard Bogdan saying, 'in a fine place fit for a mighty vampire. It is called the Premier Inn.'

'Well, I hope there are some Premier Inn-ocent humans we can feast on there,' said the Vampire King.

'Ha ha, very good, Your Majesty,' said Bogdan.

'So I can get them Premier Inn-side me, Premier Inn-stantly,' the Vampire King went on.

They heard Bogdan chuckling politely, then two doors slamming shut, an engine starting and a car driving away. As the sound faded to nothing, another noise broke through the hush inside Lower Donny village hall. The sound of a teenage girl thumping down hard against dusty wooden boards. It was Mo, fainting in a heap on the floor.

# 46

When Mo Merrydrew woke up, exactly eight seconds later, she saw two faces directly above hers, smiling down.

'There she is,' said Luca, beaming.

'Oh, Mo, you're alive,' said Lou, smothering her in kisses and then pulling a *yuck* face. 'Wow, you stink.'

'It's mainly carpet cleaner,' Luca explained.

Mo watched the two of them sleepily, her head resting in Luca's lap.

'What happened?' she asked, her voice a thin whisper.

'You fainted, but only after you totally convinced the Vampire King that you're a vampire,' said Luca. 'It was amazing.'

'And you did it by telling him you're a human,' Lou said excitedly. 'I couldn't believe it, Mo. You were so brave and so out there – you showed him your neck! I thought he was going to kill you, right in front of me. I would have hated that. I would not have recovered, ever, just so you know. But he didn't. Did you have that worked out all along?'

Mo shook her head. 'I didn't have anything planned,' she said. 'I was just, I don't know . . .'

'You were majestic,' Luca said, beaming again.

'When you smashed that glass bottle down with all the weird stuff in it,' said Lou.

'Blended worms,' Mo muttered.

'Yeah, well, that was wild,' said Lou. 'And you attacked him. It was like when you went for Danny Harrington in the market square, only much more powerful. You actually sent him flying! It was brilliant.'

'Lou's right,' said Luca. 'Such strength and daring. I knew you had it in you.'

'I didn't,' Lou said.

'Thanks a lot,' Mo laughed.

'No, I mean, I wasn't sure you could outsmart him, even though you're so brainy, and I definitely didn't know you were such a risk taker. You risked your own life to save us. *Soooo* cool.'

'I liked how you defended me, when you yelled, "Leave him alone!"' Luca said. 'I liked that a lot. It made me feel . . .'

'Made you feel what?' Mo asked, sitting up.

'Really, really good,' he said slowly.

She gazed at him and he gazed back. She leaned towards him and he leaned towards her . . . Mo heard Lou breathe in sharply, and then she closed her eyes.

The kiss, when it came, felt to Mo like freedom, as if the last trace of stress, of fear, effort and pretending evaporated off her and disappeared. She melted, like chocolate buttons in a child's warm hand. Some moments later, Lou's excited squeal brought Mo back to reality. She looked at her friend, and then back at Luca, and blushed.

'Told you he liked you,' Lou said. 'I knew it all along, and now you two are together.'

'Are we?' Mo said, looking at Luca.

'One hundred per cent,' he replied.

'Oh wow,' Lou said. 'I hardly recognise you, Mo. Fighting off vampires and kissing hot guys. I don't think anyone could call you a neek now.'

Mo laughed. 'I guess not,' she said.

'This will blow Tracey Caldwell's head off,' said Lou. 'You have totally Caldwelled Caldwell to the max! She's going to absolutely hate it.'

'Too bad. I'm not scared of her any more,' Mo said. 'Can't believe I ever was. And besides, if she's got a problem with who I am, if anyone's got a problem with who I am, you know what they can do?'

Luca and Lou looked blank for a few seconds, but then Mo pulled down the neck of her T-shirt a little and grinned. The grin crept across their faces too and together they shouted, at the top of their lungs, 'Bite me!' before collapsing into laughter.

The laughing lasted for ages, a delicious release. 'This is hurting my bruises,' Lou winced at one point as her sides shook with it all, but still she couldn't stop.

'OK, come on, let's get a grip – think of Lou's bruises,' Mo said eventually, squeezing the words out through ripples of giggles.

The other two nodded and, slowly, their laughs ebbed away to chuckles and sighs and big, exhausted smiles.

Mo stood up and looked around her, a little stunned. 'What do we do now?' she asked.

'Can we eat? I'm starving,' said Luca. 'I haven't had any dinner.'

'You nearly were dinner,' Mo said.

'We've got Mini Battenbergs,' Lou said, passing the box to him.

'I've never tried one of these before,' he said.

'What did he say?' Lou asked, outraged, turning to Mo. 'Never eaten Mini Battenbergs before? Mo, finish with him. This second. He's not right.'

Mo laughed.

'You love these, don't you?' Luca asked, picking up a cake.

'Yes,' they both replied together.

'And eat them all the time?'

'Yes,' they replied.

'OK,' he said, taking a bite and chewing thoughtfully.

'You look confused. What is there to be confused about?' Lou asked. 'This is the best thing you can eat in your life.'

'It's all right, I suppose, but honestly? I don't really get it,' he said.

Lou whacked Luca with her crutch, laughing and spluttering, 'How can you say that? Mo, how can he say that about the cake I love?'

'I don't know, Lou, but please stop hitting my boyfriend,' Mo said.

She stepped in front of him, arms outstretched to protect him, but he slipped his hands around her waist and pulled her into him, kissing her neck.

Mo laughed and wriggled and felt waves of new joy pulse through her bones and veins. She had never felt like this before, so awake and tingling and just so searingly happy to be alive. The bunting's pastel shades now glowed like embers, the strip lighting seemed to shine like the June sun. Mo felt as though she'd woken from a long sleep and was now ready to soak up all the air and life and colour around her.

She broke away from Luca, ran to the door and galloped out into the cold evening air. The stars were strewn across the November sky and the moon glowed with a pale blue light. Mo ran for several minutes, unaware of where she was, breathing deeply. She could hardly remember the last hour, could only sense it – the fear, then the fire, the rage, and finally the power to hold her ground and stare the Vampire King down. Her body still tingled with it all, but her mind felt as quick and light as clean sheets on a washing line.

'Hey, get back in here and wipe up these worms!' Lou shouted from the doorway, and Mo laughed and dashed back in, where she found Luca dabbing at the puddle with some paper towels.

'Oh, Luca, stop, you don't have to do that,' Mo said.

'Familiars clean up after their masters,' he said.

'Not tonight,' she said. 'Let's do this together.' She grabbed some towels.

'Watch out for glass,' Lou said, pointing a crutch at a shard of broken bottle. 'And try not to chun, Mo. You've gone really pale.'

'It's so gross,' she muttered. 'Liquid worms.'

'You should try actually blending them,' Luca said. 'I'm going to have nightmares about that for years.'

'I'm sorry, Luca,' Mo said, reaching out and squeezing his hand, her eyes swimmy with gratitude. 'You've done so much to support me. Thank you.'

'All right, enough of that,' Lou said, banging her crutch loudly on the ground. 'We'll never get out of here if you keep on breaking off to stare into each other's eyes and snog.'

Mo giggled.

They cleaned up the mess, took down the bunting, put the chairs and the table away and left.

'What are we going to do about the broken loo door?' Lou asked, as they walked away.

'I can fix it tomorrow,' Luca said. 'I'll borrow some tools from your dad's shed.'

'I don't think we should meet there any more,' Mo said. 'It's not secure.'

'Well, we don't have to, do we?' Luca said. 'Bogdan's gone, the Vampire King's gone, you can go back to your house. I can meet you there.'

'No more skulking around at night,' Mo said. 'Of course, I still need to work as Vampire Queen. I need to meet the other vampires, keep them happy, make Great Britain into a vampire stronghold so the Vampire King stays away. There's lots to do . . .'

'But you'll manage,' said Luca. 'You're the Chosen One.'

Mo smiled.

'Apparently so.'

'Now can we eat?' Luca asked. 'That tiny cake really didn't do it.'

'Let's go to mine,' Lou said. 'Mum's cooking pasta. She makes loads and she'll be made up to have us all there. And Nipper – he'll be excited too.'

'Does he ever, you know, live up to his name?'

'What, bite? Only now and then,' said Lou. 'He was OK when you visited the other day.'

'He might have gone off me since,' Luca joked. 'I hope he doesn't bite me.'

'Ha ha,' said Mo.

'What?' said Luca.

'Bite me! You said, "I hope he doesn't bite me."'

'Oh yeah, bite me!' Luca said, then he shouted it out – 'Bite me!' – grabbed Mo's hand and ran with her up the road.

'Bite me!' he roared.

'Bite me!' Mo shouted back, and they laughed as they raced off, charging through the cold night air, with Lou giggling and shouting, 'Wait for me,' as she bounced along on her crutches behind them.

*To be continued . . .*

**Jo Simmons** is an author of funny fiction. *I Swapped My Brother on the Internet* was shortlisted for the Lollies Book Awards 2020 and has been translated into several languages. Jo began her working life as a subeditor on magazines in London and later became a freelance journalist. She started writing for children when her two boys were young and hungry for daft and silly stories to make bedtime more fun. She lives in Brighton with her family and a small, scruffy dog who leaves hair absolutely everywhere. *The Reluctant Vampire Queen* is her first novel for teenagers.

# HOT
# KEY
# BOOKS

Thank you for choosing a Hot Key book.

If you want to know more about our authors
and what we publish, you can find us online.

You can start at our website

## www.hotkeybooks.com

And you can also find us on:

**We hope to see you soon!**